RANÉE S. CLARK

Tight Ends & True Crime

HOUSTON PUMAS SPORTS ROMANCE

Cover design by Sweetly Us Press. Illustrator Ivanna Nashkolna

Editor: Jenna Roundy

Published by Sweetly Us Press

www.sweetlyuspress.com

To the guy who doesn't laugh (too much) when I'm certain there's a murderer living in our attic. Thanks, babe.

AUTHOR'S NOTE

If you know anything about the story behind the Houston Pumas Romance Series, you know that it's taken some time to get these stories out into the world. Carlie and Law's story was written in the summer of 2023, just before devastating wildfires destroyed the community of Lahaina, Maui. My family and I had visited that same community in 2022, and many of the things we did are the adventures I based Carlie, Law, and their friends and family's activities on. After the fires, I went back and forth on whether or not to address them in *Tight Ends & True Crime*. In the end, I decided not to, but my intent is not to be dismissive of the tragic circumstances, so I chose instead to acknowledge it here. Many in that community are still rebuilding today, and part of helping that is continuing tourism to Maui, since much of the island economies depends upon it.

The Road to Hāna – We drove part of this as a family. It's *very* twisty! We didn't go far enough to see the black sand beach in Wai'ānapanapa State Park where Law and Ivy meet his fans.

Kalepolepo Beach – We weren't able to see this beach

recommended to us by a friend, but we did get to see lots of sea turtles at a beach across from our hotel. Magical!

The ice cream that Carlie talks about getting just before they all leave Maui is inspired by Island Cream in Lahaina. Delicious! Some of the best I've ever tasted.

We snorkeled at Honolua Bay, like Ivy, and my kids really enjoyed it. It's also a pretty hike down to the beach!

Like Carlie and Law and her family, we also hiked Twin Falls off the Hanā Highway. My kids had an absolute blast at the pool, and there are a few trails to explore there.

CHAPTER 1
CARLIE

You know how they say that one person ruins it for everyone? That's how I feel about my preschool teaching career. And to be technical, it wasn't just one person. Most of the parents at the private preschool where I taught in Arizona were great. You know, the kind that show up to parent-teacher conferences with a harried smile—both of us knowing that neither of us has time for this—listen to me praise their kid, and nod along with "yeah, of course" expressions. And even the few times I had to give bad news, they're all like, "Oh, we'll for sure work on that at home."

Except when their kid is the next Albert Einstein and it's your fault for holding them back from curing cancer.

My sister Jenna laughs so hard right now at the story I just finished telling her, her husband, and his brother Jett. I had a set of parents that threatened to have me fired for allowing the cleaning staff to mop up a finger-painting masterpiece that their daughter smeared on the floor of the classroom.

To be fair, it did have a startling resemblance to *The Starry Night.*

"There's no way," Jenna says, her shoulders still shaking at my impression of the father's indignation over the whole thing.

"They couldn't believe I didn't even get a picture first.

Apparently, they also didn't realize that twelve four-year-olds participated in the destruction of the masterpiece before I even called in the cleaning reinforcements. At least two kids slipped and fell on it, smearing paint *everywhere*. There was also some puking involved. Unrelated to the artistry, and mostly due to pure dislike of cottage cheese." It feels good to laugh about this now, especially since my audience is also laughing at the incident. It's weird how entertaining someone else with your own misfortune can be cathartic.

"It sounds like after all that, you need a vacation," Jett says. His eyebrows rise in a knowing way as he eyes Devin and Jenna.

Yeah, I quit my job after more incidents like the mini Jackson Pollock than I can count, but helping out with Jenna's kids while she gets their second GetAwayHome property ready *is* like a vacation. For one, her kids are angels. It shouldn't be allowed, but it's true.

Maybe my bar is just really low at this point.

It's Jenna and Devin who need the vacation with all the stress with the second property. Jett, who's a pro football quarterback and unbelievably rich, would bail them out the second he got a whiff of trouble. He says that's what brothers do. Which is why I'm sworn to secrecy that Jenna and Devin need to get vacationers in this house as soon as possible. The mortgage on this new property is higher than the others, and it's stretching them thin without the house bringing in anything. Jett would push twice as hard for Jenna to move into the house next door to his, which he also owns. But my sister is being stubborn about it, insisting this is her business and she'll manage it how she sees fit. I think she's crazy not to take a free house that Jett genuinely wants to provide for them, but Jenna will be Jenna.

Besides, they *are* going to get a vacation. Jett's flying them out with him to Maui for his teammate's wedding celebration, and Jenna can go knowing her kids are in good hands with me.

"Why don't you bring Carlie with you to Maui?" Jett says to Jenna.

I know Jett well enough to know that he's not the kind of guy that assumes everyone can throw money around the way he can. After winning a championship with the Houston Pumas football team this year, his agent has already negotiated a monstrous new contract for him, and he's always paying for something for Jenna and Devin. Just like with the house, Jenna hates it a little bit. Like she thinks she's mooching off of him, even though I can see it makes him happy to spend the money on his family and friends.

So I laugh at his suggestion. "I'm not sure at what point you missed that I just quit my job and I'm living with my sister."

Jett returns the laugh but shakes his head. "My treat."

Jenna narrows her eyes at Jett in confusion, like she knows he's up to something but hasn't quite gathered what yet.

"That's a great offer," I say, giving him a rueful smile. "But I promised Jenna I'd babysit. I can't back out now."

Jett doesn't even open his mouth before Jenna shakes her head. "Jett," she says with a scold. Devin laughs silently, covering his face in his hands.

"Listen," Jett says, holding up his hands. "Ava and I want to help, and the resort has some great activities for kids and babysitting. They'd have a blast, Jen."

I see the thoughts swirling through Jenna's head. My sister and I are close, so it's easy to guess the track her thoughts have taken. They can't afford this right now. That's why they didn't plan on taking the kids, especially since Jenna would never ask for more from Jett than he's already giving them.

"Jett," she says again. "This is too much."

Inwardly, I want to face-palm. I've reminded my sister a few too many times how much money her brother-in-law has and how she needs to chill.

Jett barks with laughter. "Everyone in Texas knows how much money my new contract is. I could take you and the kids to Maui every weekend and it wouldn't be too much. I could buy a house for you and it wouldn't be too much," he says pointedly.

She ignores the insinuation. "You need to get some kids of your own to spoil."

Jett smiles, and the expression on his face says *soon, very soon.* "Then they'll grow up to be entitled." His smile turns to a teasing smirk.

Jenna looks over at me. I hold back my own laugh. Like I'm going to turn down a week-long getaway in Maui.

"I don't get to say no, do I?" Jenna shakes her head again. "Jett, you're too much."

Jett glances over at me, catching me grinning from ear to ear. "Carlie doesn't think so."

CHAPTER 2
LAW

I step out onto the patio of my suite, drawing in a long breath of ocean air. In the distance I hear music and laughter, probably from the restaurant here at the resort that most of my teammate, Colby, and his new wife, Gabriella's, guests are using. Between the handful of family and friends they invited and then a good chunk of the football team, we've got this whole section of the resort rented out.

Jett McCombs, the Pumas quarterback, waves at me as he and his girlfriend Ava walk past on the beach, heading in the direction of the restaurant. Ava holds a toddler, and Jett is hanging onto the hands of two older boys—his nephews and niece, I assume. I met Jett's brother and his wife yesterday, since they have a suite just a couple doors down from mine, but we were all so exhausted from flying over there wasn't much small talk.

"Ready?" Ivy asks, coming out onto the patio with me. I'm new to the Pumas, and I wasn't about to come on this trip without some backup, so I brought my best friend to make sure I had someone to hang out with. Funny, since I haven't seen her most of the day.

"Yeah." I step out onto the sand and let Ivy lead the way to the restaurant. I need to use this trip to make friends with some more guys. I played with Colby in college, so I know him well, but he's the honeymooner—basically. He and Gabriella keep insisting that this isn't a honeymoon. They already went to Bali in March. Apparently, this is in place of the beach wedding they didn't get to have because they got married in the middle of the last season.

The music gets louder as we approach, and plenty of Pumas players and their families dance on a wooden platform lined with lights that juts out from the restaurant. I smile at the sight, and Ivy tugs on my arm, hurrying me inside.

"I'm starving," she says as an excuse before turning to the hostess to give our room number.

"Must have been busy today." I raise an eyebrow at her while we follow the hostess to a table.

"I had to snorkel right away," Ivy says, plopping into the seat of a small table just off the dance floor. I settle into mine across from her as the hostess hands us the menus and tells us a waiter will be by shortly. "The Maui Snorkel Report said it was awesome at Honolua Bay."

I chuckle in response, looking over the menu. I am not a snorkeler, much to Ivy's dismay. I'm happy to chill on a beach with a book or something, which she makes fun of me for constantly, always ribbing me for not being a typical jock. She does have me convinced to take surfing lessons later in the week, though.

This restaurant has mostly American food, which is okay with me. I'll eat authentic Hawaiian somewhere other than the resort. I settle on a steak-and-potatoes meal and lay down my menu, my attention landing on the dance floor again.

A woman I don't recognize holds Jett's niece now, twirling around with her, both of them laughing at the way the little girl's dress spins. I smile as the toddler grabs at the woman's long skirt, pulling it out, obviously indicating that she wants the woman to spin too. She obliges, and I'm captivated for a moment by the woman's huge smile and sparkling green eyes. She picks the little girl up, and her waist-length, strawberry blond hair swings out behind her as she and the girl spin. Her skirt doesn't twirl as much as the little girl's did, but the toddler is still delighted, pointing at it.

Since I met Jett's sister-in-law yesterday, I know this woman isn't the girl's mother. It just reminds me that the Pumas team is tight-knit, and I note my gratitude for that. They'll accept me too, I'm sure. Playing for the Pumas was never in my football plans. I've had my sights set on the Nashville Blues for so long, grew up believing that was my destination, worked my butt off through high school and college and then on the LA Rays so my dream team would look hard at me—I stop myself. I can't go down this thought path. I'm more than fortunate to be playing for the Pumas, even though it's not something I ever planned on. Besides, anytime I speak to the media, I have to put forward the face of a total team player for the Pumas. It's way easier to do that if I don't dwell on what I feel like I missed out on.

I watch the woman and the little girl until a waiter comes by, drops off two glasses of water, and then asks for our drink orders.

"What did you do today?" Ivy asks when the waiter has gone.

"Finished that habits book you've been on me to read." I put my elbows on the table and lean over.

"And?" she asks, mirroring my movements.

"It was good. Just as motivating as you said it would be. I've already got a list of things to work on."

"A little at a time," she reminds me, pointing a stern finger my way. It just makes me laugh. Ivy has wispy, pale blond hair that's always escaping her ponytail or braid or whatever. Even when she's wearing it down, like now, there are flyaways that make it look like she hasn't bothered to comb it in a while. With her bright blue eyes and heart-shaped face, she never comes off as stern as she wishes she did. It's hilarious to me that she's a life coach, that anyone actually does what she tells them to. But maybe her cheerfulness is what motivates people to keep trying with her.

"Right. One percent better." I nod at her obediently, and she beams.

The woman and the little girl come off the dance floor, and Ivy waves at them. They stop at our table, although the little girl tugs away and runs over to Jett, who's at a bigger table more toward the middle of the restaurant. The woman watches her run over and get Jett's attention before turning back to me and Ivy.

I stand automatically, something my Southern grandmother drilled into me from the time I was little.

"Hi, Ivy," the woman says, smiling. She turns to me, nodding and smiling as well.

"Carlie." Ivy waves in my direction. "Have you met Law yet?"

Carlie shakes her head and puts out a hand, which I take, and I notice a streak of red paint down one side. "Carlie Gallagher," she says. "I'm Jenna's sister, you know. Jett's sister-in-law."

"Right. Yeah. Lawson Card." I'm still holding her hand, and her smile grows. I should let it go, but I don't.

"Yeah. The new guy."

Up close, I see pale freckles across her nose and cheeks. I can't look away from her eyes, which are such a striking color. My answering laugh to her calling me the new guy comes several seconds too late, and when I glance at Ivy, she smirks knowingly.

"That's me." I finally let go of Carlie's hand. A shiver of awareness runs through me, as though my body wants me to take note of what just happened here. I'm not a love-at-first-sight kind of guy, but there was definitely a spark.

"Jett says you're one of the best tight ends in the league, and he can't wait to really start making plays with you." She tucks her hands into the pockets of her skirt, glances sideways at Ivy, and then backs up a step.

I have suspicions right away about what that means. It happens a lot. Ivy and I are close, and I did bring her on a vacation. We're sitting at a table for two. Of course, anyone would assume that there's something going on between us. Most of my team has already. But our relationship isn't romantic in the least. I have no idea how to convey that to Carlie right now.

"He's a great quarterback," I finally say. "I'm eager to see what we can do together."

She smiles. "I'm sure it will be awesome." She casts a glance over her shoulder and turns to Ivy. "I'd better go help with the kids. I'll see you guys around." She gives me one more look and then strides away. I watch as she leans over the younger of the two boys at the table and then crouches next to him, nodding at whatever he's telling her.

"Let me guess," Ivy says as I sink back into my seat. "Make sure she knows I have no territorial claim on you."

I was so obvious about my attraction to Carlie that I'm not offended by Ivy's guess. "If you don't mind."

"I'm used to it by now. Especially the looks—like, why in the world would you *not* be dating that gorgeous football player?" She gives a faux long-suffering sigh. "I cannot get through to these women that your inexplicable love for historical fiction is the biggest turnoff," she teases.

I snort. "You're just annoyed that it's not something macho like battlefields and wars."

"Look at you!" She shakes her head in exasperation. "You have a stereotype to live up to, Law, and you're failing miserably."

I laugh, and then scoot back as the waiter arrives with our food. By the time he's served both me and Ivy, her attention has wandered around the room. She's genuinely interested in every person that crosses her path, so it doesn't surprise me that she's already met Carlie, and probably half the team and their families. That's the other reason I brought Ivy. She's outgoing and loves to talk to people. She'll help me make friends on my new team, and although I'm not shy, I always welcome her nudges and extrovert expertise.

"How do you know Carlie?" I ask, bringing her attention back to me.

"She was playing with Jett's nephews on the beach this morning when I went for my run. I stopped to chat," she says. Of course she did. "Jett paid for her and the kids to come, but he still wants Devin and Jenna to get the vacation they need—"

"Devin and Jenna?" Carlie mentioned that name earlier—Jett's sister-in-law. So Devin must be her husband.

"Jett's brother and his wife, Carlie's sister," Ivy confirms.

"Ah."

"I think she's had the kids most of today—she's a former preschool teacher—but I guess they're doing some activities tomorrow, and then Jett has them, so she'll have some free time too. It sounds like Jett is big on everyone in his family getting R&R except for him." She pauses only to take a bite of the enormous salad the waiter brought for her.

I'm not shocked Ivy gleaned this much information from what was probably a five-minute conversation. "Jett does seem like the busy type."

"You should ask Carlie if she wants to go hiking with you tomorrow."

I was going to ask a couple of the receivers I had lunch with today, but Carlie does sound like a more attractive option. "Yeah. Maybe."

Ivy wiggles her eyebrows and takes another bite and then she goes back to surveying the restaurant. She'll know something about all of my teammates and their families before the end of this week, and that's what I'm counting on to help me fit in.

CHAPTER 3
CARLIE

I'm so glad that Jett talked Jenna into this. Sitting with my sister on the small porch of our suite, listening to the water so close and a warm breeze shifting lightly around us, is pretty much heaven.

"I saw you met Law Card tonight," Jenna says from beside me.

I glance over to see her eyes closed, her expression relaxed, which is a relief. She's been so stressed about the house lately. "Briefly," I say. My cheeks warm. Thankfully, in the darkness, Jenna won't be able to see it, even if she does open her eyes.

"He held your hand forever." Jenna's voice rises with teasing, and I can't help a soft chuckle.

"He brought a woman here with him," I point out. "He must be some kind of player." But his eyes were kind. I whisk away that assessment. It doesn't matter what I *think* I know about Lawson Card. Life and true crime podcasts have taught me that the charming, pretty ones are the ones you have to look out for.

Jenna scoffs softly. "Jett would have said something. You know him. The minute Card expressed interest, Jett would have been warning you. He called her his 'friend' when we met him last night." She gives a shrug.

"Yeah." But it doesn't ease my mind. Not that I'm uneasy over Lawson Card. Not after a brief few minutes talking and the warm feelings that snaked through me when he couldn't take his eyes off me while we talked. I could flirt with a football player—just for fun. Seriously, I could. It's just my nosiness getting the better of me. Well, Jenna calls it nosy. I call it natural curiosity that she weirdly lacks.

"If I marry Lawson Card, would you let me pay your mortgage for a few months until the house is ready?" I ask, nudging her leg with my foot.

She scoffs and doesn't open her eyes, but she frowns a little. "I don't need my family members paying for my business."

"Fair." I shrug. "Could I invest? I just hate seeing you so stressed, Jen."

She opens her eyes to reach across and squeeze my hand, her relaxed smile returning. "When you marry Law Card, you can 'invest' in my business. For now, helping me with the kids is huge."

"Okay, but I bet if I put some effort into it, I could have him ready to elope by the end of the week."

She laughs. "Sure, sure. The problem is, *you* won't be. The background check would take too long." She raises her eyebrows at me, and I swat at her.

"Once bitten, twice shy," I retort.

"Fair," she imitates me, and I swat at her again.

"Maybe I'll elope with him just to prove you wrong." It's an empty threat, and Jenna's answering laugh proves she knows it.

Two figures walk down the beach in front of us, and Jenna sits up a little. "Hmmm," she says. "I thought Gab said Ford wasn't bringing his wife." She frowns. "I'm glad he changed his mind."

I'm, of course, instantly intrigued as I watch the couple. I know Jenna means Wylie Ford, a defensive player for the Pumas, but I wouldn't have recognized him in the dim lights that line the balconies around us.

"Why wouldn't he?" I ask, half knowing the answer. The couple is walking a couple feet apart, nothing romantic about their stroll along the beach except some laughter we can hear faintly from them. The need to know their story bubbles up through me. I can't stop it.

"Having some troubles." We share a sad look. Jenna's seen first-hand the toll that football took on Jett's relationship with Ava, and she hates seeing it hurt marriages.

"What better place to fall back in love than Maui?" I say optimistically. I'm almost holding my breath, hoping the couple will close the distance and hold hands. Is it football driving them apart? And what is it about the sport, if that's the case? The long hours? The traveling? I push down the spiral of questions. They're not getting answered unless I walk up to Wylie Ford myself.

A smile retakes Jenna's expression as she turns to me. "Indeed," she says, wiggling her eyebrows, and I shake my head at her.

———

The next morning, my second full day in Maui, I revel in the fact that I'm lounging on a cabana bed, with the curtains behind me fluttering gently in the breeze, and waves lapping on the beach in front of me.

"I am going to move here," Ivy says from beside me.

I never would have pegged her as someone who could just sit on the beach for the forty-five minutes that we've been here. She seems to go, go, go, right from the moment that I met her yesterday, running up the beach. But when she found me walking down to the beach from the suite I'm sharing with Jenna and Devin, I told her I needed beach time relaxation without the kiddos, and she inexplicably joined me. Maybe to keep an eye on me, just in case her "best friend" shows up. And yes, I mean those air quotes very seriously. They looked so cozy at dinner last night that I'm not sure what to think of the way I caught Lawson staring at me or how long he held my hand when Ivy introduced us. It's just me wanting to know everything. I told Jenna he must be a player, but that doesn't feel right either. Not that I've trusted my feelings in a long time.

I turn back to my phone, which I've been using to troll for tidbits about Wylie Ford and his wife. The only articles I've been able to find are old ones from their wedding just over a year ago. Ford's wife is a tall, blonde woman with ice-blue eyes, named Madelyn Wise. She works for a Houston law firm, and I can't help wondering if Gabriella Duncan knew her before she was Mrs. Ford, since she's a Houston lawyer too. That might be why she knows more about the situation than the gossip columnists do. I put my phone down and shake my head at myself. I don't need to figure out everyone's story, despite the temptation to do so.

I glance over at Ivy, another story that's nagging at me. I'm just not sure I can really believe that Lawson doesn't have a thing for her. I mean, I'm perfectly confident in my body shape. I exercise … some and I try to eat right, but I'm never giving up ice cream, which I'm pretty sure Ivy must have done to be so toned and have something like -1% body fat.

My phone rings next to me, and I pick it back up to see a video call from my twin brother, Caleb. He scowls as soon as I answer. "I forgot you were on the beach. I can't look, Car."

I laugh. "You only had to say the word and I know Jett would've bought you a ticket."

"Jenna would've killed me."

It's true. My sister is stressed more than she should be about Jett bringing her family and me to Maui. I'm not sure what she doesn't understand about 200 million dollars. Sure, that's over five years, but he's guaranteed 90 million, even if he never plays another game for the Pumas. That's not even counting all the endorsement deals that rolled in after they won the championship. Jett has plenty of money for this, and he wants to spend it on his family. For heaven's sake, he bought them a house she refuses to accept. I need to figure out if this is just stress from her GetAwayHome spilling over. Devin doesn't seem to care about his brother being everyone's sugar daddy.

"Who's that?" Ivy asks, leaning over to check out my screen and tipping down her sunglasses. "Hi!" she says in a friendly way I've come to expect from her, even in the short time I've known her. At dinner last night, she talked to everyone, it seems, like she's known them forever—even though Lawson just got traded to the Pumas at the end of last season.

It strikes me that she's probably already talked to Ford and possibly his wife. Could I find a way to bring it up?

No. I don't need to know.

"Hey." Caleb smiles at her and waves at the screen, because again, what man wouldn't with Ivy beaming at them?

"This is my brother, Caleb." I tilt the screen toward her.

"Brother?" She grins.

"Yup. What's up?" I ask him, turning the phone back toward me.

His disappointment is evident, and I try not to roll my eyes. "Wondering if you were serious about that offer to share rent someplace in Houston," he says.

"Offer?" I chuckle. I basically begged him. I'm staying in the guesthouse at Jenna's for right now, but if I want to stick around, I can't afford a place on my own. Especially without a job. "Of course."

"Mom's driving me crazy."

I bite back a chuckle. Caleb is the most amazing IT expert, and he bought our parents' house a long time ago so they wouldn't have to worry about it. He lives in a finished apartment in their basement, but he can do his job from anywhere, which is why I asked him to come to Houston.

"What now?" I put my arm behind my head to prop myself up on the cabana pillow.

"She's set me up on no less than four dates in the last week. There're more to come." He widens his eyes at me.

I let out a laugh, and I look over to see Ivy's shoulders shaking. "Are they … good dates?" I ask. I won't be shallow and ask outright if they're attractive women, but I'm curious.

"They're fine," he huffs. "But they're obviously Mom's choices. A doctor, a lawyer … one of them is a bank CEO."

I whistle at the power players Mom rounded up.

Caleb shakes his head and goes on. "She's still obviously worried that I live in her basement, and—despite buying her house—that I'm in danger of not being able to support myself."

I laugh again, but before I can answer, Ivy asks, "Would she approve of a life coach?" She smirks at me.

Caleb's eyes widen again, but this time in surprise that the beautiful woman next to me is blatantly expressing interest. And maybe I do need to rethink my attitude about her and Lawson being "just friends." Maybe this is a really good excuse to make her tell me everything she knows.

How will I work Wylie Ford into that?

"I'm old enough not to care what my mom approves of," Caleb drawls, and Ivy's grin widens.

She leans back. "Maybe I'll see you in Houston."

"Maybe." Caleb swallows, and we stare at each other, having one of those silent twin conversations. "So, should I look at some apartments?" he asks. He knows I wasn't far along in my plan to reunite us in Houston. I shoot him an *obviously* look, and he smiles back.

We chat a moment longer, and Caleb hangs up to get back to work.

"He's gorgeous, Carlie," Ivy says when I hang up.

"I'm shocked you think so," I say sarcastically. I'm okay with them flirting, but I do need more information on Ivy before I let her steamroll Caleb. The fact that I've only known her for a day or so and can already read that she has a strong personality speaks for itself. And I have to figure out what's really going on with her and Lawson.

"He looks like your sister," she says.

I nod. "There's an obvious split in our family. He and Jenna are clearly our mother's children, no doubt about it. I look just like my dad."

She doesn't move from her relaxed position on the cabana when she says, "I'm not dating Law."

It doesn't surprise me that Ivy is blunt like this, but it still takes me off guard. "Oh."

"Everyone always thinks we're dating, and I don't blame people. I moved to Houston when he got traded, and I'm in Hawaii on vacation with him, but we really are just best friends."

I roll my head toward her. It's one thing if she doesn't feel that way about him, but does he have feelings for her? Would she know if he did? "And Lawson—"

"Law. Please just call him Law. He doesn't really like being called Lawson." The way she pinches her lips says there's more to why, but she doesn't share this. At least she has some boundaries.

Unfortunately.

"No. Law doesn't have feelings for me either. Cross my heart."

All I can think is how people always say that men and women can't just be friends, and that won't leave my head. "You moved to Houston with him." It seems so crazy that she uprooted her life for someone who's just her best friend.

"Caleb's going to do it for you," she points out.

"He's my brother. My twin." It's different.

Her eyebrows jump when I say twin, probably because we don't look alike, as she already mentioned. "Law is like my brother. Coming to Houston was difficult for him, and he needed my support. Like your brother, I can work from anywhere. I'm not planning on staying here forever, but I wanted to be here for him. And he brought me to Hawaii because he doesn't really know anyone on the team yet. Also, I begged."

I can't blame her there. It's not like I asked Jett to bring me to Maui, but I made no move to talk him out of it, like Jenna probably wishes I had.

We lie there in silence for a little while before Ivy asks, "What are you doing next? Are you looking for another preschool teacher job?"

She's such a life coach. I wonder if she ever turns that off. But her interest in my life is something I can relate to, so I don't mind sharing. "I'm not sure yet." I smile and listen to the waves for a second, thinking about how just two weeks ago I was knee-deep in four-year-olds and my only moments of peace were recess. Even then, I could still hear them outside my window. "Maybe I can find a preschool on a beach somewhere, because I really like this."

"You're perfect for Law," Ivy says, but before I can respond, a waiter comes up the sand toward us, asking if we want anything. I've never been to an all-inclusive resort like this, so the free food and drinks at all times is something I'm really enjoying. Ivy and I both order virgin drinks—it's a little early in the day to start drinking, especially when I'm not sure yet what I want to do once I drag myself off the beach.

"No one's perfect for anyone," I say when the waiter leaves. I direct my gaze to the ocean, knowing that Ivy's the type of person to try and dig into that statement. "All relationships take something."

She makes a little humming sound and shrugs. "I just meant that Law really loves just relaxing on the beach, and I'm already getting a little antsy. It's perfect and all, but I can't help but need to *do*." She picks up her phone, like her last statement was an explanation. From the glance I give her, I see that she's opened an email app, scrolling slowly through a list of new emails. As I settle back into my relaxing, I can see her occasionally typing from the corner of my eye.

"Should have known you wouldn't be able to sit out here for long without working too," a voice says. Law steps around to the front of the cabana and tilts his head at Ivy.

"I have to get some things done. Answering emails while I lounge on the beach sounds perfect to me. In fact, Carlie and I were just talking about how we were going to make this our permanent office somehow."

Law sits on the edge of the cabana at Ivy's feet. "I could maybe believe that of Carlie, but not you."

Ivy scoffs. "I've got Wi-Fi, and this place isn't bad. I could do everything from here and not feel an ounce of guilt."

Law smiles and sneaks a look at me. I smile back, but I don't know if he catches it with how quickly he looks away. "What are you doing in Houston, then?" he asks her.

"You'd miss me," she mutters. She's already back to her emails.

Law turns his attention to me, though his gaze keeps darting around. "I'm going on a pretty laid-back hike in a couple hours. Want to come? I talked to Jett because it's an easy one for kids too, and they'll probably like the waterfall and pool at the end."

"I'd love to." I'm not just agreeing so quickly because I want to spend some time with Law. I'm basically the nanny here, and even though Jett told me to do my own thing today, that he had the kids, he and Ava could use help if they're taking them on a hike.

Nanny. That's a thought. I bet Jett knows some people that might be able to hook me up with a gig like that. Somewhere with a beach. The idea is really growing on me.

"Perfect," Law says. "Ivy? You want to come?"

She shakes her head. "I'm doing lunch with one of your teammates. He's interested in my services." She wiggles her eyebrows like it's naughty, but Law and I just laugh at her.

I'm drawn to both of them, and I have to admit that part of the draw is figuring out why Law and Ivy aren't dating. It's so cliché, but I like having hard answers, or at least I like knowing that somewhere there's an answer to things that I can find with enough work, even if I don't know right now. Maybe it's just a softer version of the crime stories I'm obsessed with. The murderers that are still loose or the people still missing are so far from hard answers that I should hate it all, but somehow having evidence in front of me and a trail of clues makes up for that. There'll be answers someday for everyone's case.

Like with my ex, Xavier. It took years for his past to catch up with him, but it did. That's a case I've had to shuffle to the back of my mind all the time, and I do it again now. I'm past obsessing over what he did. Also, I'm on a beach.

I'd rather figure out what's going on with these two best friends before I let Law's handsome face and broad shoulders confuse me.

"In the meantime," he says, "do you two mind if I join you?"

"Of course not," Ivy says, frowning at her phone. "You can keep Carlie company while I schedule a few consults."

Law grins at me before ducking away to grab a lounge chair and pull it up in front of the cabana.

"Has she always been like this?" I ask once he's settled in. This is the perfect way to get into how long they've known each other and answer some of the questions swirling in my brain about them. I mean, if Law's interested in me, my curiosity about him and Ivy is fair game, right?

"Yes." Law dons a pair of sunglasses, and the effect makes me want to fan my face. Keeping my distance could be hard when he looks this good. "She got straight A's through college because she never quit moving."

"I didn't have good looks and muscles to skate by on," she says, but she looks up and winks at him, probably more of an indicator to me that she's teasing than to him. I'm not sure how long Law's been playing professional football, but it still means that he and Ivy go way back.

"And you're the more laid-back one?" I guess, nodding at

Law. Which seems crazy. It takes a lot of discipline to reach a professional level in football.

"I'm better at relaxing, yes. Mostly because Ivy taught me how to do that better." He smiles.

I laugh. "Ironic. You two seem so different. How did you meet?"

Ivy glances at me, her eyes narrowing ever so slightly like she might have guessed exactly what I'm doing. She gives a soft little sigh and goes back to her phone, letting Law answer.

"Ivy tutored me, and then I guess you could say I was her very first client. She's helped me navigate a lot of complicated stuff." Law tilts his head back as he answers, like he's pretending to relax, but his shoulders pull together the slightest bit despite that.

"Tutoring?" That slips out in my surprise, but I don't know why. College athletes have a lot on their plate, and him being proactive about staying on top of it makes me admire Law.

He looks down at his hands before forcing his expression into something neutral. "My mom wanted to make sure that football didn't take over everything, just in case I didn't make it pro."

Tension hangs over his words. Between the way he talked about the complicated things Ivy has helped him with and her mention of how he doesn't like to be called his full name, it all points to a difficult relationship there. That means I'm not sure what to say next. Something benign about his mom caring about his future will feel dismissive of whatever isn't being said.

"What subject?" I finally ask.

"Stats," they answer at the same time.

"Ugh." I reach out a fist toward Law. "Who didn't need help with that? My brother Caleb is the only reason I passed. Here's to, thankfully, knowing geniuses."

He bumps my fist. "You had to take stats for your teaching degree?"

I make a face. "Yeah. So dumb, and my attitude didn't help. It was a general requirement at the school I was at."

"You have my deepest sympathies." Law chuckles and fist-bumps me again.

"Auntie! Auntie!" My nephew Hudson's voice comes from somewhere behind the cabana, and I move aside one of the curtains to see him and his brother, Ian, running toward me from our suite just up the beach. Jett follows, scooping up four-year-old Ian when he biffs it in the sand, laughing so that Ian's cries end almost instantly.

"Hey, Hud." I pull him onto the cabana when he reaches it, hugging him close.

"We get to go see a waterfall, Auntie," he exclaims. "Wanna come?"

"Of course."

"Let's go!" he shouts, pulling on my arm to get me off the cabana.

"We have to wait until after Ruby's nap, remember?" Jett says, coming up next to us.

Hudson scowls. "Oh yeah." Then he spots my piña colada on the wooden tray between me and Ivy, and crawls over me toward it.

"Hud—" Jett starts toward him, but I wave Jett off.

"Non-alcoholic," I mouth.

Jett nods but has a resigned smile. "That's what started this in the first place. Devin had one last night and let both boys drink it with him, so now they think all of them are safe. Colby had to scramble to keep him out of his last night."

I bite back a snicker at that. "I'll be vigilant. Promise."

Jett sets Ian down, and once Hudson is done drinking half of my piña colada, he scoots off the cabana to join his little brother playing on the beach. Jett drags another lounge chair toward us, and he and Law fall into football talk. I enjoy listening as I settle back against the pillow behind me. Both Jett and I have eyes on the boys as we chat and Ivy continues her work, but they're content to play in the sand for now, digging with a bag of toys that Jett brought with him.

"How long has Ruby been napping?" I ask during a lull in Jett and Law's football talk. The little boys are going to be eager to go the minute she wakes up, so I've got to go put shorts and a tank on and dig my tennis shoes out of my suitcase.

Jett looks at his watch. "About an hour."

I slowly sit up. "That's my cue, then, to go get ready. She could be up any minute. She's been off since we got here."

Jett nods, and I throw my legs over the side of the cabana bed.

"I'll see you guys in a few," I say, waving at Law before I head up the beach. A few steps later, I hear the murmur of their conversation continuing, but when I glance over my shoulder, Law is watching me walk away.

CHAPTER 4
LAW

Jett rented a big SUV, and since his brother and wife are off doing something as a couple, Carlie and I pile into it with him and Ava instead of taking the sedan that I rented. I spent the last thirty minutes trying to decide if she'd accept a ride with me if I said I was taking it, or if she'd want to go with Jett and Ava to help with the kids. I finally landed on her wanting to help with the kids, but before I could even ask for a ride with them, Jett offered with a smirk. I've never been great at hiding what I'm thinking, although Ivy's helped me perfect a more neutral expression to help with PR stuff I have to do for football. I hate wearing all my feelings on my sleeve, but when it comes to women I'm interested in, it's not always a bad thing. Ivy says that she can tell Carlie is skeptical of us just being friends, so that means I'll have to be extra obvious about how much I like Carlie. That's okay with me. I don't like games. My mom played enough with me while I was growing up to last a lifetime.

Ivy's helped me come to a neutral place about my mom and our relationship, so I can see how her less-than-perfect relation-ship with my dad, a congressman, and then his subsequent death plays a part in how much she has to control perception. Her taking over his seat on his death, and then winning reelection twice in a row, has probably cemented it all into her personality now. It would just be nice if she could lay down her act at least with me and my brother.

Carlie and I sit in the middle row of the SUV with two-year-old Ruby between us in her car seat. The three McCombs children have now all been properly introduced to me, and I can see why Jett's happy to help his brother out by hanging out with them during this trip. They're the most well-behaved children I've ever seen, although admittedly I don't have a ton of experience with kids. But my mom never misses a chance to talk about what terrors Malcolm and I were.

Carlie sings a song with Ruby as we pull away from the resort and head toward Paia. The trail will be just a little ways past the town. I can't keep my eyes off Ruby and Carlie as Ruby giggles with delight over all of Carlie's exaggerated movements. Even the boys in the back bounce around to Carlie's voice. She must have been an amazing preschool teacher, so I'm now more curious than ever about why Ivy told me she's a *former* teacher. Carlie has so much energy, and she's so thrilled by everything with the kids, that I can't help thinking about how excited she'd get on the sidelines of a football game, cheering for me.

The hike is as low-key as I was told, so the boys walk the whole way. Jett has a backpack that Ruby rides in for most of the hike. Carlie and I take charge of the boys and walk side by side, while Jett and Ava hold hands and take the lead.

"Think they'll get married soon?" I ask in a low voice, tilting my head toward them.

Carlie smiles softly and nods. "Can you keep a secret?"

I furrow my brows. "Of course."

"Look at Ava's left hand."

I squint, and sure enough, there's a modest diamond ring there. I blink in surprise. Jett McCombs is one of the most popular quarterbacks in the country. How does everyone not know? "Did that just happen since we got here?" I ask. I can't think of another explanation.

Carlie chuckles and shakes her head. "No, they've been engaged for a while. Only family and friends know. Jett trusts the teammates that are here, so she's been wearing her ring. They knew pretty much right away. They were engaged eight years ago, so it didn't take long for Jett to propose this time around."

"I'm happy for him. For both of them, that they found each other again." I watch them for longer, jealous of the way that Ava leans into him, how she stares up at him as they walk, trusting that he'll keep her from any harm on the trail, easy as it is. After everything I've been blessed with in this life, do I deserve to ask for that kind of happiness as well?

"Yeah," Carlie agrees, watching them with the same wistful expression I must be wearing.

"Ivy says you just moved to Houston." I change the subject, eager to know more about Carlie. Everyone knows Jett's story with Ava—how they broke up while he was playing for University of Nevada, and how Colby and Gabriella's wedding brought them back together again, bumpy as the road was. I don't need to discuss that during one of the few opportunities I have alone with Carlie.

"Yeah, I'm staying in the guesthouse at Devin and Jenna's for a bit, helping them with the kids while they get their new house ready. Jenna's a GetAwayHome host," she explains when I tilt my head in curiosity.

"Then you'll look for another teaching position? I think Ivy told me you teach preschool."

She shrugs. "I don't know. The place I was at in Arizona made life pretty stressful—the parents, that is, not the kids." She turns toward me with a mischievous smile. "Today I was thinking that maybe I should be a nanny to a family that likes to travel regularly to the beach."

"Not a bad career choice. I'm certainly enjoying the beach."

"And what about you?" she asks. "How do you feel about moving to Houston?"

Her expression is perceptive, which makes me guess that Ivy has said something vague to give away that Houston wasn't my first choice of teams to get traded to.

But my answer is automatic. I don't have the right to bemoan the fact that I'm living my dream, playing pro football, no matter where I am. It shouldn't bother me so much that the Blues didn't try to trade for me when my contract was up with the Rays, and I need to let it go. I'm on a championship team. I keep telling myself that's what matters, not my childhood dreams.

"I'm happy to be playing for a championship team. What more could a guy ask for?"

She studies me for a second, and I wonder if she sees through how much I have to force that. It's not a lie that this is a great opportunity, but if I continue to play at the top of my game, the chances of me getting what I've dreamed of since I was a little boy—playing for the Nashville Blues—will be slim. The Pumas won't want to trade me.

"It is a pretty big deal," she admits, but her tone is cautious.

I run through several things I have to be grateful for to banish the ingratitude crowding my mind right now, especially the bitterness that working hard hasn't gotten me exactly what I wanted. How can I not be happy with what I have? I have a good chance of winning a championship next season. Everyone believes the Pumas are only getting better.

The urge to admit to her that I was disappointed when the Blues didn't make an offer bubbles up, but I push it down. I don't want people, especially Carlie, to think of me as some rich guy whining over what he doesn't have.

Before I respond, I notice that Carlie is focused on a couple passing us on their way back down the trail. Their conversation is intense, by the looks of it. Carlie and I have been walking close enough that our shoulders brush as we walk, something I've been enjoying, but now I notice how tense they've become. The boys, jumping and playing on the trail as we walk, are fine. Ruby is singing happily from the backpack. I'm not sure what has Carlie's guard up.

"Everything all right?" I ask.

"Hmm?" She barely takes her gaze away from staring over her shoulder at the couple. "Um, do you think they're okay? Like, that she's okay?"

At the hint of fear in her voice, I stop, turning to watch the couple without making it obvious. It's probably just a regular argument, but Carlie's tone holds more than the usual concern over something like that. I glance at her, noticing how she's pressed her lips together and her brow is furrowed.

"Vacations can be stressful," I offer. I haven't been on a single one with my mom and brother in the last six years that hasn't involved at least a couple arguments. And the ones I remember from before my dad died held their fair share of my parents getting snappy with each other after long flights and little sleep.

"Yeah," Carlie agrees, but her gaze is still on them as we move slowly forward.

The woman shakes her head at the man and then starts laughing as she shoves his shoulder. "No. No, that's not how it went," the woman says, and he joins her laughter as they round a corner.

"You were right," Carlie says, forcing a smile and hurrying forward to catch up with the boys. In a couple strides, we're right behind them again. "You just never know how people really are, right?" She gives another glance over her shoulder, squinting at the bend where the couple disappeared.

It's too soon for me to ask why that's where Carlie's mind has gone after witnessing a mild argument—maybe a playful one?—between strangers, but my insides tense at the possibilities. What past experiences have her so invested so quickly?

"Ivy says you're a reader," Carlie says.

Her abrupt subject change takes me off guard, but I shake it off and then laugh. "I feel at a disadvantage with Ivy giving away all my secrets. We need to talk about you more."

She waves that away, her smile growing more genuine. "I want to know what you're reading. I love to read too, but with my job, I tend to do a lot of picture books." She chuckles.

"Even in your free time?" I raise my eyebrows, picturing Carlie curled up on a couch with *The Very Hungry Caterpillar*, as absorbed as I can be when I'm really into one of my books.

"Free time? Have you met a teacher before?" She winks and then shakes her head. "No, I read true crime for fun."

I can't stop the burst of laughter that breaks from me, and Carlie's smile widens. "True crime?" I repeat.

She shrugs, and for a second, her expression shutters before her smile breaks through again. "I got into it a few years ago, and now I can't get enough. I even had a fan blog for a little while, digging into stories that my favorite podcast did." She shrugs again, and a light stain of pink to her cheeks tells me she's embarrassed to admit that, but she did. Excitement wings through my stomach that she trusted me, even with this little bit. It has me ... hopeful.

"That's so cool. Everyone has different ways of detaching, right?"

"You're going to look up the blog, aren't you?" She covers her face with one of her hands, shaking her head.

"Will it be hard to find?" I bump her with my shoulder.

"I hope so." She bumps me back. "It's just ... my sister says I'm nosy."

"That's funny. Nosy girls are my type." I grin playfully at her, then realize what I just implied about me and Ivy. "I mean, I get along well with nosy girls," I say, trying to recover.

Thankfully, Carlie just chuckles. "I just want to know the story—about everyone," she admits with a self-deprecating shrug.

"I'm reading this book right now about historical conspiracies. You'd probably like it." I pull out my phone and show her the cover on my reading app.

She takes the phone from me, scrolling to the description.

"I've read about a lot of these." She grimaces, then forces a laugh. "Sometimes I don't take sleep as seriously as I should."

She hands the phone back and stares at the ground for several steps. I don't know what's going through her mind, but I wish I did. In this situation, Carlie certainly isn't the only nosy one. She makes me want to know everything about her.

CHAPTER 5
CARLIE

When we get to the waterfall and pool at the end of the hike, it's absolutely stunning. It's not crowded, but there are more than a few families and couples up here. Jett passes off Ruby to me, and he and Law take the boys to swim toward where the waterfall splashes into the pool. I shed my shorts and tank top to take Ruby into one of the shallower ends and glance toward Law, I guess hoping he notices me. His gaze flickers toward me, then away. It's the same swimsuit I was wearing earlier, a pair of high-waisted bottoms that does some nice things to shape my butt and a basic thin-strap top with turquoise and white stripes. Somehow it's different when I'm not lounging on the beach.

I set Ruby on my hip and wade out, finding a good spot where she can sit down and splash. Ava sits on a log that's lying nearby, setting her tennis shoes behind her and putting her feet in the water. I smile at the way she stares at her ring.

"Do you guys have a date yet?" I'm careful to keep my voice down. Jett and Law have caused a few people to turn and stare. When Jett first got into the water with the boys, I heard someone near whisper, "Is that seriously Jett McCombs?" When I glance up at them again, a man has actually approached, holding up his phone. Jett shakes his head, probably explaining apologetically that he doesn't take pictures with the boys, who are perched on Jett's and Law's shoulders, respectively.

"We talked about eloping this weekend, having Jett fly out his parents too, but this is the beach wedding that Gabriella didn't get. We didn't want to take away from that, even though she probably would have loved it, to be honest." Ava laughs. "Whatever we do will be small and spur of the moment. The family has all been warned. I don't want tabloid photographers stalking my wedding."

I scowl. I don't blame her. Jett has always been wary of social media and sharing too much of his personal life, and Ava has had her share of people trolling her and making life miserable. It's no wonder they want to keep this special moment of theirs private for as long as possible.

"That kind of sucks, not to get to plan a big wedding—especially when the groom is loaded." I shoot her a smile so she knows I'm teasing.

"Oh, it will still be a big deal." She wiggles her eyebrows at me. "I planned weddings for a while, and I know who to trust."

Ruby reaches for Ava, who scoops her up and then slides into the pool with her.

I lean back on my hands, my attention straying back to Jett and Law. "Is it hard, having everything under scrutiny?" I ask.

"It's different," Ava says, sympathy automatically crossing her expression.

I focus on the water, waving my hands back and forth. Jett and Devin are really close, so Jett is like a part of my family, meaning he and Ava know about Xavier and everything that happened. It'd be hard not to know about all of that. Xavier's arrest was huge news, and there were more than a few pictures of me.

"And Jett has always been a big deal, as long as I've dated him," Ava says. I'm glad she moved quickly past my five minutes of fame. "Even back in high school, everyone loved him. I'm used to it, mostly."

"Plus, he's so great, no one says bad things about him." I grin.

Ava scoffs. "Never," she agrees dryly, and we both laugh. There were so many memes last year when Jett threw two interceptions mere plays apart from each other. It did get brushed over quickly, considering the story that emerged later that day was a picture of Ava on the sideline with him and then the news that he'd reunited with his high school sweetheart.

I wish it was Jenna here so I could tell her how scared I am of finding out something about Law. I like him. Earlier, he took my wild imagination seriously. I don't know if he realized that he got a tiny bit protective after we saw that couple, and the concern in his voice didn't make me itch the way Ava's pity kind of does.

We all play for a long time at the pool before finally deciding to head back down the trail. The boys are exhausted now from swimming for so long with Jett and Law, so I take the backpack with Ruby, and the boys ride on Jett's and Law's shoulders.

Considering how much I'm around kids, it doesn't surprise me that seeing Hudson with his arms wrapped around Law's face both delights me and makes him incredibly attractive. Especially the way he pretends to run into trees anytime Hudson covers Law's eyes.

I see us, in my mind's eye, the way we must look. Like we're a family. Before I can be too twitterpated with that idea, it strikes me that this *should* be me. With Xavier.

"Hey, you need me to take Ruby?" Law asks, startling me from those thoughts.

"What? No. I'm fine." I pat her back. She's sleeping, which isn't surprising. It's been go, go, go since we got here.

"You looked like maybe she was wearing you out." That concern is back, and it makes my chest flutter.

"You just want to show off. One on the shoulders, one on your back." I eye him playfully.

"There's someone on my shoulders?" Law says in mock surprise. He spins around like he's trying to find said someone, making Hudson giggle.

"I'm right here!" he keeps shouting, and then Law pretends to run into another tree.

I can't help my own laughter. Is falling for a guy because he's adorable with kids cliché? Because it's happening to me right now.

————

By the time we get the kids back to the resort, they're exhausted. Hudson and Ian fell asleep for a few minutes between the trail and Paia, but stopping to get ice cream woke them up for the rest of the trip. They're still ready to crash when Jett and I bring them into the room. By the time I get out of the shower, Jenna's snuggling with the boys in their room and tells me they're all going to have an early night.

I'm about to agree that I could use that too, when my phone dings with a text from Jett.

JETT

A bunch of us are hitting up a nearby food truck for dinner. Coming?

I laugh a little. I know who *a bunch of us* is going to include. Jett's playing matchmaker, which means he approves. That's comforting. But it doesn't stop me from feeling like I need to know more.

That I need to know everything.

"What is it?" Jenna asks softly. Both boys have fallen asleep, but she hasn't moved from where she's holding them on the bed.

I flip my phone around to show her the text.

"You going?" she asks, barely holding back a smile.

"I like him," I say, dropping softly into a chair near the bed.

Jenna's brows furrow. "But?"

"How do I know he's a good guy?"

Her face tenses in anger. "He's pretty famous, Car. People would know if he's a drug kingpin."

I swallow. Nobody knew that Xavier was. Nobody knew that his financial firm was a huge front and all the money he was making was dirty. Not even me, the woman he was going to marry. The woman who thought she knew everything about him, right down to the weird way he'd brush his teeth, floss, and then brush them again.

"He's not Xavier," I say, pushing myself up, but I'm not even sure I really believe that. Maybe he's not a drug dealer, but Law must have secrets. There's the whole situation with his family that he danced around this morning when he was talking about his and Ivy's friendship. And he's not telling me everything about his feelings on coming to Houston to play for the Pumas.

I remind myself that those are all normal things that people don't share right away in relationships—family problems, work issues. It doesn't mean he's hiding some big skeleton.

Jenna tilts her head over Hudson and eyes me. "The kids are all asleep, so we could walk down to the restaurant. Devin's just watching TV." She starts shifting carefully, but I put a hand up to stop her.

"I'm going to go with Jett and Law and whoever else is included in that 'bunch of us' reference." I chew on my lip. "It's okay for me to see where this goes, even if I'm cautious about it."

Jenna smiles a little bit, her expression proud like only a big sister's can be. "What are the chances you fall for two drug dealers?" she asks in a light tone, and I cover my mouth to quiet the sudden huff of laughter that escapes me.

I go with her trying to lighten the tone of the conversation. "Maybe I have a type."

Jenna tries to hold herself still as she chuckles at that, shaking her head. "Jett likes him, and he's crazy protective."

"Jett barely knows him." I have to point that out. Nobody here really knows Law well, except maybe Ivy.

Jenna shrugs. "Have fun."

I nod and slip out of the room.

CHAPTER 6
LAW

Once we get our food at the Little Aloha food truck that's just down the street from the resort, we put together two picnic tables to fit everyone. With as many football players as we have with us, it's still a little crowded, and I wish Carlie was sitting next to me instead of between Jett and Gabriella. The silver lining is that I'm sitting across the table from her so I can watch her without her catching me—too often. I force myself to hold her gaze and smile when she does instead of looking away in embarrassment. I get a smile back every time.

"Okay," Ivy says from where she sits between me and Alec Sanford, the running back she went to lunch with today. "I want to hear everyone's most embarrassing moment."

I almost groan. This is one of Ivy's favorite things to do when she works with groups. She says it helps people be vulnerable with each other and trust more. She's trying to help me, so I give a supportive nod. One of the pieces of advice she gave me when we were working through my responses to being traded to the Pumas was to be myself—all of myself. "People will relate to you more if you show you're human and you make mistakes," she said so frequently I almost made it the lock screen on my phone. It's something I'm still working on.

It surprises me that a ripple of tension seems to dance across Jett and Carlie. She's frozen, staring down at the Spam-and-rice meal she got.

Jett glances at her. "Well, mine is pretty obvious," he says, his voice forcing lightness. "You know, throwing two interceptions during the biggest game of the year besides the championship."

I laugh with everyone else and keep it to myself that I jumped out of my chair when the Blues cornerback intercepted the one in overtime, and then I moaned dramatically enough to make Ivy laugh out loud when Colby forced the fumble and the Pumas *still* scored a touchdown.

"Wait." Ava puts up her hands and turns to her boyfriend. *Fiancé*, I think with a secret look to Carlie, but she's still pushing around her Spam and rice. "You're just going to pretend like your embarrassing addiction to salt-and-vinegar chips with guacamole just doesn't exist?" Ava asks in mock astonishment.

Colby, Alec, and the other guys around the table groan again, all exclaiming in various ways how disgusting it is, and Jett defends himself.

He turns to Carlie. "Hey, tell them about that time you *tried to seduce* one of the preschool parents." He nudges her softly with an elbow.

It wakes Carlie up from whatever was going on, and she covers her eyes. "Oh my gosh." She straightens, her expression still mixed with something I can't put a finger on. Worry, maybe fear? I'm not sure.

But she jumps in. "It started with a text from one of the only single dads of my class, asking if he could meet me after hours. That totally sounds like a date, right? Right?" She looks around the table, and it's a relief to see her face more animated, but I can't help but wonder what was happening before. And why did Jett save her like that? Because it was totally a save, going first and then suggesting something specific for Carlie to tell. She was in some kind of spiral thinking about whatever her real embarrassing moment is, and it's selfish of me that I'm a little bit jealous. I want to be the one to save Carlie.

"Absolutely sounds like a date," Gabriella says, and everyone around the table nods.

"Thank you," Carlie says. "So I say sure, and he replies that he'll be at the school at four—which, in the mindset I'm already in, I read that he'll pick me up straight from the school. It's plenty of time for me to do a quick change and refresh my makeup. And by change, I mean into my little black dress that's way more—well, not preschool teacher professional—because this guy is *so* good-looking and *so* successful."

Alec whistles from beside Ivy, and everyone laughs. I catch Carlie's eye and grin, probably a little wolfishly. I would like to know exactly what's not teacher-professional about Carlie's little black dress. Backless, maybe? I can picture her long hair brushing against her bare back and my arm around her, guiding her into a nice restaurant.

She looks away and draws a breath. It takes a beat for her to start again, and I hope it's because I've distracted her the way she distracts me. "Then he walks in wearing a pair of joggers and a T-shirt. And he asks me if I have a hot date."

Everyone, including myself, is grimacing at this point, because we all know where it's going.

"I know, I know," Carlie says, continuing. "I should have realized, but I thought he was being flirty or something, so I say, 'Yeah, but I'm wondering if I'm overdressed,' and he doesn't say anything. For, like, so long." She puts her hands to both sides of her face, and the pink in her cheeks says she's reliving that awkward moment. "I think he realized before I did what had happened, because he says, 'Did you think …' and it took me too long to be like, 'No, no, no, no. I'm going out with someone after this.'" She sits back a little and bites her lip. "Turns out he wanted to talk about his son's reading progress and what he could do to help him improve at home. So he's good-looking, he's successful, he's a great dad, and he transferred his kid out of my class the next day. I narrowly missed losing my job for hitting on a parent."

"He was a fool," Alec says, eyeing Carlie meaningfully. She blushes more. I murmur something along the same lines as everyone else, that of course she thought it meant a date, worded like that. I still can't stop thinking about Carlie, standing there in her little black dress, and that guy walking away from it. Insane. Yes, a fool.

Alec tells about the time he ended up on a date with two women, which we all rib him for not actually being embarrassing and more of a brag, and the conversation turns before anyone else has to go. But the exercise did exactly what Ivy wanted it to. Despite still being distracted by the beautiful, vulnerable, brave woman across from me, I'm interacting with the guys around me, laughing and sharing stories. This is why I brought Ivy, and it's why she decided to come to Houston. She can't help but take care of me.

I try to walk next to Carlie as we all head back to the resort, but she ends up in a group with Ivy, Gabriella, and Ava, all of them wanting pictures of the guy that turned her down for a date. At least she gives me an apologetic look as they herd her forward. That's something. I'll have to have a talk with Ivy about betraying me, though.

I walk back to the hotel with Jett, and since Colby hangs on to Gabriella's hand despite her being with the girls, and Alec has joined them as well, we're basically alone.

"I'd bet money that's not really Carlie's most embarrassing moment," I say.

Jett gives a mirthless, short laugh. "Carlie's most embarrassing moment is a lot more serious than a fun story to tell around a table of people she hardly knows." He doesn't add to it, and I don't push.

"That was nice of you to help her out like that." What I've

learned of Jett in the past few days has just made me like him more and more. The quarterback is often seen as a leader on the field, and Jett is definitely a leader off the field as well.

"Her sister married Devin when I was still in high school, so I've known Carlie a while. Our families are close. Right now Jenna and Devin have the only grandkids on both sides, so we end up doing a lot of family things together, just to make stuff simple."

I can easily picture Jett and his family having a great time together, probably without the tension that seems to accompany anything Malcolm and I do with my mom. "That sounds amazing."

"It is pretty nice."

We walk in silence for a minute, maybe both of us hoping the women up ahead of us will break up. They're laughing at something on the phone now, so that's probably a vain hope.

"I saw Ava's ring," I say, avoiding that Carlie pointed it out. I don't think Jett will care, but just in case, I don't want to throw her under the bus. "Congratulations."

He grins. "Thanks. It was seven years coming. Wishing I hadn't been so stubborn."

"Seven years is a long time to wait for the girl of your dreams." I smirk at him.

"Too long, for sure."

I wait for him to tease me about Carlie, say something like how I shouldn't wait too long for her, but he doesn't say anything for several seconds. I try not to shift uneasily. The silence isn't exactly uncomfortable, but Jett and I don't know each other well enough for it to be comfortable. We come to the entrance to the resort, and Ava breaks away from the group ahead of us, coming back toward Jett.

"Take things slowly with Carlie, okay?" he says before Ava gets to us.

I nod at him, agreeing without saying anything since Ava is

already slipping her hand into his. I look up, seeing that Gabriella and Colby are breaking away too, heading toward the beach. I hope that Ivy and Alec have made some kind of plan too, but Alec walks on one side of Carlie and Ivy on the other. I sigh. I did spend a good chunk of the day with her, and Jett just got done telling me not to rush things. I can totally do that.

CHAPTER 7
CARLIE

Jenna and Devin take their kids out on a glass-bottomed boat the next day, so I'm left with most of the day to myself. I use it wisely by sleeping in. Tonight is the main event of vacation—a special ceremony on the beach for Gabriella and Colby and then a party afterward. I tried to get out of it well ahead of time by offering to watch the kids, but everyone nixed that idea. The kids will be at the resort daycare, watching a pirate show that the resort puts on. Devin or Jenna will pick them up when the ceremony's over and put them to bed, but since the party is on the beach right in front of the building that houses our room as well as most of the rest of the team that's here, Jenna and Devin will just bring a monitor out and check on them from time to time.

That means I'm going to this party.

It's not that I don't want to. I don't know Gabriella and Colby very well, but I've spent some time here with them, given that they're good friends of Ava and Jett. And I am looking forward to spending some more time with Law. It's just … we barely know each other, so how do we get to a point where he opens up about who he is and I can start trusting myself a little more? Last night, if it was just me and him at that table and he asked about my most embarrassing moment, I think I would have told him the truth. Sure, I was super embarrassed that I misunderstood that parent, but it pales in comparison to having your picture in the news, people talking about how your fiancé is a drug dealer, and footage of you being hauled out of the apartment with him because at that point they can't take a chance you aren't part of it all.

When I do finally get up, I eat breakfast on the ocean-view deck of our suite and dream about how lovely it would be if this was my every day. Maybe I should tell Caleb to find us a place to rent in Galveston. He can totally afford something right on the beach. But the truth is, the Texas ocean isn't the same as in Hawaii.

I grab my headphones, turn on my crime podcast, and head for the beach, walking sometimes briskly and sometimes lazily up and down it while the host of the podcast—who feels like my bestie at this point—details the frustrating lack of action by the police and family members in the disappearance of a fourteen-year-old girl. All the clues point to the older boy she was sneaking around with, and I find myself ticking them off in my head like everyone didn't already know that and they still did nothing. Anger boils in my chest as I listen, but it's a feeling I've weirdly grown to like. I can tell by the way the host tells this story that the stupid nineteen-year-old boy will be caught, and everyone will know what he is. I'll get the whole story.

Sometimes I find myself thinking about how this host would tell Xavier's story and how the end would be satisfyingly tied up. *After months of compiling evidence and careful video surveillance, federal agents move in to arrest Xavier Elliot in his Phoenix apartment, surprising him on a quiet night in with his fiancée Carlie Gallagher—who the FBI would later realize was an innocent bystander caught in Elliot's web of lies …*

Listeners would feel like the story wrapped up so nicely with the bad guy in the jail and the sweet fiancée saved from his terribleness. So how come it doesn't feel wrapped up neatly like that when that's all the truth?

Surprisingly, I don't encounter Law or Ivy on my long walk. They probably went to do something fun like Jenna and Devin did. Come to think of it, I don't even know where Jett and Ava are.

I do cross paths with Ford and his wife—until I realize it's not his wife. I glance back a few times at him and the woman he's with. She's blond, like Madelyn Wise, which is maybe why Jenna thought it was his wife the other night when we watched them walk down the beach. They're walking closer this time, and after a few steps of my own, I make my decision to follow them. I turn and walk up the beach behind them, looking totally casual. If there's an opportunity to find out more about this situation, I'm absolutely going to take it.

She purposefully bumps into him while laughing and then steps away, making the way she puts distance between them look intentional. His responding smile has a definite flirtatious vibe. I pause and hold my phone up like I'm taking a selfie on the beach, waiting for the perfect moment when the woman turns to say something to Ford and I can see her face. I snap the picture and send it to Jenna.

CARLIE

I don't think Ford brought his wife …

I've followed them clear down the beach, to a new group of hotels, when Jenna texts back.

JENNA

That's probably just a friend. I'm sure Ford is a good guy.

But I can totally hear the uncertainty in her tone even over text, even without an emoji. She's my sister.

And maybe Wylie Ford *is* a good guy, and this conversation is totally innocent, and he's taking a long walk on the beach with another woman for a completely explainable reason.

She could be his agent.

She could be someone on staff with the Pumas that Ford knows well.

She could be a family member of someone else on the team that he's helping entertain.

She could be any of those things and also be *more*.

I'm totally going to find out. Madelyn Wise deserves better than someone lying to her, no matter who she is. And if Ford is innocent, all the better.

I just can't imagine that he is. This doesn't look like innocent to me.

They walk up a sidewalk that leads from the beach into a restaurant, and I hesitate as I pass the sidewalk. They've noticed me multiple times. There's no way I can go inside. I walk for another ten minutes up the beach and then turn and head back like this ridiculously long beach walk was my intention the whole time. I slow when I come to the restaurant, hoping that Ford and this woman have a table outside or in front of the big windows facing the ocean.

No such luck. But I'm already convinced. There were enough flirty vibes while I followed them to make anyone suspicious. But there's no proof until I catch them kissing or something. Then I'm going right to Gabriella.

———

I spend the rest of the day lazily, sometimes feeling guilty that I'm not off parasailing or snorkeling or zip-lining or something, but mostly just enjoying how great it is to read a book on a cabana on the beach.

When Jenna and Devin and the kids get back, Devin entertains them on the beach for a while so Jenna and I can get ready. The ceremony has a color scheme, which I'm learning is a very Gabriella thing to do. The pictures will look gorgeous, with Gabriella in her white boho gown and everyone else in shades of gray with pale coral and teal accessories. My dress was a fortunate Amazon find, since I can't afford something better, but I ended up loving it. It's a pale pearl gray, off the shoulder with a flounce neckline, and the pale teal beaded necklace I found contrasts perfectly with my hair.

When we're finished, Jenna helps Devin with the kids, and then they go together to take them to the daycare, so I head down to the beach myself. There's a wooden arch standing alone in the middle of the area roped off, draped in pale gray fabrics and flowers in the ceremony colors. There are no chairs, but Jenna warned me that the ceremony would be short and Gabriella and Colby wanted people standing, so I'm prepared.

There are a few people milling about, and when I approach the area, a resort staff member asks my name, ticking it off a tablet before handing me a small electric candle. "Gabriella would like you to turn it on at the start of the ceremony," she instructs. The whole thing will look so gorgeous when it's photographed. Ava planned their wedding earlier this year, so I wonder how much she had a hand in the aesthetics of this.

I see Law before he sees me, which I'm glad for, because he looks so good. His suit is exquisitely tailored for him and is just a shade or two darker gray than my dress. I almost laugh when I see he has a teal tie that must be almost the exact color of my necklace. We'll look like a bridesmaid and groomsman. He turns as I stare at him, and our eyes meet. His broad shoulders rise as he takes a deep breath, and he tucks his hands into his pockets, making him look more like a model, if that's possible. A slow smile spreads across his wide lips as he takes the first step toward me, and my heart flares to life, warming me all over. His gaze is not just appreciative, not just in admiration of my looks. There's joy and excitement there that makes those same feelings dance through me. I want so badly to trust that Law is a good guy, that there's no dirty skeleton in his closet waiting to jump out and surprise me, but there's something with everyone.

By the time Law reaches me, I'm grinning ear to ear, regardless of my thoughts.

"You look stunning," he says in a low voice, leaning over to kiss my cheek lightly.

"Thank you," I say, staring up at him, a little giddy over the idea that he likes me.

He holds out an arm toward me, and I take it, still grinning. "Can I stand with you?" he asks.

"Of course. I'd really like that."

We don't walk very far, and for a moment we stand, watching the sun quickly descending toward the ocean. The setting is completely magical. This is why people fall for each other quickly in situations like this, why they get involved too fast. Half of my brain is chiding me for not heeding my own advice to be "twice shy," but the other half wants to know what it would feel like to have Law wrap his arms around me. To kiss him. To feel his hands pressing into my back and closer to him.

"How was your day?" he asks.

"Good. Relaxing." I'm not about to tell him about how I followed Ford and that woman for almost an hour. I know how that looks without an explanation as to why I'd care that he might be cheating on his wife.

And what exactly is my explanation? I just needed to know? It sounds stupid in my head, and I know it kind of is, but would Law understand that I don't want Madelyn Wise to go through what I did, even a tiny part of it, by finding out the person she loves isn't what he says he is? If I can spare her that, why wouldn't I?

"How about you?" I ask instead. I also don't ask where he was or why I didn't see him, even though I've been wondering all day.

He answers that anyway. "Ivy and I took a boat out snorkeling with some of the other guys on the team. It was amazing, so much sea life and just right there." He shakes his head and pulls out his phone. "Want to see?"

I don't like the jealousy that pricks at my stomach thinking about him with Ivy all day, and I force myself to shake it off.

They probably booked that excursion before they came. Maybe he would've invited me if they hadn't.

I lean in toward him. "Of course."

He scrolls through several photos, and I ooh and ahh over all of them. He even has a couple videos, and it's delightful to watch the colorful fish dart this way and that. I try to ignore the cozy pictures of him and Ivy and believe her that they really are just friends.

"That's so cool." I don't pull away from him until he tucks his phone back in his pocket. Did I mention that he smells spectacular? It's kind of sporty, but also with the barest hint of something tropical. Or maybe that's just the air around us. I can't say for sure.

"I heard about this great beach where we can watch sea turtles. Do you want to go in the morning?" he asks.

"Absolutely." I don't have to think about that answer. Still, I cringe a little when I can't help asking, "Would you mind if the kids come along? Probably Jenna and Devin too. I promised to help with them tomorrow since I had today to myself."

His expression doesn't even drop. His smile grows wider, and I am so smitten. "No problem at all. Jett and Ava will probably want to come too."

I tilt my head. My gut says he really is this good, that I'm not in danger of anything with him, but my heart still worries. There are still clues to find to put together the story of him. Still loose threads. "Thanks."

Devin and Jenna join us, and I smile at them, but I don't drop Law's arm. I like the closeness and the warmth of him.

I just like him.

CHAPTER 8

LAW

The party spreads to the restaurant after Colby and Gabriella say their vows, and though Carlie has dropped my arm, she walks next to me up the beach. There are finger foods set up in the restaurant, but the main attraction is the dance floor. Amid laughter from the guests, the first song is a rap song that Colby drags Gabriella onto the dance floor over, and they hop up and down, joined by teammates and other guests within thirty seconds.

Carlie turns to Ava, laughing as she watches. "Tell me someone's going to post this."

Ava already has her camera up, grinning ear to ear. "Mmm-hmm. Gabriella can't put it on her account, but I'm sure it will send the right message when I post it."

Jett chuckles. "Maybe I should."

Ava widens her eyes. "Oh my gosh, would you, babe?"

He takes Ava's phone, turning it around to film him dancing with her to the song. Pretty soon they've put the phone away and head for the dance floor.

"Did I miss something?" I ask, looking down at Carlie.

"A Houston influencer blasted Gabriella last year for having this song on her wedding playlist. It was some stupid political thing that has to do with book banning." Carlie smiles as she watches everyone dance ridiculously and Colby shouting over the top of every swear word to bleep them out. "The woman implied that Gabriella approves of kids being able to listen to stuff like this without parental supervision. She was just looking for trouble."

It's an open secret that Gabriella's on track to run for Congress in the next few years. My mom has even talked to me about it. She's all for helping Gabriella make the right connections and was excited when I got the contract with the Pumas. She's been on me to make an introduction.

"Looks like Gabriella's going to be just fine." I grin. Jett has the camera up again, filming a good chunk of the Houston Pumas football team bouncing to this song, with Gabriella in the middle of them. I can't wait to see what Jett posts about it. "So," I say. "Food or dancing?"

"Food." Carlie tugs on my arm, and I follow instantly. "Always food first. But we'll dance later?" She raises her eyebrows in question.

"Absolutely. I've been looking forward to it."

We fill our plates and sit down away from the dance floor so we can hear each other talk.

"Spam again?" I ask with a smirk as Carlie picks up a Spam musubi.

"Unashamed." She grins as she bites into it. "I'm sure, as a history buff, you know all about Hawaii and Spam and World War II, right?" she says when she finishes chewing.

"Obviously."

"It would be remiss of me not to celebrate it properly." She takes another bite and then says, "I'm going to need more of this. It's amazing."

"Should I go get you some?" I scoot my chair back, ready to serve at her beck and call.

She shakes her head and waves her hand. "No. Sit down. Tell me your favorites." She nods at my plate.

I relax, grateful to have these moments with her, uninterrupted. I'm more than happy to have her family come and see the turtles with us in the morning—the McCombs kids will love it—but I hope that before we leave, she'll let me spend more alone time with her. It's hard to remind myself that Jett thinks I should take this slow. He has good reason, I'm sure, and it's only been a few days since I met Carlie. There's no reason to rush anything. Even if my desire to brush kisses over her bare shoulders says otherwise.

"It's hard to choose between these teriyaki BBQ meatballs or manapua." I break open one of the breads with the pork char siu filling.

"I thought they were just rolls!" she exclaims, eyes brightening at the meat inside. "I will also need one of those."

Her enthusiasm for the food is contagious. I have three on my plate, and I've already eaten one, so I offer her the unbroken one.

She tilts her head, but then smiles and accepts it. "Do you think we'll actually be able to dance once we're done with all this and the obligatory seconds?" she asks, motioning to the food around us.

"I hope so. I'll carry you if necessary." My phone rings, and I pull it out to check the caller. I frown. It's Chad. "I'm sorry." I scoot my chair out. "I think I should take this. It's my neighbor, and it could be something with my house."

"No problem. Easier to stuff my face without you watching me." She waves me away with a reassuring smile.

I stand and move away from our table before I answer. "Hello?"

"Law. Thank you so much for answering." Chad's voice sounds equal parts exhausted and grateful. "Can I ask a huge favor?"

"What's up?" I'm relieved that he's not calling about my house flooding or on fire or something, but I do hope he makes this quick.

"I need someone to watch the girls last minute. They couldn't stop talking about you last time you helped me out, and I need someone ASAP. Is there any way you could swing it?"

I grimace. Chad's wife left a couple months ago, and he's been treading water ever since. He has a demanding job that requires him to be available at all hours, but he's a devoted dad too. "I really wish I could, Chad. I'm in Hawaii with my teammates, though."

"Oh yeah. Forgot about that." Chad sighs, and I hold back a chuckle. It's not like I expect him to keep up with my schedule. "I need to just give in and get a nanny. But it's just one more thing on the list that I keep meaning to get to."

My gaze strays to Carlie. Ivy has taken my seat at our table, and they're laughing together while Ivy eats the food from my plate. Normally, I wouldn't care at all about that, but what signal is it sending Carlie? I've already noticed how she's aware of everything around her, and there's a look in her eyes when she studies me and Ivy. I think she believes Ivy and I are just friends, but this won't help if there's any niggling doubts.

I shake my thoughts back into place. "I might actually be able to help you there. I know someone who might be looking, and she's got some great credentials."

"Is she in town?" Chad asks.

I grimace again, wondering if I'm helping at all. He sounds so hopeful. "Um, no. She's here in Hawaii too. She's friends with some of my teammates, but she used to be a preschool teacher at a fancy private school in Arizona."

"Oh." Chad sighs again. "Well, if she's interested, I'd love to interview her when you guys get back. I need to start getting my life back together, and I have to admit that I need help with my girls. They're my priority."

"Have you been talking to Ivy?" I can't help asking. It sounds so like her.

He laughs, the first time this whole call. "She brought over cookie-decorating stuff for the girls the other day, and we might have chatted for a bit."

"I'll talk to my friend. In the meantime, call Shelby's mom. She wants to help, and she doesn't blame you." I say the second part gently. His mother-in-law, for now, has dropped in a couple times when I've been around. She's careful, something I picked up on right away thanks to growing up around my mom, but in a different way. She doesn't want to step on Chad's toes, and her expression usually holds the guilt I suspect comes from being the mother of the woman who left.

He blows out a breath. "You're right. Thanks, Law. I'll talk to you when you get back."

"Anytime. See you, Chad." I hang up and head back to my table.

"What was that about?" Ivy asks, making no move to vacate my chair. We might have to have a talk about proper wing-woman skills. She took off with Carlie last night, and even though she came to the rescue to entertain Carlie while I took that call, she doesn't look like she's leaving any time soon to give me alone time.

"Chad needed some help that unfortunately I couldn't give him."

Ivy frowns and sighs in sympathy. "Chad is Law's neighbor. His wife left recently, and he's been struggling to deal with his demanding job and now being the full-time parent. I think he's used to being the guy on top of everything, and he's struggling not to have gotten things together," she explains to Carlie.

Carlie nods. "That's hard. I can't imagine not being around my niece and nephews as much as possible, so leaving my kids is unfathomable. But you never know the other side of the story, right?" She shrugs, and her thoughtfulness for what Shelby might have been going through steals more of my heart.

"Amen," Ivy agrees, picking up one of the BBQ teriyaki meatballs from my plate.

"And speaking of all that, what would you say if I might

have gotten you a job?" I ask Carlie, leaning against my former chair. Her eyebrows rise in interest, and I continue. "Chad needs a nanny. He doesn't live on the beach …" I shrug at her, and she feigns a disappointed sigh. "But his girls are cute, three and five, and he's desperate. He wants to interview you when we get back if you're interested."

Her face lights up. "I'm absolutely interested. I loved my teaching job, but I'd also love to try my hand at something different too. Thank you so much for thinking of me, Law." She reaches toward me and takes my hand, squeezing it.

I want to hold on to it, feel the warmth of it in mine for the rest of the night. "Of course. You're the only potential nanny I know, and I couldn't keep letting Chad down in that phone call," I say.

She drops it as she laughs, and I miss it instantly. I give up on getting my chair back and find another one to scoot close to the too-small table. On the upside, I'm sitting very close to Carlie, close enough that by shifting my right leg I can rest it next to hers.

Bonus, she doesn't move away.

"Why did his wife leave? Do you know?" Carlie's gaze darts between me and Ivy.

"Not a lot," I say. "I only met her a couple times after I moved in before she left. There was some definite tension between them, but they seemed like a normal married couple to me." I shrug.

Ivy shakes her head. "Law doesn't actually know what a normal married couple is." I freeze, and Ivy instantly sends me an apologetic look, which I nod at. I get it. Carlie does already feel like a close friend, and that Ivy would slip and say something like that makes sense. "I think Shelby was overwhelmed," Ivy says quickly to cover up what she said, but I can feel Carlie's gaze on me even though I'm avoiding looking at her.

"Are the girls difficult?" Carlie asks, which I don't blame her for. And I'm also glad she doesn't push for more about why Ivy said what she did.

Ivy shrugs. "It's hard to say. We haven't spent a lot of time around them. They act out, for sure, but I get the feeling it's out of upheaval and trauma right now. Chad's job requires him to be away a lot, something that's also good for you to know, and I think that's probably part of it. In the few times I met her, Shelby didn't seem like she enjoyed being a mother." Ivy smiles sadly.

"Not everyone wants that, but there's a lot of expectation around that kind of thing, isn't there?" Carlie picks up some fruit from her plate and says, "It's so sad, though," before popping a piece of pineapple into her mouth.

Ivy and I both murmur agreements, and I can't help but think more about how unhappy Shelby seemed the couple of times I saw her. That happens in marriage. It's not all rainbows and sunshine one hundred percent of the time, but Ivy's always telling me I don't have high enough expectations for relationships. *No*, she would say, *it's not realistic to expect bliss all the time, but you can expect happiness most of the time.* I think she's too optimistic for her own good. Isn't that how life coaches are supposed to be?

I hold out a hand toward Carlie. "Should we go dance off some of this food so we can get some more?"

"Genius," she says, widening her eyes in appreciation and putting her hand in mine.

When we stand, I don't let go, using it to lead her toward the dance floor. Thankfully, the song changes to something slow as we approach.

I glance back at Ivy at our table, and she holds up her phone and mouths, "You're welcome." Of course she's already made friends with the DJ.

Maybe she's not such a bad wing woman after all.

CHAPTER 9
CARLIE

How soft the sand is on beaches in Hawaii never ceases to amaze me. It's almost like a powder. I abandoned my flip-flops just a few steps onto Kalepolepo Beach, and now I'm sitting back watching turtles slowly make their way toward the ocean. It's enchanting.

The whole gang is here, of course, because I couldn't stop my mouth from inviting them when Law suggested it. Jenna wouldn't have cared if I spent a few hours with him before helping her with the kids. But something about being alone with him scared me a little bit, and my words got the best of me.

But watching Ruby point and giggle and stomp her little feet in excitement is a lot to pass up on, even if Law probably did want alone time. Devin and Jenna have their kids in a little group with them as we watch, and they're sitting far enough away that it almost feels like Law and I *are* alone. They could be just another family on the beach. Except for the part where Jenna keeps looking over at me and wiggling her eyebrows.

Sisters.

"This is really cool," I say in a hushed voice. In fact, except for the few times Jenna has caught my eye, I can't take my gaze off the turtles, no matter how slow their course down into the water.

"It's amazing." Law's already taken several videos, and of course pictures of us posing in front of the turtles. He's sitting with one of his arms bracing him behind me. It would be so easy to lean into him. Last night when we danced, I couldn't get enough of his arms around me and his hand in mine. We danced for a lot longer than I expected. He makes hanging out with his new team look easy, even though I know it's anything but for him. He says things about being the new guy all the time, and it surprises me that a successful pro football player can be insecure about it. What's the story there?

I didn't know a lot about Law before he came to the Pumas. I've really only started watching football since Jett went pro. So I've probably seen Law play when his old team played the Pumas, but I didn't take note. I've since googled videos of him, and watching him makes me think he can do it all. I gasped loud enough at one point when he hurdled another player that Jenna had come over to me on the couch to look over my shoulder. Pretty soon we had Law Card highlights playing on the TV in the suite.

I turn to watch him while his gaze is still intent on the turtles. He has a small, entranced smile, so similar to the one Hudson is wearing that I almost snuggle right up to him. And listening to the caring way that Law talked about his neighbor last night solidified even more that he's a good guy, but my own insecurities are real and not something I can just dismiss.

My brain can't stop bringing up the fact that Xavier seemed that way too. He was caring. He was kind. He loved to randomly pay for people's groceries in line ahead of him, always acting like it was some big contest to win when someone racked up a bill over a hundred dollars and he got to pay. I thought it made him sweet. Now I'm certain it was just guilt—him trying to balance his sins when that wasn't even possible. I haven't talked to him since they arrested him, so I have no idea how he justified any of it.

"Carlie?" Law's voice breaks me from my thoughts, and I realize I must have been staring at him—only I know I'm scowling, because he's frowning back and his eyebrows are furrowed.

"Sorry!" I hurry to smile back. "I was just thinking."

His expression smooths out, but he still raises his brows at me. "About?"

I want to tell Law more, but it still feels too soon. Like, what is the protocol for admitting that your ex-fiancé is serving twenty years on drug charges? Besides, my nephews and niece could interrupt at any time, or anyone else who came with us, for that matter. Telling Law about my felon ex is a conversation when I know we can be alone.

"I have a stupid ex," I say carefully. "And the experience with him has left me kind of irrationally cautious."

He nods slowly. "Jett did warn me to take things slow."

I groan and shake my head. "That's such a big brother thing, right? I mean, he's not really, but he's acted like it since Devin and Jenna got married."

Law smiles. "He sort of feels like everyone's big brother. A little bossy, expecting a lot, but protective."

"Yeah, that's Jett." I'm grateful Jett said something, even if it's a little embarrassing. Maybe it means that Law won't give up on me quickly if I have a hard time advancing the developing relationship between us.

I can sense that Law wants to know more. I would. I *do*. The comment that Ivy made about Law not knowing what a normal marriage looked like was intriguing, basically a siren call to my nosy heart. Probably something to do with his parents' marriage, and I want details. That's not out of the ordinary for someone I'm considering dating. Plus, despite Law's behavior toward me, I can't shake how close he and Ivy are. It's unfair, and probably jealousy. She's such a good friend to him. I can see that. If I had more details about them, it would probably soothe some of my jumpy nerves over this.

"I have a real brother," I say. "A twin, actually."

Law smiles, accepting what I can tell him about myself. "Ivy might have mentioned him." He chuckles. "I have a brother too. Malcolm. He lives in Nashville, near my mom."

"Are you from Tennessee?" I ask.

He nods. "Yeah, I grew up in Nashville."

I widen my eyes. "You're a Blues fan, aren't you!"

He laughs and makes a show of putting his arm around me, pulling me against him like he's trying to keep me quiet. "Why don't you announce that to my whole team?" he teases.

I scoff at him. "Jett's the only one here." I try to nod down the beach where he and Ava are sitting.

Law shakes his head and lets me go, but I keep my position right next to him.

"I can't believe you're a Blues fan," I say in a whisper. "Is that why you had such a hard time moving to Houston?" I hope he knows I'm teasing.

"Ha." His laugh is a little forced, but his eyes dance. "Of course that's why."

There's more there. I can feel it. Are we good enough friends that I can push this? Maybe that's also a conversation for when we're alone. When we know each other better. It's only been a few days, after all. So I change the subject instead. "And your dad?" I ask.

His jaw clenches, and I realize I assumed too much. My parents are still happily married, so all too often I expect everyone else to have a happy family life. I should have known better, considering the hints that have been dropped from both Law and Ivy.

"I'm sorry. I shouldn't have—"

Law holds up a hand. "It's a natural thing to ask about my family. Not prying. I want to get to know you better too." He pins me with a knowing stare, and I nod in acknowledgment of what he's saying. *Soon*, I promise in my head. "My dad died about six years ago," he says.

"Law! I'm so sorry for bringing that up." I put my arms around him in a side hug. "Forgive me."

He smiles, looking down at me with an expression I didn't expect. Understanding and kindness play across his features, and my heart says I'm being paranoid. He's perfect.

"It's fine, Carlie." He shifts, moving the arm that was braced behind me around my waist, and gently pulls me closer to him. "We weren't close. He was a senator for Tennessee for as long as I could remember, or in politics, at least. He was gone a lot."

I put my head on his shoulder. "He was still your dad. Your feelings might be complicated, but you still have them."

He rests his head against mine. "Yeah. I do."

We watch the turtles quietly for a while, and I'm so content here with his arm around me.

"And your family?" he asks. "Any more siblings besides Jenna and …" He looks embarrassed not to remember Caleb's name, which is silly. I didn't mention it, and if he knows it, it's because of Ivy.

"Caleb. And no. Just us three, and my mom and dad." I offer that last almost apologetically, making sure he doesn't have to make awkward guesses.

"Do they all live in Houston?"

I shake my head. "No, my parents live in Dallas. Caleb actually lives in their basement, but not in the way you think." I have to laugh. "He's in IT, and he bought my parents' house from them several years ago to make sure they're secure. The apartment is fully furnished and nicer than anything I've ever lived in."

"Ivy said he's thinking of coming to Houston?"

"You guys really are besties, aren't you? So you talk to her about everything?" I tilt my head back a little so I can see his face as I laugh about this.

He gives me a fake cringe. "I do. But in all fairness, it's really hard not to talk to Ivy about everything. She has a vibe that just makes you want to spill your guts."

"She's probably a really good life coach, then."

"She is. So, Caleb's coming to Houston?" Law isn't letting me off the hook here, and that's fine. Talking about my family is easy.

"I hope so. He wants a break from living with my parents, and I don't blame him. Plus, if I want to get my own place, I need a roommate. He's a good option. We can afford something a lot nicer if he's paying … *most* of the rent." I break into laughter.

Law joins me, and I like the sound of it from here next to him. It rumbles in his chest in a happy way that warms me.

We chat about the easy things until the turtles have all made their way into the ocean, and even then, no one rushes to leave the beach. Hudson and Ian play in the sand, and Ruby has fallen asleep on the beach blanket that Jenna brought for them to sit on. Sometime during the last thirty minutes, Devin has gone back to the rented Suburban to get the beach umbrella to shade the blanket. Jett and Ava meander up and down the beach, holding hands and stepping in the shallow waves.

And I cuddle with Law. These last few days, every chance I've had to spend time with him has been perfect. But that's one thing that happens on my true crime podcast a lot: the host pointing out that "their life seemed perfect," which is probably why I can't stop worrying about when the bubble will burst.

———

I spend the day helping Devin and Jenna entertain the kids, mostly on the beach, but we also take a trip to a nearby park so they can just run around and be their normal selves for a little bit. When we go to dinner, Law and Ivy are there, and we all sit at a big table together. Law sits next to me, and when everyone is mostly finished and we're all sitting back and chatting, he moves his arm to the back of my chair. I love every second of it.

Law walks with Devin and Jenna and me back to the suite, and my sister makes it too obvious that they're rushing inside to leave us alone to really set the right mood for a goodnight kiss. Besides, I'm just too nervous. Despite the great times we've had together today, I'm not quite ready for that step yet. If I let myself fall for Law too quickly—and I *know* my heart will be gone once I kiss him—it just means a bigger chance of getting my heart broken when I find out that he really is too good to be true.

He seems to sense the mood isn't right either, and he leaves me with a hug that I melt into. Yeah, kissing him is going to be so good. I can already imagine the way he'll have to curl over me, how his arms will lift me up into him, and how steady his firm chest will feel.

I must be the only woman on the planet who wouldn't dive headfirst into love with a guy like Law Card—a tall, strong, kind professional athlete, for heaven's sake, who also happens to be good-looking as all get out.

He pulls away and smiles softly at me. "Night, Carlie," he says, and his understanding expression somehow says that he gets it even without knowing.

Okay, it might be too late. I might already be falling, kissing or no kissing.

I watch Law stroll off in the direction of his hotel room, unable to wipe a contented smile from my face. But that's also how I notice Wylie Ford and his "friend" walking up the beach together. I drop my sandals next to the door of our suite, and step off the patio and into the sand.

Right away, I notice their hands keep brushing as they walk, and the looks between them have surpassed flirty vibes at this point. They're also obviously headed for the Blue Mermaid, the resort bar. A lot of the football players that came on this trip are family men, so there probably won't be very many hanging out this late at the bar, which is the reason Ford and the woman might not be acting just friendly anymore. This is totally my chance to find out more and get the proof I need to show his wife he's lying to her.

I pull out my phone and pretend to be paying attention to it as I meander behind them toward the bar. I don't know the woman he's with, and between me and Jenna, we're pretty sure she's not with the team either. Did Wylie meet her here at the resort?

They walk through an archway ahead of me that leads to the entrance of the bar. One thing that has struck me about the resort is how everything is open. Archways lead right into the tiled hallways that house everything from restaurants to offices. There are few doorways that lock, except those at the front of the hotel.

Two palm trees flank the doorway of the bar, growing up through the gap between this building and the next. The woman leans up against one, pulling Ford toward her by his lapels. I hold my breath to see if he resists, but he gives her a slow smile and leans in. I walk casually past, and then I hold my phone up like I'm taking a selfie with the palm trees, careful to see if Ford notices me. I'm wearing the dress from the celebration last night. I put it on for dinner because it's cute, even dressed down with a pair of flip-flops, and I wanted to wear it again. I don't know when the next time I'll get the chance to wear it will be once we get home.

The problem is that this dress might give me away as being with the football team, and Ford might recognize me and realize I know the people he's here with. If he spooks, I won't get a picture for evidence. Is there a chance he'll remember me from the day I walked up the beach behind them?

He and the woman are too busy kissing now to notice me, TBH. I angle the phone, trying to figure out how to get Ford's face in it. Frowning, I realize I have to walk around them, back where I came from, since that's the direction Ford is facing right now.

"Terrible lighting," I murmur, in case anyone is paying attention to me, and then I sidle around so that my back is now to the palm tree and the woman. I can definitely see Ford better now, so I snap a few pictures, but I need to get closer. I shuffle backwards, fiddling with my phone like I'm trying to get more of the palm tree in my picture.

Then my back slams into something, and I hear glass tinkling. I whirl around to see that I've run into a waiter, and glasses are rolling this way and that.

"I am so, so sorry," I squeak to the waiter, who crouches to gather things.

"Oh my gosh!" the woman with Ford says, and I duck my head, since I've totally called attention to myself.

From the corner of my eye, I see dress shoes join us, and I glance up to see Ford crouching down next to the waiter to pick up the scattered glasses as well. His gaze strays to my phone, which I've set aside, clearly in camera mode. Is he going to put two and two together? I was doing a good job of pretending to take a selfie with the front of the bar in view, so hopefully he bought that. And I don't think he's gotten a good look at my face, so maybe he doesn't know who I am. We've never actually met, just hung out at a few of the same gatherings with the team.

I grab my phone and straighten, leaving Ford to help the poor waiter, and hurry away from the mess I created, ducking inside a door around the corner. I shut it behind me, noting the tile floor of the bathroom, pressing my hand to my heart. It's thumping so hard I have to take a deep breath and hold it to see if I can slow it down. I've likely made Ford think more about me by fleeing the scene when he might have dismissed me if I'd just stayed to help like a normal person, but the drive to make sure he didn't see my face was just too much. I groan quietly and push open the door just enough for me to peek out and see if Ford and the woman are gone.

"It might be easier if I go out and see if the coast is clear for you," a voice says, and I jump, barely stifling a scream.

I whirl around. "Law!" I whisper-shout. "Wha-at do you mean?" Does he know I've been spying? How can he know what I was doing? And what is *he* doing here? I watched him walk toward his room.

He gestures around him, a big grin on his face, and I notice for the first time the wall lined with urinals. A small "eeep" escapes me as I realize I ducked into the men's bathroom to hide. I slap a hand over my forehead. This can't get much worse, can it? And why did it have to be Law who saw me?

"Ivy has gone into men's bathrooms on accident more times than I can count," he says with a chuckle. "Usually because she's following me and talking and not paying attention."

"I …" This is a much better explanation than telling him I was spying on his teammate and trying to escape from getting caught doing it. "Yeah," I finish lamely.

Law steps closer. "I'm happy to go see if the coast is clear so you can sneak out of here with no one the wiser."

My answering laugh is full of air, and odd enough sounding that Law tilts his head a little bit. "My knight in shining armor." I swallow, trying to get a hold of myself.

"Your wish is my command," he says, and his voice goes slightly husky. Man, if we weren't standing in a men's restroom, this might be the right time to kiss him. Only to distract him, of course, from reading too much into my weird behavior.

He pushes open the door and walks out, and I peer out after him, keeping the door open a sliver. He walks back toward me after only a moment. "There's a waiter around the corner mopping up something, but no one in this hallway."

"Is there anyone outside the bar entrance?" I ask.

He shakes his head. "The women's restroom is just there." He points down the hallway. "I don't think anyone will notice where you came from."

But Ford will definitely notice me if he's anywhere in the vicinity. "Okay." I slowly emerge from the restroom, hesitating and peering around me like maybe I don't quite believe I'm in the clear. "What are you doing here? I thought you went back to your room," I ask once we're standing together in the empty hallway, hoping I sound casual.

He nods toward the bar. "Their fries are amazing. Ordering some to take back to my room, and I'm just waiting on them now. Want to share with me?"

And go into the bar, where Ford and the woman will *definitely* notice me given how strange I acted? "I'm sorry." I grimace apologetically. "I actually have to get right back." I scramble for a good lie. "Jenna and I have a date to binge-watch some *How I Met Your Mother* episodes. It's our favorite. We never really get to do that anymore, so it seemed like the perfect vacation thing to do, you know?"

Law nods slowly at my rambling. I sweep my hair up into a bun on top of my head, using a black hair tie I keep on my wrist next to my watch. It'll change up my appearance a little so that Ford and the woman hopefully don't notice me. The walls of the Blue Mermaid are glass, and if they're sitting at a table, they'll have a full view of my exit. Law doesn't say anything about my hair change, but that's probably because even though it's getting dark, it's still warm and humid outside.

"Thanks for the rescue." I give him my most genuine smile.

"Anytime."

"So," I say. "Good night again."

"Good night." He leans over to hug me, which actually does a lot to calm my racing heart. After the way I acted on the hike the other day, and now this, he's probably rethinking if he wants to see me again.

I walk around the corner, shrugging my shoulders so the elastic on my off-the-shoulder dress slides up my arms, giving my dress what looks like a completely different neckline. I don't look back to see what Law thinks about that. Hopefully he's already heading into the bar to get his fries.

As I hurry my steps back toward my suite, I whisper the motto of my favorite podcast to calm myself. "Don't be afraid of standing out, especially in a bad situation." The host is all about making sure women know it's okay to turn down men who make them uncomfortable, or to do things that mean you'll be remembered by people, in case something happens to you. That's what this is, I remind myself. Wylie Ford is putting his wife in a bad situation, and I may stand out a little bit, but it's all about making things right.

CHAPTER 10
LAW

Ivy booked us a tour on the Road to Hāna today. It's just the two of us with four other people we don't know in a tour van on a winding, twisty road. There are multiple stops, and the scenery is breathtaking. Though I wish Carlie could have been included on the trip, it's one of the excursions Ivy scheduled before we left. Still, I'm glad to get to see so much of Maui. I miss a couple calls from my mom, but I text that I can't talk and will call her this evening. She doesn't check in often, and she knows I'm on vacation right now, so I'm curious what sparked the call.

"So, you got some time alone with Carlie yesterday?" Ivy asks when we stop at a black sand beach in Wai'ānapanapa State Park. It's one of the longest stops, which I'm sure is why Ivy decides to bring up Carlie now.

"Kind of." We were mostly by ourselves at the beach, even though her family was there. Later that evening, we had dinner together with her family, but we were always surrounded by people.

"But you had some opportunities to get to know her better?" Ivy takes off her shoes, holding them loosely in her hand as we explore the beach and meander toward the sea arch this spot is known for.

"Yeah, there's more to the story of her ex—maybe a lot more —but I don't blame her for not getting into it. We haven't had real alone time for that kind of confiding, and maybe we don't know each other well enough yet. It's only been a few days. She mentioned things were bad with the ex, so I wouldn't be surprised if she has some trust issues."

I sigh. How can I blame her for holding back? She told me all about her family while I said as little as possible about mine. And when she teased me about being a Blues fan, I wanted to tell her that moving to Houston was more of a struggle than my joking answer made it out to be. Will she see me as an entitled athlete if I tell her that I'm not as grateful as I should be to play for the Pumas? Sometimes she looks at me with such hope that I don't want to burst that bubble.

Two boys run past us through the sand, one of them turning to look at me over his shoulder as he follows the other boy.

"Just keep listening," Ivy says, about the same time the boys huddle together, one of them pointing at me. They're probably ten or eleven, and it's hard holding back a grin at them possibly recognizing who I am.

"Yeah," I say distractedly, which I realize is kind of ironic. "Of course," I add, trying to sound genuine. Ivy raises an eyebrow.

One of the boys comes trotting back toward me—not the one who did the double take over his shoulder. "Hi," he says, smiling.

"Hi, there." The grin is itching to break out. I remember being ten years old and how excited I was any time we saw a Blues player around town. I studied the faces of every player on the roster, just in case. Any Blues player was good enough for me. One good thing I do remember about my dad was the time he took me along with him to a photoshoot with the team. Jordan Wake, their all-star wide receiver, spent ten minutes talking to me about my future in football. I told him then I was going to the pros. When I got drafted by the Rays, Wake called me to congratulate me. I want to be just like him.

"My brother—" The boy points back to the other one, who drops his gaze when we all look at him. "He thinks you're Lawson Card."

I smirk and raise one eyebrow. "What do *you* think?"

The boy beams. "I think so too." He's practically bouncing now, his grin wide-toothed and identical to the one I must have worn when Wake sat down next to me while my dad was taking pictures with the Blues owner and general manager. I love interacting with kids like this. I've spent a decent amount of time with kids through football. The service projects and football camps we do have given me a bunch of opportunities, and it's one of the best parts about my job—aside from the fact that I'm playing my favorite game and getting paid for it, of course.

"You both think right," Ivy says to the boys. She beams too, looking between me and the boy. She doesn't always love when fans interrupt time we spend together, but we're both suckers for the kids.

The boy turns around, waving at his brother. "It's him! It's him!" he shouts.

Ivy and I share a look, barely holding back our laughter.

The other little boy runs up. "You're really Lawson Card?" he says.

"You can call me Law." Lawson is a snooty last name, not somebody's first name, and my parents chose it for the future president of the United States, not a football player.

"You're from Nashville too, aren't you?" The first boy—the older brother, I assume—says, squinting up at me.

"I am. Are you guys from Nashville?" I put my hands in my pockets, hoping they don't mind chatting for a bit. This is the best part of the tour.

"Yeah, we are," the little brother says.

"Is it all right if you guys tell me your names?" I ask.

The little brother turns toward the way they were running. A man walks toward us, and when he sees me with the boys, he starts to jog. "Dad!" the little brother says. "Can we tell Lawson Card our names?"

"Law!" The older brother nudges him in the side.

"Oops, sorry."

I chuckle. "No problem."

The man reaches us and looks surprised to discover that it is, indeed, Lawson Card standing on the beach with his boys. "Uh, yeah. You can tell him your names." He laughs nervously.

"I'm Logan," the older brother says, sticking out his hand. I give him a firm shake.

"I'm Gabe," the other one says, sticking his hand out as well.

"Max Hunter," the dad says, but he just nods at me. He's definitely more nervous than the boys, which is why ten-year-olds are so cool.

"So," I say, folding my arms and looking between the two boys. "Do you guys think I could get a picture with you or something?"

The boys erupt into excitement, and I can't hold back the laugh anymore. Ivy's shoulders shake. She grabs the dad's phone and I hand her mine, and she gets busy snapping a few photos. The boys go first, and then we coax their dad into the picture with us.

"Thank you so much," Max says when we break apart after the pictures. He nods his thanks at Ivy too, who hands back his phone.

"Of course." I turn back to Gabe and Logan. "So, are you guys football players?"

"Yeah, we are," Logan answers for both of them. "We're going to play for the Blues someday."

I grin wider, but I can't help the prick of pain in my chest. At that age, I thought the same thing. I thought I'd be able to control it all, that if I played my heart out, I'd get what I wanted.

"How come you don't play for the Blues?" Gabe asks.

It's like a punch in my gut, considering how badly I've

wanted that most of my life. I force out a laugh and share a look with their dad. He opens his mouth, but then falters.

"The Pumas don't think they can win another championship unless they have me." I shrug, pushing away any bitterness leaking in because I keep wondering the same thing. These boys don't want to see a jaded football player.

"The Blues are going to win this year," Logan says authoritatively. "The Pumas will never beat them."

I clamp my lips together to keep from laughing, but it's Max who answers. "They beat us last year," he points out.

Gabe drags two hands down the side of his face in a scary imitation of the Blues coach on the sidelines of that game. I'm not going to be able to hold my laughter at bay for much longer, especially with Ivy laughing silently behind my back.

"We *had* that game," Gabe says mournfully. "Jett McCombs threw *two* interceptions!"

I can't help thinking about how Jett told that story as his most embarrassing moment, and I chuckle. "Believe me," I say, "Jett McCombs knows it." I wink at them.

"You know Jett McCombs too?" Gabe cries.

Logan nudges his brother again. "Of course he does. They're on the same team now."

"Oh yeah."

"Come on, guys." Max puts his hands on their shoulders and nods at me politely. "Your mom's waiting for us."

"Not a football fan?" I say under my breath, looking up the beach to a woman who's taking pictures of the ocean.

"She'll probably have to ask the boys who you are," Max whispers back apologetically. "Thanks again," he says in a louder voice, and he squeezes the boys' shoulders.

"Thank you!" they both echo excitedly.

"One more thing," I say, pulling off the Pumas T-shirt I'm wearing. "You got a Sharpie?" I ask Ivy, already knowing the answer. She always has a Sharpie. I always say it's because she's the one with a purse. She says I should have to carry one because I always have legitimate pockets.

"Of course." She pulls it from the bag she's been carrying over her shoulder.

"Turn around," I tell Logan, and he obeys. I put the shirt on his back, using it to sign my name across the Pumas logo. I hand it to Logan and grimace a little. "Sorry, wish I had two."

"Holy smokes!" Gabe cries, looking over his shoulder at the T-shirt in awe. "Thank you!"

"This is so awesome." Logan holds up the T-shirt in front of him in awe. "Even if it is a Pumas T-shirt."

Ivy snorts with laughter behind me. Max looks mortified and opens his mouth, probably to lecture Logan about gratitude, but I wave him off. "I get it, man," I say under my breath with a grin.

As Max leads them back toward their mother, the boys keep glancing over their shoulders. I wave every single time while digging through my backpack for the swim shirt I brought along, and then pull it over my head.

"They're adorable." Ivy loops an arm through mine, and we finally continue our walk to the sea arch.

"Yeah. They remind me of me at that age." I look over my shoulder again, and this time it's Logan and Gabe waving back at me.

"Jordan Wake would be so proud of you." Ivy bumps me with her hip, looking up at me with her own proud smile. "Plus you handled their Blues questions like a champ." She smirks. She coached me so much after it was announced I was going to the Pumas.

"Ten-year-olds are easy compared to sports journalists."

"Touché." She chuckles. "But I think you should use that answer next time you get asked, the one about the Pumas not being able to win another championship without you. That's gold."

"Yeah, I bet Jett would love it."

"Too bad Carlie wasn't here to see the show," Ivy adds with a smirk.

"Me showing off to ten-year-olds or me taking my shirt off?" I ask.

"Both," she says, wiggling her eyebrows. I shake my head at her.

I open the photos app on my phone and flip through the pictures Ivy took of me and the boys. I can't wait to tell Jett about it. That's when I realize that I *am* friends with Jett McCombs, and maybe being a Puma isn't going to be so hard.

CHAPTER 11

CARLIE

It's my shift to watch the kids while the rest of my family gets packed for our red-eye flight tonight back to Houston. That's what I get for only taking thirty minutes to gather up all my own stuff. Packing cubes—that's my secret. Everything stayed organized.

As usual, it's easy to keep an eye on the kids. Ruby and I play at the water's edge, and the constant movement of the waves has kept her attention for a while. The boys dig in the sand, something it feels like they could do every day of their lives and never get bored. Every once in a while, they run down to the water and scoop up wet sand for whatever their project is.

My phone dings with a text, and I pull it out from the pocket of my shorts. I expect it to be from Gabriella, but then I remember that I decided not to send her the pictures I took the other night of Ford and his friend yet. Jenna told me last night that his wife is a good friend of Gabriella's, so that's who I'm going to send the pictures to so that Madelyn can hear the bad news from a friend. But not until Gabriella gets home from Hawaii. I don't want to ruin her special vacation.

The text is from my grandma and in a group message with

me and Jenna that we started when I first moved back to Houston.

> G
>
> I'm glad you'll be coming home soon, but I'm sure you girls are sad your vacation is almost over. It looks like you've had a wonderful time.

I always love how Grandma's texts sound like a letter she's sent me.

> CARLIE
>
> We had the best time. Thanks, G.

G is the nickname we gave Grandma when we were teens and insisting that she needed a cool grandma nickname, like one of Jenna's friends who called her grandma Nana.

> G
>
> I can't wait to hear all about that young man you met.

Grandma adds a winking emoji that makes me snort. How can a seventy-year-old woman use emojis so on point?

Ruby takes my hand and drags me to a new spot to dig in before plopping down, so I sit next to her while I type out the answer.

> CARLIE
>
> Well, how the tables have turned. Jenna tattling on me.

Grandma sends a picture of Law she must have googled. It's after a game, and he's wearing his football pants, but he's taken off his pads and shirt. Underneath is a tight black tank that exhibits his defined shoulders and arms. His hair is standing on end, but it's still a jaw-dropping picture.

And G drops it into the chat without even a comment.

Heat dumps into my cheeks the same time Jenna sends several laughing emojis and then one with stars for eyes.

"Looks like you're not the only one who could live on the beach."

I recognize Law's voice and look up, then fumble my phone and dump it into the sand. He reaches down to grab it, and I scramble to beat him to it. The last thing he needs to see is that my grandma is texting thirst-trap pictures of him to me.

But he has long arms and gets there first. I understand how the guy Law robbed of an interception in a game last year feels. You think the ball is just about to fall into your hands, and he slips in there and snags it right back.

He hands the phone back to me with a wide grin. "Who's G?" he asks.

I think the day just got about twelve degrees hotter at least. As if last night's embarrassment wasn't enough. "My grandma," I squeak.

Law snorts with laughter before he straightens his face. "She seems nice."

The way his eyes dance with laughter is killing me. My face is on fire. "She's very good at googling for a seventy-year-old." My voice is tellingly two octaves higher than normal.

"I see that."

"Oh my gosh," I whisper. I shove my phone into my pocket, ignoring the way that Law chuckles in a low, sexy way. That sound is not doing anything to help the heat in my face—or the warmth in my chest, for that matter. "So, uh, what was it that you were asking me? You know, when you first came up?" I ask, hoping we can just change the subject.

My phone dings again in my pocket, and Law looks at it pointedly. There's no way I'm looking to see what Grandma or Jenna has texted now. Not in front of Law. She and Jenna have probably both googled multiple thirst-trap pictures of Law in the last minute or so.

"Do you need to check that? It could be really important." How he keeps a straight face while saying this, I have no idea.

"Nah, it's fine." I'm going for nonchalant, but I doubt Law buys that. Judging by the still-high temperature of my face, I don't think I'm selling it very well.

Law smiles at me for a few moments longer, obviously enjoying my discomfort at being caught with that picture of him, before he says, "I said earlier that it looked like you weren't the only one who could live on the beach. Every time I see your nephews and niece, they seem perfectly happy to stay all day in the sand."

"Oh, yeah." I chuckle, hoping that my blush will diminish soon. Definitely not, if my phone keeps dinging in my pocket like this. I hurriedly pull my phone out to silence it as I say, "Jenna always tells me that she loves taking the kids to the beach because they're endlessly entertained. How was the tour today?" I haven't seen him all day, and it's no surprise to me that I'm disappointed about that.

"Gorgeous. I wish you could've come." He steps closer, hands in the pockets of his plain black swimming trunks. He's wearing a white swim shirt, which is probably fortunate, because if he was showing off any of the biceps I saw in that picture G sent plus abs, I'd probably be incoherent.

"That would've been fun. I've been with Jenna and Devin most of the day. We took the kids ziplining, so I don't regret that either." Their faces were priceless. Hudson declared it the coolest thing he's ever done.

Law's eyes widen. "Kids? Ziplining?"

I laugh. "It was a pretty tame course, perfect for them. They had a blast. I'll show you some of the pictures later."

His smirk returns. "Why don't you show me now?" he asks teasingly.

My cheeks burn, even if my lips are twitching. "Sorry," I say, trying to sound light-hearted but mostly just coming off as breathless. "I'm watching the kids." I shrug in a what-can-you-do way, and Law laughs again.

He leans in closer to me, and my fingers tingle with the effort it takes not to put a hand on his chest and at least *feel* the muscles I can't see. "When are you guys leaving?" he asks.

"The flight leaves at eleven. We're hoping the kids sleep for most of it." It will definitely make the flight easier. Although with five adults in our group and only three kids, our ratio is good. Plus Jett got us all first class. The flight over was uneventful. If we're lucky, the flight home will be too. I'm preparing for a few hiccups. The kids have been on the go so much that they're bound to be short tempered. Even that's relative for Jenna's kids.

"They'll be great," Law says, echoing my thoughts.

"I sometimes worry that her children being so great means that I'm the one who'll get monsters," I confess.

Law grins. "Luckily, you're perfectly equipped to handle them. And speaking of …" He grimaces.

"What?" I ask. Ruby lifts her hands toward me, and I move to pick her up, but Law gets to her first. She grins and claps his cheeks softly, the move she reserves for people she likes the most.

"Traitor," I mutter, but I smile. But daaang, this man is hot—and a baby in his arms? I can't even right now. "What's the look for?" I ask, distracting myself.

"Chad, ever the overachiever, got your name from me and called your old preschool for references. He's over-the-moon impressed with whatever your boss told him. He tried to get me to schedule a FaceTime interview with you tonight, but I reminded him that he might want you to meet the girls before he makes a big decision like this." He chuckles. "I'm sorry if he overstepped and if it was too soon for that move."

I shake my head, waving Law off as we begin to walk slowly down the water line. We don't go far before turning back around, since I need to keep the boys in sight. "It's fine. It sounds like he's in a tough spot, and I don't blame him for getting ahead of himself. Hopefully it means he cares about his girls. And it's good to know that Naomi still has good things to say about me." Also, it feels good to have a lead for a job. I'm happy to help Jenna for right now, but I need new employment sooner rather than later.

An amused expression crosses Law's face, and I can tell he's thinking about the story I told when we all went to the food truck the other night. "Hopefully she didn't warn Chad that you might hit on him."

I burst into laughter. "Naomi wasn't the one that insinuated that I'd better not cross the line with a parent again or I'd get fired. She was assistant principal then, and when she heard my side, she laughed a lot—and sided with me. But she wasn't happy when I told her I was quitting. Especially since it wasn't to take another job, but just to leave."

"From what Chad said, that's because you were, hands down, the best teacher she had." Law leans into me.

"That was nice of her to say." I put my arm through his and lean in close. He smells perfect, as usual, that sporty scent that's probably a requirement for athletes, and there's a definite hint of the ocean on him.

"Can we go out when we get back to Houston?" he asks.

"I'd love that." The time I've had with him this week has been perfect, but we've never really had alone time. I'm looking forward to finding moments for us to share the things I know we've both been holding back. "When do you start training camp?" Hopefully we'll have a few weeks to get to know each other before his life gets crazy with football.

"Full camp is in July, but I'll be doing some mini-camps and some training this month and next." He shrugs. I'll have to ask Ava how busy Jett is in the off season. "You on duty with the kids tonight?"

"Yeah." I look up at him apologetically. "The couples want to try this ice cream place nearby. Alec told Jett it was the best ice cream he's ever eaten."

"He told us about it. Ivy and I went when we got back from our tour. I agree." His turn to look apologetic, which makes me laugh.

"Jenna promised to bring me back some," I assure him. I hope he asked if I had the kids tonight because he wanted to spend a little bit more time together here in paradise, so I throw him a bone. "They'll be sleeping. You want to come hang out?"

He beams. "Yeah. That sounds great." He nudges me with his elbow. "Maybe we can see if you know how to google as well as your grandma."

I slap him softly on the arm and shake my head. His laughter is contagious, though, and even if I can't help the embarrassment that makes me blush again, the warmth of his laughter takes it over.

I decide I might as well just own this. "Actually, I'm a lot better." I smirk.

————

By the time I'm settled in my seat next to Ian on the plane, I still have a smile on my face. Nothing big happened with Law, but our couple hours together before I left were great. I turned the tables on him and googled all the cool plays Jenna, Devin, and I had been watching a few nights before. Though he was flattered, he was also clearly embarrassed to have the spotlight on him. I ended up showing mercy, and we played a card game that brought us both to tears of laughter multiple times. I'm looking forward to spending time together in Houston, getting to know him better, and finding the trust I've been looking for since Xavier was arrested. Just before Law left the suite, I thanked him for giving me time to know him, to work toward the trust. He smiled and gathered me up in a hug.

I can't wait to see him again.

CHAPTER 12
LAW

I made the mistake of telling Chad that Carlie was getting home a day earlier than me. At least I've held off passing along her number until I hear from her. They didn't get into Houston until almost eight a.m. Even if the kids were perfect on the plane, she's definitely still sleeping. It's only ten now. So I send her a quick text that hopefully doesn't disturb her.

LAW

> Chad wants an interview today if possible. Text me when you wake up and if it's okay to pass along your number.

I add some laughing emojis so she knows I'm not pressuring her.

I'm in the air before she answers. She uses some laughing emojis of her own.

CARLIE

> I understand his impatience. Go ahead and give him my number.

I text Chad her number, and less than five minutes later I get a single laughing emoji from Carlie. Chad, of course, wasted no time.

I can't deny that I have selfish motives here. With Chad's job and the unpredictability of when he gets called in, I'm pretty sure he'll want Carlie living with them, probably in his guesthouse in the back. That means I could end up with her as my neighbor, and even though her job as Chad's nanny might get intense, I can make excuses to see her often. The time I got to spend with her in Maui makes me crave more. I do want her to open up about why she's taking her time with us, but her thanking me for letting her go slow made my night. Even Ivy was asking what my grin was about when I got back to our suite.

I have missed calls from my mom when I land, and that's when I remember that I didn't call her last night after Ivy and I got back. I had gone for a walk after we got back from the tour to make the call, knowing the beach would be calming. I never know what conversations with my mom will hold. Then I ran into Carlie and the McCombs kids and all thoughts of calling my mom flew out of my head.

My mom will have to wait even now, though. Ivy took a Let's Ride home, so I'm "alone" in a private car, but I don't want to have a conversation with my mom with a driver listening in.

I do call her the minute I step through my front door. Waiting any longer is only going to upset her more.

"Hello, son. Is everything okay?" Her tone is light, but false concern says everything about how she feels about me ghosting her last night.

I bite back a sigh, already wishing I'd ghosted her for a few more hours. "Everything is fine. You know how vacations can go. I was with friends last night and didn't have an opportunity to call, and the time change makes it tricky."

"Of course." But her voice is tight.

I wait. Whatever she wants, she'll have to come straight to it. I just don't have the energy to dance around conversationally with my mom, and thoughts of relaxing have me feeling impatient even only a few minutes into the conversation. Despite the fact that my flight wasn't a red-eye like Carlie's, traveling all day still has me wiped. I'm going to relax in my hot tub with the new book I started on the plane. Ivy would certainly make fun of me if she knew, asking if I'd gotten out candles or something.

"There are pictures of you in some tabloids."

I can't help that a laugh escapes. That's what was so pressing? "There are pictures of me in tabloids pretty regularly."

"There's a woman," she says shortly.

Carlie's been caught in pictures with me, probably, and I realize that I didn't even think about that. Since my trade to the Pumas, people seem more invested in my social life. I've lived most of my life under a spotlight, first with my dad in politics and then my mom. This new scrutiny doesn't bother me, but it might bother Carlie.

"Ivy?" I ask anyway. I've instructed my publicist to stop acknowledging when reporters even ask questions about our relationship. I may understand why people always think it's more, but I'm done answering questions about something I've clarified over and over.

Mom lets out an exasperated sigh. "Would I be calling you over pictures with Ivy?" At least one person believes we're just friends.

"Then I assume they are pictures of me with Carlie Gallagher."

"Yes. I've discovered some concerning things about her. This is not the type of woman you should be associating with, Lawson." If anyone ever needs evidence as to why I don't like being called by my full name, they just need to hear my mom say it once and they'll understand. It holds all the tone that being called by a pretentious name does, with a layer of *I expect far better of you.* Maybe even in some snotty, refined Southern accent.

"Mom, please stay out of my social life. And I disagree. Carlie's exactly the type of woman I'd like to associate with. Kind, thoughtful, great with kids ..." Just like any other mother,

Mom wants grandkids, so I'll use that to my advantage as often as I can.

"The girlfriend of a drug dealer," she snaps.

I reel back, even though we're on the phone. The first thing that comes to mind is how Carlie told me she had a stupid ex that made her irrationally cautious. The next is the way she froze up when Ivy asked for embarrassing stories, and how Jett told me Carlie's story was more serious than most people's.

I'll give her the benefit of the doubt. My time with her recently has earned her that. She's everything I just told my mom and more. "That's not what it looks like."

My mom takes a beat. "Then you knew."

"I know enough." That's not exactly a lie. She told me about having an ex that made her distrusting. I trust that eventually she'll tell me the rest. We just haven't had a chance to talk more about it.

"Lawson." This time my mom takes a conciliatory tone. She's handling me. "This doesn't look good. Perhaps she is a very sweet woman, but—"

"This is none of your business." I make my tone final. "I'm not a politician, and I don't need to worry how this looks. If it's a problem for you, I'm sure your staff will find a way to spin it for your good."

"Lawson—"

"Mom, it's been a long day, and I've made myself clear. Have a good night." I hang up before she can protest more.

I drag a hand down my face. Carlie would have told me if we'd had more time alone together in Maui. I'm sure of it. I figured she had baggage from an ex, and I want to give her opportunities to tell me on her own.

So I push aside the doubts my mom's words created and take a deep breath. I channel the way I handled it on the phone with my mom—I'm sure Carlie will explain everything. Hopefully soon.

CHAPTER 13
CARLIE

I talk Chad Harrell into giving me time to shower and change before coming over to his house. Even though I suspect I have this job in the bag if I want it, I still choose my favorite work pants. I love dresses, but working with four-year-olds makes pants a better choice. These ones are flares and look fancy on the outside, but they're stretchy and easy to move around in. Plus, they're lightweight. It's already hot in Texas, but that's nothing new for me. My whole professional wardrobe is built for Arizona heat. I choose a sleeveless, lightweight top with floral design and lace details at the sleeves and neckline. And dressy sandals, of course.

Mr. Harrell and Law live in a gated community in the River Oaks part of Houston, but Mr. Harrell has already texted over his guest code for the gate. When I pull down his long driveway, I park on the empty pad of a four-car garage with two double doors. I text Jenna that I'm heading into the interview. Law has vouched for Mr. Harrell, of course, but I'm still going into the house of a man I've never met before. She reminds me to send her one of the grinning face emojis if I get into trouble. It's our code word whenever I'm out with guys or something, and I once accidentally sent it during a date. Jenna called me in a panic, and she already had Devin's phone on hand, ready to dial 911. It took a lot to convince her it was an accident, that I really was fine, and that I wasn't saying any of it under duress. It's possible I've talked about a few too many true crime stories in front of my sister involving women getting murdered on dates.

I push open the door of my tiny four-door car, which looks comical in the huge driveway, and head to the front door. The man who answers is tall and good-looking, with dark hair that has a few strands of gray just showing up. He wears black scrubs and his feet are bare, making me feel overdressed.

He smiles at me. "You must be Carlie."

"Good to meet you, Mr. Harrell." I take his outstretched hand and shake it before following him inside.

"Please, call me Chad." He leads me to a sitting room just off the front door.

Chad and I take our seats—Chad in a gray chair and me in a matching loveseat situated perpendicular to it.

"Thanks for coming right over," Chad says. He sits on the front of the chair, one leg bouncing before he notices my attention and stops. "Law has probably told you how impatient I am to have someone to help with the girls."

"I'm glad I'm in the position to help out." I sit back against the sofa I'm on but keep a straight posture. I'm hoping Chad can relax with me. With everything going on, it's no surprise he has a nervous, agitated aura around him. I'm sure that's not helping his girls adjust to the absence of their mother.

"Your references are great," he goes on. "I hope you'll forgive me jumping the gun and checking those out right away."

"No problem." I clear my throat. If Chad has checked me out, it means he knows about Xavier. I need to broach it just in case, so it doesn't surprise him later if he doesn't know. It's easier to assume the worst when someone keeps information from you on purpose. "Do you mind if I ask if you googled me?"

He smiles, which is reassuring. "I did. I know about your ex, and I have a friend in law enforcement that did me a favor and checked out what I couldn't find out from the news. He assures me you're innocent as far as anything they could find. Is that true?"

I nod. "I had no idea. I just didn't want you finding out later and thinking I was hiding things."

He claps his hands together, obviously ready to move on. "How about I run through a few things I'd need from you, and if you think you can do the job, I introduce you to the girls?"

This is the easiest job interview I've ever had, but I guess since Chad did so much legwork up front, that's kind of expected.

"I'm a trauma surgery consultant, and my hours can sometimes be really erratic. I'm on call basically all the time. I'd need you available at pretty much all hours." He grimaces, and I force myself not to react. Law did tell me that Chad's schedule was demanding, but I guess I just expected late hours a few times a week.

"Isn't that illegal for a doctor or …"

"Trauma surgery consultant," he corrects. "Not a doctor. I advise doctors on what hardware to use and the best surgical practices for that hardware. With the company I work for, me and three other guys cover about five hospitals in Houston. Someone always has to be available to consult on the surgeries, and we don't have the same rules as doctors about how much we can work." He shrugs at me. "It's very lucrative but time-consuming."

"I see." I keep my reaction minimal. No wonder he needs a nanny ASAP. And the very lucrative part explains why he's living in such a nice house with a pro football player next door.

"So you can see why I think it would be best if you lived on site. I have a guesthouse, and you can park in the garage," he goes on. "We—I've used the guesthouse as a rental unit until recently, so it's ready for you to move in. If you need to get out of a lease agreement, let me know and I'll take care of that."

I shake my head. "No, I'm living with my sister right now."

"I'm also willing to offer a salary that takes into account the erratic hours, along with some benefits." He picks up a piece of paper from the side table between the furniture, handing it to me.

I keep my calm as I scan the numbers, but he's offering a salary that blows my old salary out of the water, plus medical and dental benefits and retirement savings. Yeah, definitely lucrative if he can afford to pay me this.

"You'll also see that I'll pay overtime for anything over forty hours in a week and for holidays." He leans forward again, his expression eager.

"This is very generous, thank you," I say.

"Do you have any questions for me?" he asks. His leg starts bouncing again.

"Yeah, I guess." I jotted down a few on my phone before I came over, and I pause a moment to remember them. "What kind of responsibilities would I have around the house? Like cleaning. Would you expect that?"

Chad shakes his head. "Nothing beyond basic stuff like having the girls pick up after themselves and straightening things up in the living areas and kitchen. I have a housekeeper who comes twice a week, so you're mostly off the hook there. Your responsibilities will be only the girls."

"Okay. What about backup care for the girls in case of an emergency with me? And how would sick days work, you know?"

He's not surprised by the question. "I know my description makes it seem like I'm going to rely on you a lot, and I will, but I promise I'll also have backups for those kinds of situations. My family has been helping a lot, and I think it would be a good idea for us to also find a backup childcare provider as well."

I relax a little at that. He needs so much from a nanny, it was easy to think I was *it*. It's fair that he'll need a little more time to get everything back in order. "That's all good to know. I know it will be tricky to work out, but what about regular time off and vacations?"

"You'll have one full day a week off, and I'm open to a reasonable amount of vacation time. I'll need plenty of notice, of course, to arrange things, but once we're in a routine, I'm sure that will be easier. How much paid vacation did you have at your last job?"

"Two weeks." It was so stressful to arrange subs that I never used all of it, but I make a mental note not to do that with whatever time Chad can give me. I'll need the downtime if this gets intense.

"I'm good with that," he says immediately. "I'll need twenty-four hours' notice or more for one day, and at least two weeks' notice for anything over three days. Is that acceptable?" He has that apologetic look again, and it must be because of how stressful his job is.

"Totally understandable." Everything else I can think of is information I'll want once I've accepted. "I might have more questions if I accept the job." I take a deep breath. Why in the world would I turn this down? Sure, the hours might turn out to be horrible, but it's also the middle of the day and Chad is home. It might be a trade-off. "Do you mind if I step outside to consider some things?"

"Of course not." Chad stands, and I follow suit. "I understand what I'm asking of someone. I never thought—" He shakes his head and cuts himself off. "There's a garden area in the back if you'd like, and the guesthouse is unlocked. You're welcome to take a walk in that direction and check it out."

"Perfect." I nod and follow him out into the entryway and then through a large kitchen and family room area to a back door. He gestures to the yard, and we step out onto a path.

"The house is just through those trees." He points to some cypress trees. "Hopefully that will give you some privacy as well so you can have your own space."

So basically my own apartment with free rent in a gorgeous

neighborhood. There's a lot of stuff to make up for the strange hours this will require.

My thoughts swirl as I head down the pathway in the direction Chad pointed out. I'm seriously considering this even though part of me says that's crazy. But every time that part of me speaks up, another part shouts about the free rent, the great salary, and the benefits, for heaven's sake!

As I approach the trees, I pull out my phone to call Jenna.

"How did it go? Are you already done? Hold on, G's here. I'm going to put you on speaker," Jenna says.

"G can't be objective about this," I tease. "She'll lose her roommate if I take this job."

Grandma gives a *psh*. "The same could be said for Jenna, losing you as *her* nanny," she retorts.

We all laugh, and then someone on the other end yawns, probably Jenna. She didn't get to sleep in like I did. Even though I offered to help with the kids after we got back, she shooed me home. The kids slept almost the entire flight, so I doubt they wanted to go back to bed this morning. Still not enough sleep, though, and I'm guessing they're cranky—well, for Jenna's kids.

"Well, what do you think?" Jenna yawns again after this sentence.

"He hasn't asked me anything," I confess. "So I get the feeling he's already done all the research he needs to on me."

"Plus he's desperate," Grandma adds with a chuckle.

"There's that. He's a trauma surgery consultant, basically on call around the clock. So essentially, I'd be an on-call nanny." I lay out the biggest con on my mental list.

"Ooof," Jenna says the same time Grandma gives a soft *hmm*.

"Yeah, but he's offering me a house to live in, separate from his but on his property. A very high salary, and even benefits, all to make up for it." I give them the numbers from the paper Chad showed me.

"Wow." Jenna draws out the answer. "So, do you think it's worth it?"

I sigh. "It's so hard to say. Like right now, it's the middle of the day and he's home, so there will definitely be times when I have great hours. But there's also definitely going to be some truly terrible hours."

"True. But also sometimes when you're 'working,' so to speak, the girls will be in bed," Jenna says. It doesn't surprise me that Grandma's contributions to the conversation have mostly been sounds of agreement or consideration. She's always listened more than given advice. Jenna, on the other hand, is a true older sister.

I nod to myself, mulling. "You think it's going to balance out?"

"Maybe," Jenna says, sounding confident that she means yes.

"I don't know anything about him," I admit. "Law has only known him a couple weeks. He could be a serial killer."

"Or a drug dealer," Jenna says dryly, and we all laugh. "I googled him since I knew you didn't really have time." I hold back a snort of laughter at how well my sister knows me. "And I've been stalking everything I can on social media. From what I can see, he's everything he says he is."

"Sometimes we just have to have a little bit of faith, be careful, and do the best we can," Grandma says gently. "You can't know everything about everyone."

I feel like that's easy for her to say. She comes from a different time. But maybe people weren't any more trustworthy. Maybe they just hid it better. "I know, G," I say.

"Have you met the girls yet?" Grandma asks, and I smile.

"No. I'm looking at the guesthouse, and then I'll ask him. I'm thinking seriously about saying yes." My voice rises at the end. I want them to answer for me. Even if I don't know everything, Grandma is right on a certain level. I'll have to get to know Chad, just like it will take time to get to know Law. But is that a good idea?

They both pause, and I can picture them sharing a look. "I'm sure you're just what the doctor ordered," Grandma says, chuckling. I burst into laughter the same time Jenna does.

"I think that's a good choice," Jenna says. "It's going to be crazy, but so was your old job. This is just a different kind of crazy. Plus, think of how much of that ridiculous salary you'll save with free rent. And if it doesn't work out, you can walk away."

With all her housing worries right now, it's not surprising that's where Jenna's mind went. "True."

We say our goodbyes, and I hurry ahead toward the beautiful modern farmhouse-style cottage in front of me. It's separated from the park behind Chad's by more trees and a fence, making it feel like its own little yard. It has a covered porch with some outdoor furniture arranged on one side, which makes me fall a little bit in love right away. Without my permission, my brain pictures cuddling with Law on this furniture. I glance to both sides of the yard. I'm not sure where Law lives. The front doors of the guesthouse are two French doors, adding to the charm of the small home. I step up one step to the porch and cross to the doors, pushing open one.

The front portion of the house is an open living room and kitchen area, with a loft above the living room on the right and vaulted ceilings, making the room seem a lot larger than it is. The kitchen is modern, white with stainless steel appliances and navy-blue accents. A small, circular café table is in one corner in front of a large window. The living room is cozy with a loveseat and a chair, both in light gray with the same navy accents. The floor is a dark gray barnwood. Up in the loft is a bed, maybe a full or a queen, sitting low on a pallet frame, and a small dresser next to it.

I head down the hall to inspect the rooms behind the two doors on each side of the hall. The one on the left is a bathroom. It's all white, like the kitchen, with a small, clawfoot tub and shower, and a pedestal sink next to the toilet. I walk inside, turning on the faucet, flushing the toilet, and turning on the tub and shower, like I'd know if anything was wrong with this.

I cross the hallway to the other door. I'm already a little bit in love with this place. The other room is a bedroom, and it's pretty tiny, but it has a big bed, a tall dresser, and a decent closet running along the wall closest to the hallway. The walls are white paneling, with some abstract art that follows the blue theme in the house. The linens are all white, and there's a gray knit blanket folded across the end of the bed.

I'm more than happy with the house. With the loft, Caleb could still come stay with me—with Chad's permission, of course. I go back down the hallway and sit on the couch for a moment to really mull. I think I'm going to say yes. I just need to meet the girls before I make a final decision on this.

When I return to the backyard, Chad steps out from the sliding glass door we came out of earlier, clearly waiting for me. "Well?" he asks, his smile hesitant and hopeful.

"It's pretty and perfect," I assure him. "Do you mind if I meet the girls before I give you a final answer? You can introduce me as a friend or whatever if you don't want to get their hopes up."

"Of course." He nods. "Come inside and make yourself comfortable. I'll go get them."

I follow him inside and then take a seat on the large sectional in the family room. There's a basket full of toys at the end of it, a few scattered on the floor, and that makes me smile. The kitchen is a little messy, with dishes littering the countertop and a few in the sink. This looks like the hectic, lived-in kitchen of a family. Other than the random clutter, it's spotless.

Chad did tell me that his sister's been helping him out the last couple months, but she has kids of her own and the evenings can be hectic. So yeah, he's in desperate need of a nanny, and these girls are probably in desperate need of some routine. First their mother leaving, and then being shuffled from house to house every time their dad has to go to work.

Footsteps sound from the entryway, where the stairs are, and

Chad comes into the family room holding the hands of two girls. Their eyes are on me the entire time they walk across the room until Chad stops a few feet from the couch.

"Girls, this is my friend Carlie. Carlie, this is Scarlett." He shakes the hand of the older one. "And this is Zoey." He wiggles the other girl's hand gently. Despite an obvious age difference, the girls could be twins. Both have white-blond hair, very different from Chad's dark brown hair, and bright blue eyes. I would guess they look like their mother, but I realize that I haven't noticed any pictures of her around.

"Hi." I wave at them. "It's so good to meet you. How old are you?"

Zoey holds up three fingers the same time Scarlett says in a quiet voice. "I'm four, but I'll be five in …" She looks up at her dad.

"Three months," he finishes for her, giving her a proud smile. Chad loves these girls. That's evident by the tender way he's still holding their hands and the adoring expression he has every time he looks at either one.

"Are you in school?" I ask them. With them clinging to Chad, and him obviously staying right here with us, I won't get a good idea of their behavior. Law didn't seem to think they were too much trouble, even if he did mention acting out, and it sounds like he's watched them a couple times for Chad. I love thinking about him hanging out here with the girls, and the way he's talked about it, he's totally comfortable doing it. It makes my insides fluttery. I think about the light in his eyes when he told me about the little boys who stopped him on the beach to talk. He was smitten, and it made me fall a little bit more for him.

"Not in the summer," Scarlett answers, pulling my brain away from thoughts of Law.

I nod and gesture toward the Legos in a bin nearby. "Can you guys show me how to build some things?" I ask.

The girls look up at Chad, who nods, and they walk slowly toward me. Zoey sits closer, more trusting in her younger age, and Scarlett keeps her distance. I ask them quietly about the colors they're choosing and the little house they help me build. They're shy and don't open up quickly, but Zoey's clearly warming up. Scarlett's hesitancy tugs at my heart. They're making my decision easier and easier with every second.

After several minutes, I thank them for playing with me and look to Chad with a nod.

He crouches next to the girls. "Will you two go upstairs while I chat about a couple things with Carlie for a few minutes? Then we'll have lunch."

They nod, cast a few looks my direction, and then hurry out of the room. I hear their footsteps lightly tapping against the wood of the stairs.

Chad turns to me. "I don't want to rush you. I know this is kind of a big decision, but you do understand that I need an answer soon. The sooner, the better."

"Of course." I stand up. "I'll let you know by this evening at the latest." The truth is, I'm going to say yes. I just want to sit on it for a few hours. And also google Chad and do some stalking myself.

"Thank you." His answering smile is genuine relief. Perhaps he can tell I've already decided and it's going to go his way. The truth is, I can't say no. He and those girls need me.

CHAPTER 14
LAW

I don't want to tell Carlie I know about her ex in the middle of some crowded restaurant, so when I ask her if I can see her tonight, I suggest a quiet dinner at my place. She says she'll pick up food on her way over. I busy myself with cleaning up my kitchen and dining room and getting plates and silverware out for when she arrives.

An hour later, my phone alerts me that Carlie has used the gate code I gave her, so I head outside to meet her. She smiles at me when she gets out of the car and holds out a bag from a place I don't recognize.

"I already miss the island," she says with a little laugh. "Hope you don't mind Hawaiian barbecue."

"Sounds fabulous." I pull her into a long hug, which she returns, bags in her hand and all. I take one from her and lead her into the house.

I ask her about the interview right away, so we spend the next few minutes as we pull out containers and dish things up chatting about the salary Chad offered, the beautiful guesthouse he's offered for her to live in, and the girls.

"It was hard to get a read on them just in the few minutes I met them," she says. "Do you have anything to add?"

She's already going to say yes. I can see it in her expression as she talks about all of it—her eyes dancing with excitement, the subdued smile as she tells about what the girls said and did, and the "how can I say no" widening of her eyes when she tells me the salary. "They can be spoiled, and that's gotten a little worse since Shelby left. Shelby never really said no to anything, and now Chad *can't* really say no to a lot. He feels bad about Shelby being gone, about the girls missing her and being confused about the situation, and most of all his demanding job. And they sort of freak out when he leaves them, so that will be an adjustment."

"Understandable," Carlie murmurs. "I had a student last year whose grandpa passed away suddenly. They were very close, and my student flipped a switch. He cried every time his mom dropped him off, and then sobbed with relief every afternoon when she came to pick him up. That was a rough few weeks."

"Yeah, that sounds super hard. I can't decide if Shelby finally calls or something, it will be a good thing or just make it worse." I shrug. I still can't wrap my brain around what Shelby did, just walking away like that. I, of all people, know that families can be hard and complicated, but as difficult as my mother is, I can't imagine her ever just leaving us behind and never looking back, even when that might have been easier.

Carlie tilts her head at me. "Wait. She hasn't called or anything?"

I sigh. "Nope. Well, at least according to Chad, right? But I don't think he'd lie about that. You said it: the girls are his world. If Shelby called, he'd make sure they got to talk to her, to know she's alright. That's half the thing with the girls—all Chad can tell them is Mommy had to leave for a little while. He has no answers."

Carlie scowls. "That's horrible."

There's something more going on in her brain. She's already admitted to me that she's nosy and she's always curious about people's stories. I bet not knowing more about Shelby is making that mind of hers whir into action. She's even zoned out a little, pushing around the macaroni salad on her plate. It's as good a time as any to tell her what my mom told me.

"So," I say, taking a deep breath. "There was a picture of us in a tabloid." I looked it up after my mom left, and it's benign. Just a cell phone shot from someone showing me and Carlie sitting snuggled up on the beach when we were watching the turtles.

She lets out a short laugh. "I know. I saw." When I tilt my head in confusion, she swallows. "I have alerts set for if my name shows up online anywhere." She presses her lips together. That has to be because of her drug-dealing boyfriend. I didn't look anything up on that. I really want her to be the one to tell me, in her words, what happened.

"I see." I clear my throat. "So, my mom actually has something similar set up. Well, her staff, I guess. And when she saw the picture, they automatically did research on you. Very in-depth research. She likes to be ahead of any possible scandals or whatever." I rush to explain why she would be looking Carlie up. Especially to the level she has.

Carlie's shoulders slump as she realizes what I mean. "She knows about Xavier." She puts her fork down and steeples her fingers above her plate. "I was going to tell you. Soon. But we just never had any time in Maui. It's a conversation that I wanted to make sure wasn't interrupted."

I hold up a hand. "It's fine. We haven't known each other long, and I wouldn't have expected you to open up about everything right away, especially a hard experience like that must have been. I just wanted you to know that I know. Or I know some things. I didn't look anything up, because I want you to be able to explain exactly like you should have been able to."

She manages a smile. "That's sweet, Law."

"Whenever you want to. No rush or anything." We're sitting kitty-corner from each other at my large table. I had to buy it to fit the space, but I wanted our dinner to be more intimate, so I set us up close to each other on one end. I reach across the corner of the table and squeeze her hand.

She smiles at me again, her expression soft, and I hope she knows how much I want her to know she can trust me. "I really have been meaning to tell you for days, so now is as good a time as any." She draws in a long breath. "Xavier and I were engaged."

I shove a bite of the teriyaki chicken into my mouth to keep from gasping. She was going to marry him.

"I had absolutely no idea," she goes on, spearing some of the macaroni salad that litters her plate. "He had a whole separate life—another apartment, another phone. The only redeeming thing, maybe, is that somehow he protected me from all of it. The people they took down after they arrested him, they had no idea about me." She puts the bite in, chewing slowly and not looking at me. "I was with him the night they arrested him, at his apartment. They broke down the door and all these cops came in with guns and everything. It was the scariest thing that's ever happened to me." She stabs at more macaroni, her hand trembling, and I reach over and take it, pulling the fork away from her.

"It sounds like a nightmare," I say in a soft voice.

She squeezes my hand, and her eyes shimmer. She's turned in her chair so that we're facing each other, and I turn mine too. "It was. It was awful. At first I thought it must be some huge mistake, but they just kept showing me all this evidence." She looks me right in the eye. "I don't know if I've really trusted myself since then. I definitely haven't had any serious relation-ships in the last few years since it happened. I'm sorry, Law. I'm just not sure how to trust that you're everything you say you are."

She falls forward against my chest, sniffling, and I wrap my arms around her. How can I blame her for second-guessing herself? One minute her life was headed for happily ever after, and the next the rug got completely yanked out from under her.

The man she would have pledged her life to lied to her. Lied about everything. It also explains why she's always looking for the answers, always wanting to know the details.

I scoot my chair closer so her leaning into my arms isn't as awkward, and we sit like that for a long time. I don't know if she's crying—I can't tell. But she breathes deeply, and I'm happy to just be here for her while she finds some calm.

Irritation toward my mom prickles at me. Carlie is a victim in this, and I hate that Mom tried to sow doubt about her with me. That she acted like Carlie might be a co-conspirator. I get that Mom has to keep her life pristine or her political opponents pounce—and Mom is doing some good in politics, fighting the good fight and all of that—but I'm getting tired of keeping up with perfection.

After several minutes, Carlie draws in one more long breath and sits up. "Okay. Thank you for understanding, Law." She plants a kiss on my cheek and then blushes as she stands up. "I'm going to get more macaroni salad since I have mutilated this." She scowls at the plate, and I smile.

"I picked up brownie and peanut butter chocolate ice cream on my way home. It's my favorite, but if that's not your thing, we can go get something else." I dish out some more rice and chicken onto my plate.

"That sounds amazing," she says.

I made the decision a while ago that Carlie was worth waiting for, was worth going slow for. I'm doubly sure now. I want to be the man that Carlie can trust will never let her down. Not even on the ice cream.

CHAPTER 15

CARLIE

The next few days happen in a whirlwind. Once I tell Chad yes, he wants me to move in as soon as possible. That's not difficult. I sold all my big furniture before I left Arizona, and the few boxes I have left are mostly still packed. Chad's guesthouse is furnished, so Jenna lets me keep those boxes in a closet at her house.

Two days after accepting the job, Chad has me come over for dinner to introduce me to the girls as their new nanny. And then he has to explain what a nanny is.

"A babysitter," I say, interrupting his complicated explanation. I understand there's a lot more to it, and other nannies might not appreciate me boiling down their careers to that, but that's what Scarlett and Zoey will understand. "I'm going to be your very special babysitter who comes to help you when your dad has to work."

"Like a new mommy?" Zoey asks. Chad looks horrified.

"Not quite. Mommies are pretty special. I'll be like the substitute for a little bit, doing some of the things mommies do, but not all." I shrug at Chad, hoping that's an okay explanation for him. He nods, but his cheeks still look red.

The girls know about the guesthouse, but we walk down there with them to show them where I'll be living, and then back to the house to show them the room I'll stay in when I need to sleep at their house. I've already separated some clothing to put in the dresser there so I can be ready when that happens.

The first night I'm going to spend at the guesthouse, Jenna comes over with me to bring the last of my stuff.

"You shouldn't be wasting time helping me drive stuff over," I chide her when she parks behind me in Chad's driveway.

"It wouldn't have fit in your car." She winks at me as she pulls out one of the two huge suitcases she put in the back of her SUV.

I scoff. She laughs, because it would've been a tight fit in my little Kia Forte. The trunk space is sort of a joke. It took a lot of creative thinking to get as much stuff as I did in this car when I moved from Arizona. I had to ship more than I wanted to. But it gets amazing gas mileage, so there's that.

"Well, it would've taken you so many more trips, hauling it all from the driveway and down the path." She points ahead of us to the path that skirts around the garage and down one side of the yard before circling the back of the yard to go through the trees to the guesthouse.

"I know you need to be working on the new house." I adjust one of my bags on my shoulder so I can grab a second one.

"It's fine," Jenna says, making her way toward the side of the garage. The way her shoulders tighten as she leads the way says otherwise. Or it could be the strain of the two suitcases. Hard to say.

But not really. Devin's been working extra late hours this week, and Jenna's been taking advantage of the last of my time with them, staying at the new house until two or three in the morning and then getting up with the kids. At the least, she should've stayed home and gotten some extra sleep tonight.

"Okay, well, since I have this amazing salary now and I can't help you like I planned, let me 'invest' in your mortgage payment for a few months to give you some breathing room." I trip on a rock, and the number of bags I have distributed between my arms and the backpack on my back threatens to have me tumbling to the ground. I stop to try and right myself and shift all the bags back into place.

Jenna looks over her shoulder at me and laughs. "No need, Car. I promise. It's fine."

I hurry to catch up with her. How is she making such good time rolling those suitcases over the uneven ground? Is this like a big-sister superpower? "I was supposed to come and help you until you got the house ready. That was the plan," I say.

She shakes her head. "The plan was for you to move out here and help out, and it was always in the plan that you'd look for a new job here."

I didn't expect that to happen for at least a month. In fact, I wasn't even going to look that hard until Jenna was closer to finishing. I have enough savings to chill for a bit and help my sister the only way she'll let me: by living in her house for free, watching her kids, and helping out Grandma. But I can't even do that now.

"Yeah, but now that I'm not going to be able to live with you while I work, I messed up the plan, so let me help. Seriously, you know the numbers. It's not a big deal, and I know you'll pay me back as soon as you can."

She shakes her head. "Carlie, it's fine. I have a friend who's going to watch my kids a few times a week in exchange for a couple nights at the beach house for her and her husband. She's even letting me get away with nights that aren't already booked, so I'm not losing money. See, it's fine." She's repeated that it's fine so many times that it has me doubting how fine she actually is. I've barely seen her this week, and her calm demeanor now is an act. Or she could be annoyed with me. Again, hard to say.

"Guess I'm going to have to move faster with Law than I really wanted …" I mutter.

Jenna laughs, hauls the suitcases up the two steps, and sets them by the door, turning to wait for me to lumber up behind her.

"Hey." I point a finger in her face after I set down a couple bags so I can dig the keys out of my purse. "You promised that if I married Law, you'd let me invest in your business."

"Sure, sure." She holds her hand up in surrender, but she's smirking. "I one hundred percent believe that you're going to jump right in with him, considering how recently you were reminded of how some men can be scum."

I grimace. "Has Gabriella said anything?" I just sent the pictures a couple days ago, since Gabriella and Colby spent extra time in Hawaii after everyone else left. It's not really my business to know what happens between Madelyn and Ford, but after being the one to catch him, I'm dying to know.

Jenna shakes her head. "No. But it sounds like it's the last straw."

I frown and stick my key in the lock. "It's too bad."

Jenna hums in agreement and follows me inside once the door is open. "If it helps at all, Car, I do think that Law is one of the good ones."

I sigh. "So do I." The problem is convincing my brain.

———

I start my new job the next day at a completely normal time. Chad calls me at about eight a.m., saying he's been called in. I'm already dressed and working on a loose schedule for the girls to get back into something normal. I had planned on going down to spend time with them again around nine anyway. Chad and I have talked about me being around during the day most of the time, with a lot of leniency when I have to come over at nights. We both agree that the girls need more structure, and I'm glad he's on board with that.

I hurry over, and when Chad leaves, he's got the first real

smile I've seen him wear. Something flutters in my chest at being able to provide not only stability for the girls, but relief for him. That's not the type of feeling I got to experience teaching ten upper-class kids from relatively stable homes.

The girls are still sleeping, probably because Chad let them stay up too late—something he admitted to doing because bedtime is too much of a chore when they're not exhausted. We're going to work on that too. I decide now is a good chance to explore the house. Chad gave me a tour, but I want to familiarize myself with the house, especially since I know I'll be here at night a lot. An unfortunate side effect of being obsessed with true crime is that my imagination is vast when it comes to things that can go bump in the night. The more familiar I am with this house and its quirks, the easier it will be for me to dismiss strange noises. Mostly.

Plus I want to snoop. I can't help myself.

The front room is pretty basic—clean and unused. I straighten up the kitchen and family room as I go through them, but I don't spend much time there. When I've been with the family so far, it's been in these two rooms, and I feel familiar with them already. The housekeeper will be in tomorrow to clean. Chad made me a long list of helpful information, full of phone numbers and household details like that.

I head down the hallway behind the kitchen. There's a bathroom, as well as a large laundry room and mudroom that connects to the garage. It's a mess of shoes and jackets flung all over, so I straighten up here too.

After that, I head upstairs quietly. The girls' bedroom doors are closed, so I'll inspect them closer later. There's the guest bedroom where I'll sleep when I need to be here overnight. I've already brought over some of my things to keep in the dresser to be more efficient. There's an office up here, and I push the door open to look inside. This is the first room I'm a little anxious about. Chad showed me it earlier without pause—this is where the computer is kept, so if I need that, he told me I'm welcome to use it. He's already even set up a guest account for me and given me a password.

There are a couple of frames on the desk, and I walk in to get a closer look. I'm dying to know what Shelby looks like. So far, I haven't seen pictures of her around. But these are pictures of Chad with the girls and then one of the two of them in cute, themed Halloween costumes that must be from last year. They're characters from a show Ian and Hudson watch too, so I recognize them and smile.

There are more pictures of the family in the front room downstairs and in the family room. Maybe I just somehow missed the ones with Shelby in them. Curious, I go back downstairs and inspect all the photos closer.

There are none of Shelby. They're all of the girls, and a few of Chad with the girls. One of them is a professional one that has to have been done recently. I've gathered from Law that Shelby left just two months ago. He said the other night that Shelby hasn't contacted them at all, so it's weird that Chad has already erased her from their home. Is this supposed to be easier?

I have mixed feelings about it. Maybe Shelby told him she wanted nothing to do with the girls when she left. Or is Chad cutting off the relationship because of what Shelby did? This is a complicated mix of things I didn't think about. I'll have to approach Chad about how to talk about her.

I go back upstairs to listen for the girls and remember the master suite. When Chad gave me a tour of the house earlier, he pointed at the doorway at the end of the hall and just said that's where it was. He didn't take me in, and that didn't surprise me, but I really want to see it. In a house this nice, it's got to be awesome.

I hurry down the hallway and carefully push open the door. Maybe the pictures of Shelby are here, in his private space.

The room is spacious, with floor-to-ceiling windows on one

side. The shades are drawn, likely because Chad was rushing from the house this morning, so the room is dim. A huge bed occupies the far wall, and in one corner are a couple of cozy chairs and ottomans. A blanket is draped over one, but it looks unused. Maybe that was Shelby's space. On the wall next to the door is a wide dresser, but it's clear on top except for a tray with a couple candles and some spare cash and change. No pictures here.

The master closet is massive, and jealousy inducing, and the doorway next to it is an equally impressive bathroom. It has a huge, glassed-in, tiled shower as well as a large soaking tub. The long countertop has double sinks, and it's clear of any items too. I can't help myself; I peek into some of the drawers, looking for reminders that Shelby lived here. She can't have taken *everything* from her bathroom. Three of the four drawers are completely empty. There's no sign of her belongings in the cupboards either. She must have packed a massive suitcase. I do note that there are women's clothes in the closet, though it's emptier than I would expect for one so large.

The doorbell rings, making me jump and hit my head on a shelf in the closet. I swallow back a cry of pain and pull up the doorbell camera app that Chad gave me access to while I rub the back of my head. It's just the FedEx guy dropping off a package. I frown and head downstairs, contemplating Chad's situation. I open up the front door and pick up the package, setting it on a table next to the door for Chad.

I'm not surprised that Shelby's leaving stirs up my curiosity. I have questions. Who wouldn't? Why did she leave? Has Chad really not heard from her? How does someone walk away from two sweet girls? What kind of relationship did Chad and Shelby have to contribute to it?

I force all the questions out of my mind. They're none of my business. I'm here to help Chad and the girls get through a rough time, and I don't need to know about their family matters to do that—for the most part. This is a situation where I recognize it's important for me to respect boundaries. I might be nosy, but I can also be professional when I need to be.

It's just really hard.

Still, I send off a text to my old boss, Naomi. She has a doctorate in child psychology, and she's the best person I can think of to ask advice about how to handle the fact that Shelby has completely disappeared from the Harrells' life.

CHAPTER 16
LAW

Though I hate doing it, I call my mom a few days after my date with Carlie to pass on what she'd told me. In any other circumstance, that's a story I'd keep to myself, but Mom and her staff will keep digging if I don't make sure she knows there's no reason to.

"It looks bad," Mom says when I finish telling her Carlie's side of the story. "There's no way she didn't have some clue that he was into something shady."

She, of all people, should realize how easy it is to put on a façade to the world that's completely fake. I swallow a huff of annoyance. "He had a separate apartment and a different phone, and he was very careful not to intermingle his worlds."

She lets out a scoffing breath. "It's better safe than sorry. You're a public figure—"

"*You're* a public figure. I'm a football player, and no one will care if my girlfriend's ex is in prison."

There's a long pause, one in which I know Mom is breathing deeply to keep from snapping at me over the phone. "You're not going to play football forever, and the image you curate now will follow you for a long time."

"I'm well aware that my football-playing days have an expiration date that I have no control over. I also know that I will never want a political career."

The frustration between us is almost tangible. My dad was in politics, and my grandfather was in politics. It's practically a dynasty, Mom likes to remind me. But unless she talks Malcom into it, it ends with her.

"Don't cut off your options out of spite, Lawson. You never know how you'll feel about this in a few years … or ten years, even."

"I know." Time to end the conversation. "I have to go now, Mom. Please tell your staff not to invade Carlie's privacy any more." I hang up before she decides to press forward with more arguments.

Thankfully, a text from Carlie is waiting when I hang up the phone.

CARLIE

Do you want to come over and see my awesome house and meet my brother? I'm off for the afternoon.

Well, you know. As off as I can be. Chad could get called in at any moment.

LAW

I'm on my way.

Carlie has popped in here a couple times since she started working for Chad, once with the girls as a distraction. It sounds like the first few days have been rough for them. They're used to their aunt or grandma being the ones to swoop in. But they like Carlie—who wouldn't? That was evident by the shy smiles they gave her every few minutes while they were at my house.

There's a gate in the fence on Carlie's side of the trees in Chad's backyard, so I use that. She's sitting on the small porch with a man that looks more like Jenna than her when I approach, and she waves, sitting forward when she catches sight of me. The man sets aside a laptop on the outdoor couch he's sitting on and sits up too, eyeing me.

"Hi, I'm Law," I say, putting my hand out when I reach them.

"Caleb, Carlie's brother." He smiles when we shake hands, no protective big brother vibe that I can detect.

"You sleeping in the loft?" I ask, nodding toward the house.

He chuckles and shakes his head. "Carlie thought that maybe having a weird guy around the yard might be too much for the girls right now."

"Chad told me I could use the guesthouse as though it's my own apartment when it comes to guests—as long as I'm protecting the girls, of course—but it seemed like a good idea to wait on this."

"Probably," I agree. It's also good to know that Chad's not going to be a stickler about me hanging out with Carlie over here.

"I'm staying in her old room with my grandma," Caleb says. He picks up his laptop when he sits down, indicating I should sit, which I do. It's hot outside, but the shade from the trees makes it bearable and almost nice to sit outside and enjoy the day.

"We're trying to decide if leaving Mom's basement to room with Grandma is a step up or not," Carlie says in a teasing tone, grinning at her brother.

"She's not setting me up with Dallas's top executives, so I'm calling it a win." Caleb holds up his hand for a fist bump.

"I figured you'd be over here!" a voice calls out from the gate, and we all turn to see Ivy striding toward us. There's a slight shift to the way Carlie's sitting—not tension exactly, but maybe caution. She can't still think that there's something between me and Ivy, can she? Or is it the way that Ivy is zeroed in on her brother? No protective big brother vibes, but maybe some protective sister ones. I like it.

Caleb stands again as Ivy approaches, smiling.

"You must be Caleb," Ivy says. "Nice to meet you in person."

"And you're Ivy?" he guesses, taking her hand and holding it for several seconds longer than he did mine. I turn to share a smirking look with Carlie, but her gaze is intent on Caleb and Ivy.

"Yep." When Ivy pulls her hand away from his, she still smiles up at him for a moment, before looking between me and Carlie. Instantly, Carlie's expression transforms into a smile. "I came over to see if you guys wanted to go grab something to eat," Ivy says. "Carlie? Law? And of course we want you to come, Caleb."

Carlie shakes her head. "I need to stick around here. Chad got called in last night and was gone until around nine a.m. He's going to need to sleep eventually. I already planned on going over to do dinner with the girls."

Ivy glances at me. The look in her eyes says she wants me to play wingman, but Carlie and I haven't really spent time together since we had dinner at my house. Plus I have a mini training camp next week, and I won't have much time to hang out. I really want to get our relationship off the ground. Right now it feels like we're friends on the precipice of something more, but still just friends.

"I'm out. I'll keep Carlie company until she has to go."

Ivy's face falls, but Carlie speaks up. "You should go with her, Caleb. Law and I are clearly party poopers." The siblings share a look, probably communicating silently the same way I do with Ivy. I hope Carlie understands that Ivy really is like a sister to me.

"Yeah, okay," he says. "I'm in."

Ivy suggests a couple places, and Carlie adds in her ideas. I watch Carlie and wonder if the other two see that there's a very slight edge to her smile. They tell us goodbye and head back through the gate toward my house, where I assume Ivy's car is parked. I pat the seat next to me once they're gone.

"Actually, you want to go inside? It's getting really hot out here." She stands and leads the way into the house. When she sits down on the couch in the living room, I sit right beside her.

"Everything okay?" I ask, looking pointedly toward the door and the direction where Ivy and Caleb just left.

She sighs. "Yes. Totally fine." She adjusts so she's facing me, her legs crossed in front of her. "No offense, Law, I just don't really know Ivy yet. She's probably great."

"She is," I promise her.

"And Caleb wanted to go."

"I wondered what that silent conversation was about." I smile at her.

"Oh, I'm guessing similar to the one you and Ivy had a few seconds before," Carlie challenges.

I laugh. "She was begging for a wingman."

"And look at what we maneuvered instead." She puts a hand on my knee. "Alone time. Although I did kind of want you to hang out with Caleb. But there'll be plenty of time for that."

Maybe she's just thinking about how Caleb will be here for a while, but I like how it's a given for her that she and I will have plenty of time as well. "How were the girls today?" I ask.

She frowns but then shakes her head. "They were better, for sure. They're getting used to me, and that's good. I want to take them over to Chad's sister's sometime this week for dinner or something. Give them a little of their old routine."

"Chad says they're in love with you, so I'm sure you're going to have them behaving like angels in no time."

She nudges me softly, but beams. Then her face goes serious again. "Can I ask you something about Chad?"

"Of course." I make sure my voice is neutral. I've gotten to know Chad pretty well since I moved here back in February. He was helpful and friendly right from the get-go, inviting me and Ivy over for dinner and barbecues or just to watch some kind of game. Looking back now, I see that he needed—still needs—time to decompress from a stressful job and a stressful marriage. Maybe more so because of the latter.

But that doesn't mean I know everything about him, and what if I let Carlie walk into a dicey situation just to be able to hang out with her more?

She brushes at nonexistent lint or something on my shorts, smoothing out wrinkles and not looking at me. "He never talks about her, about Shelby, and I get that. But …" She pauses and chews on her bottom lip. "He's erased her from that house. No pictures anywhere that I can tell—and I'll admit that my curiosity got the better of me. I was thorough. Do you think that's normal?"

That wasn't what I was expecting, so I have to take a second to gather my thoughts. "When my brother's girlfriend broke up with him last year, he completely ignored any mention of her. And from what I can see of his life, he's erased her too. Deleted her number, no pictures on his phone, you know." Not saying her name feels kind of like a lie, even though it's normal that I wouldn't mention Malcom's ex by name. Maybe it's because it almost feels like I'm doing what Malcolm did. Ignoring her. But that whole thing is complicated, and I don't need to bring that into what Carlie's concerned with now.

"But did they have kids together?" Carlie asks.

I have to laugh. "No. They didn't."

She lets out a long sigh. "That's why I keep going back and forth. On the one hand, it seems kind of like a normal way to grieve a relationship, right? But on the other hand, it can't be healthy for the girls, pretending like she doesn't exist."

"Probably not." I have to agree on that, but I hate the frown that's still pulling down on Carlie's expression. "Hey. Maybe he talks about her when you're not around. Maybe he's just really private about all this." I get that Carlie's intense interest is a response to her own past and also because she cares about the girls, but I don't want her to get stuck on this.

She nods, and some of the tension in her face releases. "Yeah.

Maybe. I hope so. That would make sense." She leans toward me more, and after a moment, a real smile takes the place of the concern. "So, you're in training camp next week. Are you excited or dreading it?"

A part of me latches on to the idea of dreading it. New team. My rivals, if I'm being honest. I quickly push that all away. "Excited." I nod decisively.

She raises her eyebrows, and not since I first met Ivy has someone been so intuitive to my thoughts. My smile was good, wasn't it? "You sure about that?" Her tone is teasing, but her eyebrows are still calling BS.

"Of course. I'm ready to really get to know my teammates and get out there and start figuring things out. Jett's going to make me a star, no doubt." All truths that I believe.

"But you're still a little nervous." She pokes me gently in the side, and even though it feels like a friendly gesture, I remind myself that initiating contact like this is a flirty move.

"Maybe a little, but not much. I've already done a few team activities with these guys, so it's not really like the first day of school or anything." I lean back further into her couch and pull her closer, so she's resting under my shoulder. She doesn't resist at all, only shifting so she can tilt her head up to look at me. My heart rate ratchets up with hope and expectation when she wraps an arm around me, going full-on snuggle.

She laughs. "Team activities? Like trust exercises and meetings and stuff?"

"No. OTAs are like low-key practices. No contact, getting used to each other."

She frowns again, but her eyes sparkle now. "So no potluck picnic?"

"No, unfortunately. But I wouldn't say no to someone organizing that." I look at her pointedly.

She waves her hand around her house. "I'm sure fifty or so burly guys could totally squeeze in here."

"Fair. How about a potluck picnic for two sometime?"

The way her eyes light up sends a zing through me. The delight there is catching. "I love that. Tomorrow? We each bring something."

I choose my words very carefully. "It's a date."

CHAPTER 17
CARLIE

Is it weird to be excited about a potluck picnic date? Is it weird to be having a potluck picnic date?

The grin on my face every time I think about it feels like it's not weird but kind of great. Law said he was bringing the meat for our potluck, and that meant I got sides and bread. I went with easy and just made some basic rolls last night after I had dinner with the girls and Chad, but the side I chose is my grandma's amazing potato salad recipe. I can't stop thinking about what he's going to bring and making guesses.

"Froot Loops!" I call out to the girls, who are coloring quietly at the table. Once I bought them Bluey coloring books, this became their favorite after-breakfast activity this week.

Scarlett giggles but then shakes her head vigorously. "That's not meat, Carlie. He can't bring Froot Loops."

The other fun game they like this morning almost as much as I do? Hearing me make silly guesses about what Law will bring to our potluck. "Good point," I say, and go back to wiping off the counter. The girls seem to have found comfort in the ritual of me straightening up after breakfast, and it makes me wonder if their mom did that. I've been careful not to ask them about her. I haven't found the right way to discuss that with Chad, even though Naomi thinks the girls would adjust better if they had more information about Shelby. But how do I approach their dad and question his parenting decisions?

I pull open the dishwasher. Chad and I have an unspoken agreement that he loads it at night—unless he's called out before dinner—and I unload in the morning. To be honest, it's helped me out a lot in searching through the kitchen and finding things. I've acclimated to this house a lot quicker because of it. The girls also laugh over the way I line things up above the dishwasher when I can't find the home for it and the girls can't help. Which is often.

"A vacuum!" Zoey suddenly shouts, and I have to keep myself from beaming proudly. Neither girl has offered up their own suggestion in the game we've been playing. She begins giggling uncontrollably, even when Scarlett shakes her head and cries, "That's not even food!" Then they both just giggle harder.

I can't help staring at them as they laugh together. They've been so shy around me. I haven't seen them let loose like this.

"What, Carlie?" Scarlett asks. Her giggles are calming, but she's still smiling widely.

I think fast. "Pancakes."

"No!" they shout together, and they giggle more.

I go back to unloading the dishwasher, still grinning to myself. Their giggles fall away, and they go back to coloring, but they're interspersing it with chatter that I love listening to.

I pull a spoon out of the dishwasher that seems very disproportionate. It's got a regular-sized head but a long, thin handle, and I've never seen it before.

"Girls?" I ask, holding it up. They both look over, then shrug and shake their heads. "Is it for a T-rex to eat his cereal?" I ask with faux innocence.

"No!" Zoey cries, laughter trembling in her little voice.

"There's no T-rex living here," Scarlett says, shaking her head at me and smiling.

I shrug and set about exploring the kitchen, seeing if I can find matching utensils or something similar. After several drawers, I come to the junk drawer, which I haven't come across yet. I smile to think that there's a junk drawer in this gleaming kitchen full of stainless-steel appliances and cool gadgets.

I start to push it closed when I notice a phone sitting on top. Why is there a phone in the junk drawer? I tap at the screen, but it doesn't light up. It looks like a nice phone, newer than mine, and I can't figure out why it would be in the junk drawer until I turn it over.

The case is custom, a picture of Chad and a woman I can only assume is Shelby. She's an older version of the girls, just like I guessed. I swallow. This can't be Shelby's phone, though, right? No one leaves their phone when they take off. It must be her old one.

"Hey." I hold the phone up for the girls to see. "Is this a phone you play with?" I figure that's why it's in here. The housekeeper or someone stuffed it in the drawer when they were straightening up.

Scarlett's eyes light up. "That's Mommy's phone!" She hurries forward, taking it from me and tapping on the screen, frowning when nothing happens. "It's dead. No wonder we can't talk to her."

She stares at it for a moment, and I don't know what to do. In the week or so that I've worked here, I've just felt innately that I'm not supposed to mention Shelby ever, and now Scarlett's staring at her mom's phone and realizing that her mom can't call.

I take it back and set it gently back in the drawer. "Let's put it away, and I'll talk to your dad about it when he gets home."

Scarlett nods and goes back to the table to color, but I keep the drawer open, staring at the phone. It feels like something's stuck in my chest, filling it up. Why would Shelby leave her phone?

———

Chad gets home around four, making for the most normal day I've had with the girls since I started working. I text Law that I'm done and ask if I can come over early. We planned on five tentatively, but with the unpredictability of when I'll need to work, the real time was up in the air. He texts back that of course I can come over whenever I want. I go home first to pick up my contributions to our potluck dinner, and then I head over.

"Hey." He smiles at me when he opens the door, and my heart skips a little. He leans over and kisses my cheek, and part of me wants to put my hand up and tilt his face so his lips land on mine. I love that Law is taking this slow, just like I asked him, so is it wrong that I want to skip to the part where we're kissing? *Listen, I can't trust you completely yet, but let's make out.*

"Potato salad and rolls." I hold up the containers I brought the food over in. "A bit predictable for a potluck, but I promise you won't be disappointed."

He puts his hand on my back as we walk toward his kitchen and dining room. "I was a bit predictable too. Smoked pulled pork." He points to a foil pan on his island.

"It smells amazing. And it will be perfect to eat on these rolls," I say.

He picks up the plates and utensils he had sitting on the island with the pork and moves them to the table.

"Shouldn't we be using paper plates and plastic forks?" I ask. "I mean, for the right vibe?" I pick up the glasses he has on the counter and move them over as well. He's setting up the table like the first night we had dinner here, our place settings kitty-corner from each other on one end of his table so we can sit closer together.

"This is an upscale potluck." He moves the meat to the table to join my rolls and salad. Then he holds out my chair for me.

"Because you're rich and famous?"

He chuckles and takes a seat. I scoot my chair closer and slide a foot near his. He's always so warm, and something about it soothes me. I've been anxious over finding Shelby's phone all day. She must have had another one. That's what I keep telling myself. She probably had an affair and used another phone to communicate with her lover, and then that's the one she took when she ran off with him.

That makes total sense. So why doesn't it sit right with me? I'm guessing it's just because I don't know the "real" answer and my curiosity is killing me over this.

"Were the girls tough again today?"

I look up, realizing that I was zoning out while Law dished food onto our plates. "Uh, no. They were great today. They're coming out of their shell a lot more, so progress."

Law puts down the foil pan of pork and leans over his plate. He's so tall—six foot six, his bio on the Pumas' website says— that the move puts him only a few inches from my face. He runs his thumb softly over one side of my lips. I catch my breath at his touch, which has set my face on fire.

"Then what's with the frown?" he asks in a whisper.

I shake my head slowly. "It's really not important." Definitely not with his lips this close to mine.

His hand shifts so that he uses one finger to tilt my face closer to his, and he pauses, his gaze darting between my eyes and my lips, waiting.

"Yes," I whisper to his unspoken question. The fact that he wants to make sure I'm ready has melted me even more toward him. He's not just "probably" one of the good ones, like Jenna said. I can kick him up to "almost assuredly," which is likely the highest I can go, being me. Short of a CIA-level background check and twenty years together, I don't know if I'll ever be totally sure about him, and even then … I've listened to stories about women who've been married to serial killers for years and never even realized.

I stop myself. Now is not the time.

Law closes the distance slowly even still, so that by the time his lips reach mine, I'm hungry for the touch and fully present in the moment.

It's electric, just like I thought it would be. His lips are soft, and his chin is so smooth. He must have shaved right before I came over. The soapy scent of shaving cream even lingers a little bit. I lean more into the kiss, putting my hands on his arms. His skin is warm, and his muscles feel exactly how I thought they would.

It's not convenient to be kissing over the corner of a table, but I can't stop myself. So I slide out of my chair, coming to stand next to his. I giggle a little bit at the fact that I'm only a few inches taller than him, even standing over him like this. His arm comes around my waist, pulling me closer, and I lean over to kiss him more, cupping his face in my hands. All the anxious knots in my chest disappear. Every worry I have about why Shelby's phone is at Chad's house or if Law is really the nice guy he's proven to be every step of the way—it all flits off, leaving me in this moment, my lips on Law's, my heart entirely in his hands.

———

We give up on the table.

When we finally pull away from each other, Law picks up our plates and takes them to his family room. We sit on the big, fluffy couch together with our plates on the coffee table in front of us, talking and kissing and sometimes eating. It takes us forever to finish our food, and when we do, Law turns on the TV, flipping to a movie that's already halfway over. It doesn't matter. It's mostly background noise.

For all the … talking we're doing.

It's late when my phone rings, and I pull away from Law to see that it's Chad.

"I'm getting called in," he says as soon as I answer. "The girls are already in bed."

"I'll be there in a few minutes," I promise. I'm disappointed, but it's probably a good thing. Time away from Law after we've taken a big next step in our relationship will keep me thinking clearly.

Law pushes himself off the couch as I hang up. "I'll walk you over."

We gather up my food containers, dishing out some for Law, and he adds some of the smoked pork to my containers to take with me. He carries the containers in one hand and holds my hand with the other as we walk down the sidewalk from his house over to Chad's.

"Friday is my day off no matter what," I say as we approach the front door. "Chad will take the girls to his mom or sister if he gets called out." We're still working on some kind of backup childcare with the kind of flexibility Chad needs.

"I'm glad you have one solid day off. Always being on call for him would burn you out too quickly." Law leans over and kisses the top of my head. I let the shiver of excitement run through me, even though doubts are trying to pile in my head. I don't want them.

"We could go out for dinner or something," I say, turning to look up at him.

"Are you asking me out … again?" He wiggles his eyebrows.

"I am."

He leans over, our height disparity even more apparent now, and kisses me briefly. "Absolutely yes."

I grin, tapping quietly on the front door before letting myself in. "Night."

"Night." He waits until I close the door, and then through the windows on either side of the door, I see him hurry down the steps and jog across the lawns.

Chad appears in the hallway that meets the entryway and separates this area of the house from the kitchen and family room. "Front door?" he asks.

I nod toward Law's house. "I was with Law."

Chad smirks, and my cheeks heat. "Girls are in bed. I'll see you later." He strides down the hallway toward the mudroom and the door to the garage.

I put away my containers in the fridge and then stand in the kitchen, my eyes drawn to the drawer where I found Shelby's phone. I hurry over to it, and with a glance over my shoulder at the garage, I pull it out and plug it into the charger Chad keeps in the kitchen.

CHAPTER 18

LAW

I don't pay Ivy for coaching anymore, but she still makes me do sessions with her anyway. I'm dragging my feet the day after my potluck date with Carlie.

It went so much better than I expected. I would rather focus on that, on how great everything was between us, on the way I can't get enough of her and how it seemed she couldn't get enough of me. I don't want to think about things that might be holding me back. It doesn't feel like anything is right now.

So I try to distract Ivy. "How was your dinner with Caleb the other day?"

She looks up from her phone. She's sitting on my couch, pretty close to where I was making out with Carlie just last night. I bite back a grin.

"Which one?"

My eyebrows shoot up. "Well, I *was* talking about when you guys took off together from Carlie's the other night. It's been two days. There's been more than one?"

She casts me a sly smile. "Of course there has."

Carlie didn't mention anything last night. How does she feel about Caleb and Ivy already having seen each other multiple times? Of course, we didn't really talk a lot last night, so that could be it.

"So that first dinner must have been good, then?"

She puts down her phone, focusing on me, which is the opposite of what I want. "I'm texting him right now," she says. She claps her hands. "I have another client in an hour, so me and you need to get started. I can't get behind today."

"Another date with Caleb?" I've known Ivy for years. I know exactly how to stall her.

Except she's known me a long time too. "I'll tell you about that later." She claps her hands again, this time a little sharper, like she means business and I'd better not try a stunt like that again. "What thoughts are holding you down this week?"

I sit back against the couch and succumb to the bossy woman who's been running my life for almost eight years now. Except, unlike my mother, Ivy somehow has me convinced that everything I do is my idea.

I close my eyes and focus, a technique Ivy drummed into me a long time ago. "I can't push away the thoughts lately that Houston wasn't my first choice and that I'm maybe dreading the minicamp a little bit."

"And how are those thoughts serving you?" Ivy has a calm, melodic voice that just begs you to tell her everything.

But I scowl and open my eyes. "They're not. They're ungrateful thoughts that are just weighing me down with negativity."

She gives a soft, almost inaudible little huff. It makes me think she feels like I should know better by now. "They're neutral thoughts, Law. You're not always grateful to be in Houston. That's neutral. You're making that negative by attaching your expectations to it. Why are you making those thoughts negative?"

I *know* I'm the one giving it negative connotations. I've been working with Ivy long enough to accept that, but sometimes I still get stuck in that place I was when I was getting a C in stats and Ivy walked into the room and told me C's didn't matter. My attitude did.

"Because it just is," I say with frustration and trusting that Ivy will roll with it like always. "I have so much, Ivy. Houston, Nashville, it shouldn't matter. I'm living my dream. What right do I have—"

"To feel human emotions?" It shouldn't surprise me that she stops this particular tirade before I get too far into the spiral.

"I don't want to be the guy who's whining over the team he's playing for." I fold my arms, and I'm not sure if I'm annoyed that this has chased away all those warm, light feelings that Carlie brought with her last night, or annoyed with myself for still being stuck on this, even after four months.

"Then what should you do with that?" Ivy folds her arms right back at me.

"Accept the emotions and figure out how to make them positive." I close my eyes again, taking a deep breath. "Jett's going to put me on the map." Maybe that's something I've been repeating to myself, but I force myself to see the truth in it. If Jett makes me an invaluable tight end, if people are watching me because everyone's watching him, maybe the Blues will want me. Houston could be a stepping stone to where I want to be, and that's okay. I draw in another long breath, and maybe falling into that relaxation lets the next sentence slip out. "Carlie's here."

Ivy doesn't say anything, and when I open my eyes, she's smirking. "Good to know that you've assigned that neutral thought into the positive category. Anything holding you back there?"

Not really, anymore. I smile, and Ivy's smile widens.

"Do you want to talk about how things are going with Carlie?"

I just laugh. "I think you're taking advantage of your position as my life coach and best friend."

She waves her hand. "You're not paying me. I feel no ethical obligations to you."

"You make a good point for me to start paying you again."

She shakes her head and taps some things into her phone, probably her notes app. She uses a tablet and stylus with other clients so they don't think she's texting in the middle of their session. "Fine. Should we talk about you dreading the mini-camp, then?"

Maybe I *should* talk about Carlie more. I settle in to get comfortable with my thoughts. "Sure."

CHAPTER 19
CARLIE

Chad's late-night call blended into another one that lasted through the day, so when he got back late in the afternoon, I sent him to bed and stayed with the girls. I'll have the whole day off in a couple days anyway, and besides, this is what he pays me for. Still, the girls are happy to see their grandma, Shelby's mom, when she stops by that evening.

"Hi," she says, smiling carefully at me, even though the girls are hanging off her arms. The genes in this family are strong. She has the same light blond hair as the picture I saw of Shelby and of the girls, though this woman's has the faded look that comes with age.

I recognize her from a few of the pictures on Shelby's phone, which is about all I gleaned from it. The girls knew the very basic password, so they probably played on it a lot. No state secrets on that thing. No texts explaining where she was going, and way too few photos. It's alarming how few pictures of her and Chad there are on that phone. I've already taken more with Law in the short weeks we've known each other. It strengthens my theory that Shelby had another phone.

"You must be Mimi." I give the woman a genuine, welcoming smile. Law says she's been hesitant to overstep with

Chad, given what Shelby did. "I mean, I know that's not your actual name …"

She laughs, some nerves falling away in the few seconds it lasts. "No. I'm Liz, but you can call me that or Mimi, whichever you think is best. You don't mind that I just stopped by?"

"Of course not. Chad's upstairs sleeping. He had a long night and day, so the girls haven't seen him much. They'll be glad to spend time with you."

She relaxes even more. "I brought dinner. I left it in the car just in case you'd already started something."

I reach out and squeeze her arm. "That's so great. We were just going to do boxed mac and cheese tonight. I'll go grab it for you."

She beams and nods, and I hurry down the steps toward her car. When I glance back, she's already bending over, smiling and laughing with the girls. They're ecstatic.

There's a casserole dish in an insulated bag sitting on the passenger seat. I grin. When she'd said she'd brought dinner, I'd expected takeout, but she actually brought real dinner.

I basically chill while Liz takes care of dinner and the girls. Her face is alight with joy with them, and I can see that she hasn't gotten to be with them near enough. Should I talk to Chad about that? I still haven't even found a way to bring up if he's talking about Shelby with the girls. But the girls are happy, and so is Liz. I'll just have to force myself to ask Chad if it's okay if I invite Liz over more.

The opportunity comes sooner than I think. As Liz is reading with the girls after dinner and getting them ready for bed, Chad comes down in his scrubs. Liz stiffens as she looks up, then looks to me.

"Liz brought over dinner, and the girls seemed really happy to see her," I say in explanation.

He nods, forcing a smile. "That's great. Thanks, Liz," he says.

She relaxes a little and gives him her own forced smile. She goes back to reading with the girls, but she keeps glancing up as she reads.

"Can I talk to you for a minute?" I ask Chad, walking out of the kitchen and into the hallway.

"Is it quick? I'm sorry, I just got called back in." He put his hands in his pockets, tilting his head as he watches Liz and the girls through the opening of the hallway. He smiles, and I take that as a good sign.

"Yeah, I can be quick. I just want to ask if you're okay with the girls spending more time with Liz. They were really happy to see her, and they've been in heaven all night, but I didn't want to push boundaries if you're not okay with that." I speak quickly and quietly.

Chad takes a deep breath, rubs his forehead, and then nods. "Of course. Liz wants to help. I just didn't want her to feel obligated because of—" He clamps his mouth shut and looks at the ground.

"I don't think she does." I breeze past the way he cuts off before he says anything about Shelby. "She seemed happy to be able to spend time with them. She even brought a homemade casserole with her." I laugh a little, wanting to lighten the mood.

He chuckles. "That sounds like Liz. Are you okay staying again?"

"Of course. That's the job. Besides, they'll just be sleeping anyway."

He nods and heads into the living room to say goodbye to the girls. The last few times they've seen him this little, they usually break into sobs and cling to him, but tonight they hug him, get a little teary, but let him go with ease and find comfort in their grandma's lap. Chad's even smiling when he waves and heads down the hall to the garage. Lightness spreads in my chest. I'm doing something right. This job has been hard and different from what I was used to, but the accomplishment tonight—even if I didn't really do anything—makes up for the crazy hours.

Liz puts the girls to bed and joins me in the kitchen, where

I'm cleaning up. "Let me get that," she says, taking the casserole dish from me and buzzing around the kitchen to find containers. "I'm sure you could use the leftovers here. They'll go to waste at my house."

"Thank you. It was so good for the girls to see you tonight." I put my hand on her shoulder as she scoops out the chicken-and-rice casserole from the dish.

"Thank you for letting me come in and take over." She gives a nervous chuckle, avoiding my eyes.

I round the island and take a seat facing her. "Gladly. Besides, it made the girls so happy. That's my goal."

Liz takes the now-empty casserole dish over to the sink, adding some soap and water to wash it out. Her staying a bit longer means I can ask her about the phone.

"Did you know that Shelby left her phone here?" I ask softly.

Liz nods, turning to look at me with a half-hearted smile. "She told Chad she didn't want anything tying her here."

She told Chad. "So you didn't talk to her before she left?" Surprise colors my voice. Liz is so nurturing and loving. I can't imagine her not being close to her daughter.

Liz lets out a harsh laugh. "Of course not." She doesn't say anything more as she scrubs at the pan.

"Let that soak. You can come pick it up later," I say meaningfully. "Rice is a beast to get out of those glass dishes."

Liz stops and turns to me. She offers a sad smile and then fills the dish with water. "Yeah, I can come get it later."

I rest my elbow on the island and lean into my hand. "It's just so weird to me that she left her phone. I can't imagine going anywhere without my phone."

"I'm the same." Liz dries her hands on a towel and leans back against the counter. "I think I took about a hundred pictures just tonight." She arches an eyebrow at me. "I can see the wheels turning in your head, trying to figure out what happened here."

My cheeks heat. I have been digging into Shelby since I got

here. It's kind of my thing and it's right in front of me, but being called out like this feels like I am pushing past boundaries, even if that's not how I meant this. "I don't mean to—"

"We all have," Liz says. "To be honest, I didn't think I was going to get grandchildren. Shelby told me all her life she didn't want to do the family thing. She didn't want to be tied down to anything. She never really understood that being tied to a person isn't a prison. I don't know where I went wrong there." She shrugs, but she twists her lips together like that can hide the emotion. "I worried when she married Chad, and then when they had Scarlett, and even more when they had Zoey. I worried he pushed her, and I worried she'd do exactly this." She adds, smiling in a sad way, "If he did, I know I should be mad about that, but … I'm not sorry. Those girls are my heaven."

"Have you heard from her?" I ask quietly, and surprisingly, it's not about trying to untangle the mystery of Shelby just up and leaving. It's about the sadness weighing Liz down. I want Shelby to be better than the woman Liz is describing, for Liz's sake.

Liz shakes her head. She runs her hands down the front of her pants and then straightens. "I'm going to get out of your hair. If … if it's okay, call me for anything."

I slide off my seat and come to stand by her. "I will." I take her hands and then lean in to hug her. She wraps her arms around me quickly and then pulls away with a look of gratitude.

Once she's left, I settle down with a book, but my thoughts turn back to Shelby and her phone and the fact that she hasn't even contacted her mother. But then I think about it—Liz never really answered when I asked her that, and why would she confide in me? I'm new to this family. Maybe they have talked. Maybe she's explained everything to Liz.

I try to shake my thoughts away from this, loosen the hold of my curiosity. This is not some random story on a podcast. This is a family I'm beginning to care deeply about, and letting my nosiness make this into something more than it is isn't fair.

But I'm still bothered. Shelby seems to have disappeared right off the face of the earth, especially from this house. Could something have happened to her? No one here would even suspect.

I swallow hard as a thought hits me. Could Chad have done something to her?

I shake my head, but he's so sure about her leaving and not coming back. And Liz said that Chad was the one to tell her that Shelby left. Chad's been the one to tell everyone that she's gone.

My phone dings, and I screech in surprise, jumping and landing on the edge of the couch cushion so that I slide right off. I clap a hand over my mouth to keep another cry of pain from escaping and roll my eyes at myself.

Maybe the fact that I'm even considering that Chad might have done something is a sign that it's time to lay off the true crime podcasts. I shake myself and check my phone. It's from my brother, Caleb.

CALEB

Are you coming home soon?

I cringe as I get up from the floor. I landed on one of Scarlett's Barbies. Surgeon Barbie, possibly? She's holding something that looks like a scalpel, and I think it stuck right in my back.

Caleb must be at my house. He loves hanging out with Grandma—says she's a lot less demanding than Mom—but she's a chatterer. He comes over to see me at least once a day if I'm around. He's probably been working at my house most of the afternoon.

CARLIE

No. Chad just got called out again.

CALEB

Do you mind if Ivy comes over so we can hang out?

CARLIE

Of course not.

I chew on my lip. Caleb's texts about Ivy have been excited, and I want him to be happy. Law thinks the world of Ivy, so I can't put a finger on why I'm cautious about her. Because they're moving so fast?

Because I have issues? Sigh. First Chad, and now my brother.

CALEB

And …

CARLIE

And what?

CALEB

I know there's something more you want to say.
Twin ESP.

I laugh. He reads the tone of my texts better than anyone I know, and twin ESP is really the only thing I can think of to explain it.

CARLIE

Just wondering why you guys aren't going to Ivy's so you can be alone.

CALEB

She doesn't have a TV, smh. We want to watch a movie, and your TV is actually nice considering how tiny this house is. Better chance at staying alone here than at Law's or Jenna's. Here's hoping Chad's out for a while.

CARLIE

May the odds be ever in your favor.

I love seeing my brother happy, but something still gnaws at me. Probably jealousy. They've been together every day since they met here in Houston, and I just haven't been able to see Law as much. That's probably it.

———

I'm exhausted, so I text Law for a little while but then go to bed early. When I wake up around seven, I have a text from Chad.

CHAD

Got in at about midnight. I've got the girls this morning.

Knowing that my sleep is disjointed enough if I have to be called over for him, this has become our routine so he doesn't have to wake me up when he gets home in the middle of the night. I quietly grab my bag, make my bed, and slip out of the house, eager for some time in my own space. Maybe I'll invite Law over for breakfast later. We have a date set for tomorrow night, and it is nice to know that our time tomorrow will be uninterrupted, but that doesn't mean I have to wait to see him.

The morning is perfect, sunny but not too hot yet, and I enjoy the walk through the yard to my house. As I'm stepping out of the trees, I stop suddenly and take several steps backward.

Caleb and Ivy are kissing on my front porch. Caleb's in a pair of sweats, no shirt, and Ivy looks … disheveled—messy bun on her head and wearing one of Caleb's shirts over her denim shorts. She pulls away, waving at him as she hurries down the steps and through the gate that separates my yard from the path between my house and Law's, where she must have parked her car. The path leads to the common area of the neighborhood with a park and a pavilion. It's the reason Chad had a gate put in back here, so the guesthouse has easier access without having to walk into the main backyard to get to it.

Caleb goes back into my house once the gate is closed, and I step out of my hiding place, hurrying the rest of the way so I make sure to catch Caleb before he sneaks away too.

"Hey," I say when I come in, startling him from where he stands at the tiny kitchen counter, making coffee.

"Carlie." He turns toward me, his expression sheepish. "Did you see …"

"Yep. I definitely did." I put my bag down next to the door and eye my brother. He barely knows her, and this is just too fast. Too much commitment for someone he met just five days ago.

He turns back to the coffee. "I moved out of Mom's house to escape this kind of disapproval."

I sigh. "I'm just worried. You barely know Ivy."

He pours himself a cup and moves to the table. "I'm a big boy, Car."

I hold my hands up in surrender. "Okay, okay." I pick my bag back up and head for my room. "I'm going to take a shower," I call.

"I'll have breakfast ready," Caleb calls back. So he clearly feels a little bit bad.

I can't help but wonder what Law thinks of this, so I grab my phone as I head into the bathroom.

CARLIE

So I just caught Ivy leaving my house …

LAW

Awkward. I can't unsee this.

If anything convinces me that Ivy is more like a sister than anything else, it's that text. I chuckle and turn on the shower.

CHAPTER 20
LAW

I texted Carlie earlier that I'd be picking her up despite the fact that she asked me out, so five minutes before six, I head through the gate to her house. I can't help picturing Ivy sneaking though here yesterday morning, and I groan softly. I didn't ask her about it. Ivy and I are close, but we don't talk about stuff like that. Is Carlie going to expect me to know something from Ivy's side of things? I couldn't read the tone of Carlie's text about them, but based on our conversations about this before, she's probably bugged by Caleb and Ivy moving so fast.

And to be honest, I'm worried too. Ivy's dated a lot the past year, but as far as I know, no one seriously like this. And it has to be serious. I can't imagine Ivy hooking up just for the fun of it. Carlie is right. It's fast.

I tap on Carlie's door when I arrive, and she calls for me to come in. She pokes her head out of one of the rooms down the hall when I come in. "I'm so sorry. I just need two minutes."

I smile as she ducks back inside the room, her long reddish-blond hair swinging in loose curls behind her. Five minutes later, she comes out dressed in a calf-length skirt and a fitted Pumas graphic tee, which I have to grin at.

"Go Pumas," she says softly, coming forward to put her arms around my waist.

Mmmm, this is definitely a positive of playing for Houston. And still, I kinda want to buy her a Blues T-shirt, just for fun. I lean over and kiss her, then take her hand in mine as I pull away.

"Sorry about the delay," she says, as I lead her out of the house. She pulls away to lock the door, and then she slides her hand back into mine as we walk back through the gate to the path.

"Delay?" I snort. "Ivy is perpetually late to everything. Ten minutes on a good day. Fifteen normally. Except for with her clients. I will never understand how she can be right on time for anything to do with work, but never at the right time when she's supposed to meet up with me."

Carlie laughs. "Maybe I should warn Caleb, although I don't think he'll care." I wonder if she means because they're in too deep already until Carlie adds, "He's very chill about that stuff. He works on his own schedule, and he sort of extends the same courtesy to everyone else."

"Kind of him." We arrive at my car, which I left parked on the street so we wouldn't have to walk all the way up my driveway to the garage from the path. I open the door for her, holding it as she slides in. "You okay with them?" I ask when I get in.

She shrugs. "Sure. Just worried. Caleb doesn't do stuff like that. So it threw me off."

"Neither does Ivy," I assure her.

She takes a long breath and turns toward me. "I don't know if it makes me feel better that they're so … into each other that they're jumping in feet first without really thinking this through. Caleb isn't going to stay in Houston forever. He owns a house in Dallas, even if my mom lives there and drives him crazy. And Ivy, is she going to be here forever?"

"Probably not," I admit. I hold back the fact that I don't even know if I'm going to be here forever. I can't get rid of the hope that in a couple years the Blues will come calling. "But ..." I say carefully. "We should let them worry about stuff like that."

She laughs. "You're right. They're adults, and I don't mean to be protective." She gets a mischievous look. "But maybe you should warn Ivy."

"About?"

"Caleb can make reckless decisions when he gets dumped, and he's very, very smart." Carlie is laughing as she says this, so I know she's not serious, probably just trying to lighten the mood of our conversation about them.

"There's a story I need to know here."

She grins. "He dated a TA in his American History class his freshman year of college. I know, that was dumb, right? To get involved with someone who had control over his grade. She broke up with him, but I guess it wasn't amicable by any means. She switched a paper he turned in for one that was obviously written by AI. When the teacher confronted him about it, he emailed his original paper to him ... along with the website history from the TA's computer showing that she'd written and switched the papers."

A snort of laughter escapes. "Brutal."

She laughs with me. "He has this vigilante side sometimes. He wanted to mess with Xavier too. He found a couple accounts of Xavier's in South America and was going to drain them so Xavier couldn't pay for his fancy lawyers anymore until I talked him out of it."

"Sounds like I better watch my back too," I tease.

"Really, we all should." She chuckles. "So, where are we going?"

"To a place Jett recommended in Kemah. You good with that?" It will mean a little bit of a drive, but I welcome the extra time to spend with her.

"Of course." She reaches over to put a hand on my arm, staring out the window for a moment.

"So, can I ask about your dad?" I glance over at her, hoping that the Ivy-Caleb thing isn't bothering her too much. We can talk that out if she really needs to.

"Oh, of course. What about him?" She smiles, the worried look disappearing.

"You just keep mentioning that your mom drives Caleb crazy and that he lives in your mom's basement …" I prod.

She laughs. "Oh yeah, he lives there too. But he doesn't drive anyone crazy, and my mom's always been the dominant personality, so all of us have always said 'Mom's house.'" She tilts her head and grimaces a little. "They have a lovely, happy marriage. He's retired and plays golf a lot. Maybe if he made my mom come with him when he golfs, she'd stop trying to marry off Caleb." She turns so that she faces me as we drive, her shoulder against the seat and her head tilted into the headrest. "What about your brother? You haven't told me a lot about him. Are you guys close?"

"Not really." I shake my head ruefully. I don't think Carlie will understand. She's close with both of her siblings—worrying about Caleb and always confiding in Jenna. "We have pretty different lives."

She nods, frowning apologetically. "What does he do?"

"He works on my mom's staff. He's one of her policy advisors." We're passing the chemical plant between Houston and Kemah, and I can't help glancing out at hundreds of lights around us.

"Wow. Do you think he'll go into politics too, like your parents?"

I shake my head. "He says no, that he prefers the backstage stuff. Since I keep telling my mom I don't have any intention of going into politics either, she'll start pressuring him eventually." He might give in. He knew Dad better than me, and he won't want to disappoint either of our parents. Mom has just always assumed I'll be the one, since I already have a life in the spotlight and visibility would be easy for me.

We keep talking about our families the rest of the drive. I pull up to a restaurant that's right on the bay and take Carlie's hand as we walk up to it. "Can we have the closest table to the water?" I ask the hostess.

"Of course." She grabs a couple menus and leads us around the edge of the open restaurant, which reminded me immediately of Hawaii when Jett told me about it. The hostess takes us upstairs to a deck that juts out above the water and to a table right next to the railing. The ocean in Texas isn't the same as in Maui—it's more gray blue than the bright turquoise blue of the water there—but it's still the ocean, and we can hear waves lapping below us.

"It's not Maui," I shrug, but I can't help smiling.

Carlie's looking out across the water. The sun is behind us, low in the sky, and she has a kind of halo around her reddish-blond hair. "I love it." She turns back to me. "Although, if you want to fly me to Maui on a date sometime, I'm not going to say no."

I hold her hand across the table. "Would that be moving too fast?"

She leans toward me. "Definitely." But she smiles. "Let's not bring any kids this time." She pulls away to pick up the menu and study it.

"Oh, come on," I have to tease. "They were half the fun."

She nods. "They are pretty great. I've missed being able to see them the last couple weeks."

"How about we swing by after this?" I suggest.

Her smile widens. "They'll probably be in bed."

I hadn't thought of that, and she laughs more as she sees that in my face. "Okay, how about I text Jett and we go hang out with all of them after this? I know you miss your sister."

She puts down her menu, resting her elbows on the table and putting her chin on top of her hands. "That's not really very date-like."

I grin back at her. "You're off the whole night, remember?"

She bites her lips as she turns to her menu. "That sounds fun." And when she glances back at me again, her expression is grateful. Even though I might want to keep Carlie to myself every minute I have with her, her family is important, and seeing that smile on her face makes it all worth it.

CHAPTER 21

CARLIE

The girls spent the night at Chad's sister's when he got called in Friday evening. I volunteer to go get them on Saturday, since I'm headed to the grocery store anyway, but Chad texts that he got home before midnight and he's plenty rested. They're still gone when I drop the groceries off at the house and put them away, so I head back to my house.

I walk slowly through the thin stretch of cypress trees that separate the two yards, admiring how well landscaped the whole yard is. It shouldn't surprise me. My salary, this house, all of it points to the major bucks Chad must be making doing what he does. I hope so, for his sake.

There's no grass between the trees that grow closely together, and I pause when I notice a strange mound that I've never noticed before. My chest seizes. From here, it looks exactly like the type of mound where someone might bury a body.

Oh. My. Gosh. Is there a body in my yard? Okay, well, not exactly my yard. It's between the yards, really. I walk toward it and then gently nudge it with my foot, hoping that it's just a pile of leaves or something that got covered with dirt … somehow.

It doesn't give.

I swallow and then run straight for the gate and Law's house.

———

"You think Chad killed his wife."

I have to admit I probably deserve the dumbfounded look Law's giving me right now. The only thing I've mentioned about how weirded out I am by Shelby's disappearance is when I asked if he thought it was strange that Chad has taken down all the pictures.

"No!" I cry. But then, "Well, maybe. Why is there a body in my backyard?" I hold up my hands and notice they're shaking.

Law blows his cheeks out and closes his eyes. I think he's trying not to laugh. He opens his eyes again. "It's probably a dog, Car. Chad's lived in that house since he and Shelby got married, and to be honest, she really struck me as the type of woman to have a dog. Maybe a purse dog."

I pin him with a hard stare. "That's not a purse-dog-sized mound." I point in the general direction of the mound.

"Shelby left," he says patiently, but the humor is not gone from his expression. His eyes are actually twinkling.

"And I thought that all financial planners had late-night meetings to talk their clients out of stupid money deals." I put my hands on my hips.

Law sobers instantly. "Is that why you think Chad killed his wife? Because Xavier was a drug dealer?" He's so gentle, but I want to punch him in the face for thinking I'm jumping to conclusions about Shelby because Xavier was a big fat liar.

Yeah, okay, my experience with Xavier colors everything in my life, but that might not be a bad thing now. It means I know that even nice guys like Chad might not be all they say.

"No." I shake my head. "No one has heard from her—*at all*. Not even her mother. She left her phone. Did Chad even report her missing or anything?"

Law holds up his hands. "Okay, yeah, that looks suspicious when you say it like that, but why would he report her missing? Shelby told him she was leaving."

I've listened to enough true crime to spot that there's way more than suspicious stuff going on. "Were you there to hear Shelby tell him that?" I ask, eyeing Law with faux innocence.

"No. Chad told me."

I throw up my hands. "Exactly. Just like he told her mom that she left her phone because she didn't want to be tied to anything here and she wanted a fresh start. The only thing anyone here seems to know about Shelby leaving is what Chad told them."

Law shakes his head and presses his lips together. He might be trying not to laugh again. He comes forward and puts his hands on my shoulders. "So, are we going to go dig up her body back there?"

My mouth drops open, even as I recognize the flutter in my stomach over what he said. Yes, it's weird to get butterflies when the guy you're dating offers to dig up a dead body for you. And he might not believe we'll find anything, but he offered anyway.

I blow out a breath. "No! I'm not going to dig up a body." I squirm out of his hold, and he lets me. "What would I tell Chad?"

Law folds his arms, eyeing me with a mischievous look—the same mischievous look that won him several hands of BS at Jenna's house on Friday night because nobody was quite sure if it meant he was holding all the cards or if it was because he wasn't. Probably because it meant both. We had so much fun, and even though it cut into precious time Law and I could have spent alone together ... talking some more, I loved every minute of it.

"Well, I have minicamp next week. Monday, Tuesday, and Wednesday, so if you need the muscle to dig it up in the middle of the night, I'm just saying you'll have to wait until Thursday for my help."

"You!" But I can't help that laughter is starting to bubble up. Yes, when he says these things, it does sound ridiculous. So why does it all make so much sense in my head? Is it really because I believe the worst of people after Xavier? I start stalking down the hall toward his front door, wagging my finger at him over my shoulder. "I'm going to say 'I told you so' a lot when I'm right that there's something fishy going on here."

"Okay," he calls after me, but his voice is wobbly.

I roll my eyes and leave, forcing down my own smile. I'm not going to dig up a body, but I am going to figure out what happened to Shelby Harrell.

CHAPTER 22
LAW

I don't for one second think that Chad might have done something to Shelby, but I do have to admit that while Carlie's conclusion is skewed, she's not wrong that all the pieces look sketchy, plain and simple. Chad *is* the one who told everyone that Shelby had just up and left after they had a huge fight one night. He's the one who told me she yelled that she'd never wanted any of this and then walked out—without her phone and purse.

I knew about the purse. The phone part is new.

I haven't hung out with him since Carlie started working for him. When she's free, I've been with her, and those are the times when Chad's not working. I pull out my phone to text him.

LAW

You working tonight?

CHAD

Not yet.

He adds a laughing emoji. I smile at that. The few times I've seen Chad in passing, that desperate look has been gone. Having Carlie to help with the girls has taken a weight from him, and that all comes through in the fact that he can laugh about being called in at all hours.

I chuckle and pocket my phone to gather up my gaming stuff. My TV is way better than Chad's—given that the only time he spends using his is stolen time like this when he's not at work—but the girls are probably in bed, and he won't call Carlie to come over just so we can play video games.

When he lets me in the front door, I feel a little guilty that I'm checking out all the photos, noting that Carlie's right about Shelby being completely erased here. I don't remember a lot about before Shelby left. I was just starting to get to know Chad then, but I do remember a big family canvas of them in this entryway. The wall where it hung is bare now.

I shrug that off as I follow him back to the family room. Everything is neat and tidy in here, all the toys put away in a tall basket tucked behind one end of the sectional couch. The kitchen counters and dining table are clear and wiped off. Chad was never a slob, and he does have a housekeeper, but Carlie being around has helped bring some organization here too, whether that's Chad having more time to straighten things up with her help or Carlie doing some of that.

"You seem more relaxed," I can't help saying to Chad as I set up the console.

"Everything's been easier since I hired Carlie. She's a magician. Thanks, man." Chad pats me on the back before taking a seat on the couch and leaning back.

"She is pretty amazing." I rock back from where I was

kneeling and hand him a controller, taking my own seat a few cushions away from him.

He smirks at me and turns to the TV, going to work setting up his team while I click away putting mine together too.

"How are you doing?" I ask carefully.

He doesn't look away from the TV. "Feeling good, like we're finally back in a good routine."

I'd bet money he's not feeling good about Shelby leaving, but him relegating the grief in his life to something to get by and back to his routine reminds me of the way Malcolm would answer me when I asked him the same thing. *Mom wants to announce this new bill right away, and I'm loving digging into the work on this one.* Sure he was—it kept him from thinking too much about anything that might be wrong in his life.

"Have you talked to the girls about it? How are they doing?" I pretend my own concentration on the screen as our game starts. Chad did indeed choose the LA Rays, the team I played for before coming to the Pumas.

"They're too young to understand," he says shortly. His tone is a clear request to drop the subject.

Which I ignore. "Have you heard from her yet?" If anything will calm Carlie's mind about all of this, it will be knowing that Shelby's been in contact with someone. Well, maybe. She might point out to me again that I heard it from Chad, not from Shelby.

His only answer is a snort of derision.

I shouldn't say what I do next, but Carlie's in my head in more ways than just that I can't stop thinking about her. "You're not … worried that something might have happened to her? I mean, it's weird that you haven't heard a peep, right?"

Chad's jaw clenches as he presses buttons on his controller so Rays quarterback Eli Dash passes to a very lifelike version of me. "Nope," he says simply.

"Good," I say, but I don't know if I sound convinced. I mentally growl at myself. It's stupid that *I* let Carlie's worries get to me. I know Chad. He would never hurt Shelby.

So why am I thinking about why he's not more worried?

I mentally shake it off. He's probably still angry. I can't imagine what it must feel like to have someone walk away like that. Malcolm was a mess last year, but there weren't kids involved and a house and a whole life they'd built together.

Chad *whoops* as game-me runs in a touchdown.

I laugh and shake my head, but then I eye him. "Listen, I know the last thing you want to do is talk about this, but Ivy is a terrible influence. So when you do want to talk, call me anytime," I say.

His jaw works and he just nods before turning back to the TV and setting up for the kickoff. I nod to myself too, pretending focus on setting up my own plays. I'll do what I did when Malcolm refused to talk and none of the tactics I'd learned from Ivy worked on him. I let it go.

But this time, I can't just ignore what we're not talking about.

CHAPTER 23
CARLIE

Chad has a mostly quiet couple of days, with the only call-outs coming during the day and only lasting a couple hours each. I check in with him before driving over to Jenna's for dinner on Tuesday night, and he assures me that if he does get called in, his other neighbor, Mrs. Kay, can watch the girls for a little bit until I can get back. Even though I'm just as on-call as he is, I appreciate that he allows for some flexibility so I don't have to stay within five minutes of his house at all times.

"My long-lost brother!" I tease when I walk in and see Caleb setting the table. He smirks at me. Until he and Ivy started seeing each other, he hung out at my house quite a bit, keeping me company when I was off and using the house for quiet when I was working. I haven't seen him since the day I caught Ivy leaving.

"I have kind of been monopolizing his time." Ivy steps out from the kitchen with silverware to hand to him.

I startle a little. I hadn't expected her to be here. Jenna said "family" dinner. "Oh, hi!" I hope she can't see that my smile's forced. It's only because she surprised me. I've barely seen her too. Considering Law brought her to Maui with him, I thought she'd be more of a presence. Or maybe she's with Caleb so much, she and Law haven't been spending as much time together. I'll have to ask.

Jenna follows Ivy from the kitchen and brings a plate full of carnitas to the table. "Hey. I was crossing my fingers Chad wouldn't get called out."

I hold her gaze a moment, silently asking what she thinks of Caleb bringing Ivy, but then Caleb looks over, narrowing his eyes.

"You didn't bring Law?" he asks. He must have interpreted my and Jenna's looks. He is my twin, after all.

I look at my watch. "He's at minicamp until later tonight." Until nine, to be exact. If I don't get called over to Chad's, he's planning on coming over to hang out. He texted me a little bit about his conversation with Chad last night while they played video games. Seemed to me like he was pretty intent on convincing me that Chad's angry with Shelby and that's why he's not talking about her.

I mean, of course he's angry. She left him without a backward glance, if he's to be believed.

"Besides," I say to Caleb, "I'm not quite sure I'm ready to introduce him to the family." I keep his gaze long enough for him to easily catch my meaning. Ivy's intent on setting out the forks, so she probably caught it too. Jenna presses her lips together to hide a laugh.

"We already know Law Card," Grandma says, coming into the dining room from down the hall, probably playing with Jenna's kids. Well, hanging out in the room while they're playing and joining in the games from a perch on their beds. She comes up to me and squeezes my hand, and I lean over to kiss her cheek. "Jett's told me all about him." She winks at me. She and Jett are best buddies. It's the sweetest thing.

I smirk back. Grandma's my best buddy too. We did share a small guesthouse for almost a month. "He doesn't know *every-thing*," I say in a low voice.

Grandma gives a huff of laughter and pats me on the arm,

walking by me to take a seat at the dining room table. Jenna calls the kids in, and I help Ruby get buckled into her booster seat before sitting down between Grandma and Caleb.

"Am I too late?" a voice calls from the living room, and then Ava appears in the dining room with a small bowl. "I brought the guac."

We all laugh except Ivy, who stares at the pico in the bowl with a confused expression.

"Ava's allergic to avocados." Caleb leans toward Ivy, who nods and smiles politely.

I catch the moment she sees the ring on Ava's finger, and her eyes widen. And then I smile, because that means that Law didn't even tell his best friend what I'd told him about Ava and Jett being secretly engaged. Ivy leans quickly toward Caleb, whispering something that I can easily guess, since his gaze darts to Ava and he nods, then whispers something back.

Grandma's elbow snaps my attention back to my dinner plate, the two carnitas I put there, and the drizzle of sour cream that's starting to get out of hand. I tip up the squeeze bottle that Jenna uses for the sour cream and grimace at my plate, then reach for the pico that Ava brought.

"Something interesting you want to share?" Grandma asks in a low voice.

"They're moving way too fast," I whisper, scowling down at my plate.

"I knew I wanted to marry your grandpa the night I met him." She shrugs at me and cuts off a piece of her carnitas with her fork and a steak knife Jenna probably set out for her. I haven't seen Grandma eat tacos with her hands for a long time. Even now her hand trembles a little as she raises the bite to her mouth, and I look away from her too. I don't like being reminded that she's getting older.

"That's different," I mutter.

Grandma swallows and dabs at her mouth with her napkin. "Oh, how is that?"

"Well, it was back when …" I actually have no way to finish that sentence.

"Back when young men didn't pretend to be upstanding when they're actually drug dealers?" she says, fire dancing through her expression. She might be trying to point something out to me, but that doesn't mean she's going to pretend like she'll ever forgive Xavier for what he did. "Carlie, you're smart enough to know that the evils of the world are as old as Adam and Eve; we're just finally talking about them now. I knew your grandpa two weeks before he asked me to marry him and I said yes. That doesn't mean I wasn't taking a chance on him turning out to be something other than what he professed to be—I just knew in my heart."

"And it all worked out great." I force a smile at her. She and Grandpa were married for nearly fifty years when he died a few years ago. Her eyes glisten, like they do anytime she talks about him. I can't imagine living without someone who'd been a part of my life that long, but I also can't imagine trusting someone the way she did Grandpa. Not again.

After dinner, Grandma and I go out on Jenna's deck to enjoy the sunset. Caleb follows us out, surprisingly without Ivy, who we can see through the sliding door talking to Ava and Jenna as they clear off the table.

"Do you have something to say to me, Car?" he asks, leaning up against the railing next to the outdoor couch Grandma and I are sitting on.

"You're an adult, Caleb," I say, staring up at him. "It doesn't really matter what I think."

"You're just going to gossip with Grandma about it. And then probably Jenna later. I'm assuming you've discussed it with Law as well." He tilts his head at me.

I try not to laugh, but I'm not very successful. "Yeah, probably."

He points a finger at me. "Ivy is not—"

"Grandma has already given me the lecture." I hold up a

hand at him. She chuckles beside me. I look over at her before looking back to Caleb. "Do you know in your heart? Because that's what Grandma says will assure you that Ivy is exactly who she says she is and you're not going to get bowled over by her turning out to be a jewel thief or something."

Grandma pats my knee, but surprisingly, Caleb shifts a little. "I don't have to know anything in my heart yet," he says, his tone a bit defensive. "We're just dating."

I raise my eyebrows, but I'm not going to call out Caleb in front of Grandma. "Hmmm," I say instead, and I lean back into the couch.

Jenna and Ava come out, and Caleb goes back inside to take Ivy home. She has an early meeting with a new client that Caleb hints is a pretty big deal. She wants more time to prep.

I don't have long to talk with my sister. I can't linger. Chad is flexible, but I need to be responsible. Being available is part of the deal. But Jenna and I have both been so busy that I need at least a few moments of conversation.

"How's the house coming?" I ask, laying my head on her shoulder. Which is how I notice that her shoulders tense.

She glances over at Ava. Ava laughs. "I won't pass on any information in this conversation to Jett. Sister-in-law confidentiality." She mimes zipping her lips.

Jenna sighs. "It's fine. There's an electrical issue, so we're going to have to redo an entire floor, and Devin can't do it. Just another setback."

I wrap my arm around her. "I'm sorry, Jen. That's not what you need right now. Let me talk to Chad and see if he's okay with the kids coming over to play a few days next week. That way you can get some more stuff done."

"That's really sweet of you, sis," Jenna says, patting my leg. "I'd take you up on it, but I'm in stall mode until the guy we hired can get it done."

"Rain check," I say firmly.

She nods, which is how I know the stress is getting to her.

"Move into the house," Ava says quietly. I wonder if she's an older sister too, because there's a tone in her voice right now that holds gentle authority.

"Ava …" Jenna's tone is long-suffering, and she doesn't meet Ava's eye. "It wouldn't solve a whole lot." Ava scoffs, and Jenna hurries on. "I'd have to deal with a move on top of everything else."

"He'll hire movers. He'll put you in a nice hotel suite until it's done," Ava continues in that matter-of-fact tone. Jenna opens her mouth, presumably to protest, but Ava marches on. "Do you know how much money 200 million dollars is? He gives so much away to charities and food pantries and whatever else, but it kills him not to be able to help the one family he desperately wants to."

Talk about a guilt trip. Ava's good at this.

Jenna chews on her lip like she's actually thinking about it. I reach for her hand and squeeze it. "You said you wouldn't say anything to him," she says lamely.

Ava shakes her head. "I won't. I'm just pointing some things out. Helping you see it logically."

"I don't want to be that person." Jenna has a stubborn streak.

"We all know you won't be." Ava shrugs and sits back. "Just think about it, Jen. Seriously."

Jenna nods silently. I look at my watch, wishing I had time to stay until Ava left so I could use my sisterly powers to drive home what Ava has pointed out, but I need to leave.

Jenna and I walk Grandma back to Jenna's guesthouse, but she's mulling quietly. Grandma and I chat about Chad's girls and leave Jenna to her thoughts.

I text Chad that I'm on my way and my ETA when I'm driving back to Houston. It's funny—I've never had to communicate with a boss this much about my whereabouts or theirs, and yet for all the texting we do back and forth, I really barely know him. *Is* he the kind of guy who could kill his wife in a fit of anger and then hide her body in the backyard? From all the true crime I've listened to, anybody could be.

I turn on an audiobook for the drive—*not* a mystery or true crime or anything, since I'm trying to see things with Chad more objectively, the way Law is.

I'm about ten minutes away when my phone dings. Siri reads me a text from Chad that he's getting called in. *Liz is already here and she says not to rush on her account.* Siri even says he adds a smiley face. That's encouraging.

Liz doesn't stay long once I get there, since the girls are asleep. She's beaming when she gives me a light hug and leaves, and I'm glad she and Chad are getting past some things to allow her to be here more for the girls.

I glance up the stairs after her car pulls away, narrowing my eyes. I can't go dig up that mound in the trees without calling attention to myself, but I can inspect this house for any signs of foul play. And yes, if you're wondering, I do have a black light. In my purse.

The most likely places to find blood evidence—the kitchen and family room area—come up clean. If Chad dragged her body through here to the backyard, he was smart about it. Probably put her in a tarp or something.

And also, the housekeeper has likely mopped this floor a dozen times since. Does that matter? That's something I feel like I should know. I pause to google it and then think better of that. How's it going to look if I figure out Chad *did* do something to Shelby and I've got "can blood be completely erased from a floor" in my search history? I'm just going to assume that any evidence here—if there was any—has been thoroughly cleaned away in the last couple months.

I do a cursory search of the entryway and the front room, but no one really uses that room in this house, so I doubt that's where Chad and Shelby fought before she left. I head upstairs to his bedroom. I decide to do a more thorough search of the room than I did originally before I check for a bloodstain.

The first thing I notice is that the carpet in the room is a slightly different shade than the carpet in the hallway. I hurry from the room to inspect the carpet in my room. Same as the hall, different than the master bedroom. That's definitely sketchy. Why would they have replaced just the carpet here?

Possibly because of a huge bloodstain?

Shamelessly, I go through Chad's drawers, and that's when I find pictures of Shelby. Dozens, actually—all of them torn up and the pieces littering the bottom of Chad's sock drawer. I hold my breath as I shift everything back into place, letting it out as I close the drawer. That's creepy.

I think of how Law insists that Chad's angry. Those torn-up pictures definitely support that. Just how angry did he get?

"Carlie?"

I jump as Chad's voice rings from somewhere near. Somewhere really near.

No, no, no, no, no. What's he doing here?

I scuttle back away from the dresser, looking around frantically. I can't go out into the hallway. Chad will see me coming out of his room.

"Carlie?"

He's getting closer. Probably standing down the hall by the door to the room I normally sleep in. Thank heavens I closed it earlier. He'd be able to look in and see that I'm not there.

"She's not asleep already, is she?" I hear him mutter.

His footsteps come even closer, and I have to make a decision. Chad has a platform-style bed, so there's no frame to climb under. I dash for the bathroom, dropping into the huge soaker tub and lying as flat as possible just as my phone vibrates in my pocket.

I bite back the many swear words threatening to come out of my mouth and grab the phone, pressing it against my chest. I pick it up gingerly as I hear Chad walking around his bedroom.

The text is from him.

CHAD

The patient died in surgery before I got there.

(Should the blasé way he can just text that make me as suspicious as it does? Probably not. He does deal with this stuff on a daily basis.)

CHAD

I'm home for the night. If you're up, you can
head home.

I don't answer. That way Chad will believe I'm in my room sleeping. At 8:30 p.m.

I don't even have the excuse that I'm exhausted from days of disrupted sleep. This last week was mostly chill. Hopefully I'll think of something by the time I see Chad next.

Which might be really soon, considering I can hear his footsteps echoing inside the bathroom. *Please don't want to take a bath.*

The good news is that he doesn't want to take a bath. The other good news is that the toilet is on the other side of the room.

The bad news is that I'm lying in the bathtub, ten feet from where my boss is peeing. I squeeze my eyes shut even though I can't see anything from my position in the tub. It seems like hours before he flushes and another day or two that it takes to wash his hands.

Look at the bright side, Carlie, he washed his hands.

Of course he washed his hands. He's a medical professional.

I only relax and open my eyes when I hear his footsteps pad out of the bathroom and into the bedroom.

If Chad leaves the room, there's a possibility I could sneak out of here. Carefully, I lift my head to peer over the edge of the tub, and just as quickly drop back down. Chad's sitting propped up in his bed, opening a book.

I cover my eyes with my hand. I'm never going to get out of here. I'm going to have to wait in this tub until Chad falls asleep.

I turn my head and notice the curtains on the window.

Maybe this window opens out onto … something? The window is as tall as the ceiling, and the bottom is even with the edge of the tub. Maybe there's a way I could slither out without Chad noticing.

I carefully shift the curtains, inspecting the window. When there's no visible way to open it, I tell myself it doesn't matter. I can't get out of it without Chad seeing, and on top of that, I don't know if there would even be anything to step on. We're on the second floor, and I've never really paid attention to the architecture on the back of the house.

I do not want to admit to Law what I've been doing, but I don't see any other way out of this without tipping off Chad that I was snooping in his bedroom. And if he discovers that I think he killed his wife—

Maybe.

—who knows what he'll do to me?

I text Law.

CARLIE

911. I'm stuck in Chad's bathroom, and I need you to distract him somehow so I can get out.

The answering text is quick, thankfully, and nothing short of what I expected.

LAW

What?

CARLIE

I'll explain later. Please help!!!!

I hope the multiple exclamation marks move him to action.

LAW

Okay …

Bless his heart. In all the good ways.

Three long minutes later, the doorbell rings. Shuffling on the bed and then footsteps confirm that Chad is going down to answer it. I peer over the edge of the tub again. Sure enough, his bed is now empty.

I hop out of the tub, run as quietly as I can through the bathroom, and peer around the door. The room is empty. I run to the door and then drop to the floor so Chad won't see me sneaking down the hallway to my bedroom.

"Hey," I hear Law say from the entryway. "Didn't realize you were here. Is Carlie still here? We were going to hang out." His voice is a thousand steps away from natural, but it's the best we've got right now. I army-crawl to my room.

"I think she might be asleep," Chad says. The door shuts, so Law must be in the house now. I put my back to my door and ease it open. I can't see them through the iron railings on the landing, so I hope that means they can't see me. "I texted her earlier," he continues. "But she didn't answer."

Once my door is open, I stand up, swallow back the adrenaline arcing through me, and stride across to the edge of the landing. "Law?" I say. "Oh, Chad, what are you doing here?"

He looks up at me, and Law widens his eyes from behind him. "They didn't need me," Chad says. "I texted you."

"I was watching a show." I gesture back toward my room, which *does* have a TV. I pull my phone from my pocket and pretend to be surprised to see the text. "Oh." I frown. "That's so sad. If you're here, I guess I'll just head home."

"Want me to walk you?" Law asks, his voice still about half an octave too high.

"Sure. I'm going to grab my bag." I duck back into my room, listening to the murmuring of Chad and Law talking for a moment while I take a big, long, deep breath. The problem is, my heart rate doesn't slow. I still have to explain to Law what I was doing.

CHAPTER 24
LAW

We don't talk about what just happened until we're safely inside Carlie's house.

"You couldn't just have said you were admiring the tub?" I ask after she tells me how she was searching his room for blood evidence. With a black light. Well, not his bedroom, but the rest of the house. She hadn't gotten to the black light part before Chad came home and surprised her. "It's a nice tub," I point out.

"Yeah, maybe that's where he stowed her body until he could take it out back and bury it." She shudders, as though it's an actual possibility that she'd lain in a tub where Shelby's body was.

"He didn't kill his wife." The words come out in a sigh. Sure, Chad and I aren't besties, but I know him well enough to believe he didn't kill Shelby. It's so ludicrous that she believes he might have done something to her. I just can't believe it of him. His career is based on saving people's lives, literally. Carlie's only jumping to this conclusion because of her own experience.

She's pacing back and forth in the small space that is her kitchen and living room while I look on from the couch, so I don't think she notices the tension that has pulled my shoulders up. She's too stuck on what she thinks she's discovered.

She stops in front of the small coffee table and turns to me. "Why is the carpet different in the master suite than in the rest of the upstairs?" she asks, pointing an accusing finger at me.

I actually laugh at this, glad I have an explanation. "Oh, yeah. They had to replace it because of an incident with a robot vacuum and a diaper." I pretend to gag. "Totally ruined."

She puts her hands on her hips. "And you witnessed this? You saw the ruined carpet? Maybe you helped rip it out?" Before I can say anything, she holds up a finger. "But wait. Chad told me Zoey's been potty trained for a year. Assured me that she was totally trained, that she was easy compared to Scarlett."

I shrug. "So it happened a while ago."

"And Chad told you about it," she says pointedly. She sighs and drops her head. "Never mind."

The only way I know to keep myself from lecturing her about the way she's judging Chad right now is to make a joke out of what's happening. Then maybe she can stop and see what she's doing. "My offer to help you dig up that mound on Wednesday night still stands." I let a small smile slip. I don't want this weird thing coming between us. I want to believe that she'll come to a place where she can trust me fully and then start to trust others again. I don't want this to be something I have to worry about in our relationship. I'm falling hard for Carlie.

She rolls her eyes, and a tiny smile works its way onto her lips. "I'm not digging up the mound. I'll let the police have the pleasure."

I stand up and go to her, taking her hands in mine. "Look," I say seriously. "I know it must feel like you dismissed a hundred little things about Xavier that, in hindsight, you feel were obvious."

She shakes her head. "I didn't." She lets out a long breath and stares hard at my chest. "I mean, obviously I missed some things, but I don't know what they were. It was nothing like this. There were no clues. He never took calls he couldn't explain away. I thought he had a job that explained all the money. I never overheard suspicious conversations." She walks away from me, going around the coffee table and plopping on the couch. "The government didn't even want to use me to testify because I literally knew nothing. One day things were like happily ever after for me, and then the next, the FBI arrested my fiancé."

I sit down next to her, putting my arm around her shoulder and pulling her into me.

"You think I'm leaping to a crazy conclusion," she says into my chest. "But it's all still suspicious, Law. It really is."

When she lays it all out, she's not wrong, but she's only seeing the bad things. Is that how she sees me? "Yeah. It kind of is," I admit. I take a deep breath. "But I am still worried that this is the side of Chad you see when I just can't believe it. Have you talked to your sister about this? What does she think?"

She shakes her head. "I haven't told Jenna. You're the only one. And I'm not paranoid. This isn't about Xavier, Law, I promise." She looks so desperate for me to believe that his treatment of her is well in the past, that she's over it, and it's not affecting the way she believes a normal guy like Chad could kill his wife.

I sigh. "Okay." This is definitely about her ex, but how do I make her see that? I'll have to figure out a vague way to ask Ivy for help on this.

She sits up. "I have cookies that I made the other day. You want some cookies and milk?"

I love the playfulness on her face as she asks this, the fact that she told me something personal—vulnerable—a moment ago, and that she can also shift to teasing as easily. She trusts me, and given what she's been through, that means so much. But how *much* does she trust me? Will she jump to conclusions about me if she sees things about me in tabloids? I shake the thoughts away.

I use the hand still resting on her back to gently nudge her toward me. Her hands fall on my chest, and our lips meet. I kiss her for several moments before murmuring, "What kind of cookies?"

She runs her thumb under my bottom lip as she says, "Chocolate chip, the best kind with milk." But her touch only leads to more kissing and me wrapping both arms around her to hold her as close as possible. "I have the best recipe," she says softly as we break apart who knows-how-long later.

"I'd love some." I kiss her once more before she slowly gets up and heads into the kitchen area.

"Caleb brought Ivy to family dinner," she says, taking out two glasses and then leaning toward the small, retro-looking fridge and opening it.

"And how did that go?" I rest back against the couch, not taking my eyes off her as she moves around the kitchen, pouring milk and setting out four cookies on a plate to bring in. I hop up to go help her make the transfer, and she hands me the plate while she picks up the two glasses. I'm very happy to discuss this very normal relationship thing—awkwardness with her family.

"Just fine." She follows me back to the couch. "My grandma says she knew she wanted to marry my grandpa the night she met him."

"Jett couldn't stop talking about your grandma tonight. He seemed kind of mad about missing dinner. She must be pretty great." I set the plate on the coffee table and grab a cookie before settling back down.

"She is. They were close before, but she kind of helped him see why he needed to forgive Ava for leaving all those years ago." Carlie smiles as she settles back against the couch. "She's the reason I was brave enough to quit my job and come out here. She told me I didn't love my job the way she thought I should, that there was something better out there. I figured if Grandma, this responsible woman who did all the right things for as long as I could remember, thought it was okay if I walked away, it must really be okay."

I lean over to kiss her temple. "It was more than okay. It was the perfect decision."

She smiles. "Tell me what you think of the cookies."

I obey and take a bite, enjoying the way her smile grows as I praise her around a mouthful of a very good cookie. Her worry about how quickly she feels Caleb and Ivy are moving tells me I have to take my time. And if how great things are between us is any indication, it will be worth the care and the wait this relationship will take.

CHAPTER 25
CARLIE

I put my hands up and shake my head at my brother. "I'm never going to have time for a double date with you and Ivy and me and Law. Sorry." I turn away from where he's sitting at my kitchen table, eating a doughnut and drinking coffee from a place I know is just down the street from Ivy's apartment.

I've never been to Ivy's apartment, but Caleb's phone has been there a lot lately. He probably doesn't remember that we share our locations with each other, or he would have turned it off, I'm sure. And I googled the name of the coffee shop.

"You have Fridays off," he points out.

I keep my back toward him as I pour my protein smoothie from the blender pitcher into a tall glass. I don't want to make it easy on him to read the things I'm *not* saying. "Fridays are the one day I have completely to myself, and when Law and I can spend time together without Chad calling."

"And you don't want to allocate any of that time to the stress you think it would be to hang out with me and Ivy," he says. It doesn't surprise me that my strategy didn't work. Like the data collector that he is, Caleb has been pulling little bits of information from me every time I'm around him, and he's successfully interpreted that information as unease over his relationship with Ivy.

"Carlie," he says in a tone that makes me turn toward him. I try for a completely relaxed expression. "I think if you would spend more time with me and Ivy, you'd be able to get to know her and you could worry less."

I shake my head. "I'm not worried about Ivy being a criminal. I mean, not really." I decide to nip this right in the bud, especially because Law bringing up Xavier thanks to my investigation into Chad reminds me that everyone around me attributes my mistrust to that. And they're not wrong to, I guess. "Plenty of people lie about who they are for things much less serious than the fact that they're dealing drugs. She might have thousands of dollars in credit card debt that no one knows about because she's obsessed with buying dog knickknacks." Caleb laughs, so I have to smile. "Or she might pick her nose and you won't find out until it's too late." I shrug.

"For your information," he says, "none of those situations are something I can't get over. She's a life coach. I'm sure she can coach herself out of picking her nose." He eyes me over his cup. He takes a sip and then sets it down. "Carlie, you also know better than anyone that I could date Ivy for months, years even, and she'd still be able to hide things from me. So what's the point?"

I scowl. "There has to be a mathematical equation or something that points out that the longer you know someone, the less the likelihood of them being able to scam you is."

He chuckles. "Probably."

I grab my glass. Another mathematical equation I'm certain of is that the longer I stay here, the more likely it will be that Caleb talks me into going on a double date with them. Plus I have plans. Even though Chad hasn't called me, I'm headed over to spend some time with the girls. It's not really out of the ordinary. Even when he isn't called out, it's not unusual for me to go help out a little.

"Where are you going?" Caleb asks when I don't settle at the kitchen table with him.

"Over to the house. You're welcome to hang out here and work if you want to." I pick up my bag by the door and rummage through to make sure I've got what I need if Chad does get called out while I'm over there.

Caleb sighs. "I'm not giving up, you know. I want you and Ivy to be friends."

"We are." I plaster on a big, reassuring smile. "You forget that I spent a week in Maui with her. Basically. I'll see you later." I hurry out the door before he can heap more guilt on me for this. I wish I could shake out my worry for Caleb that something's going to go wrong. It's one thing for me to second-guess myself in the relationships I pursue. I don't want that to spill into my family's life.

When I let myself in through the back door, Chad's sitting at the kitchen table with the girls, working through the alphabet workbooks I got them. So even if he might be a murderer, at least he's sticking to the schedule I suggested. This is what I do with the girls every morning, and it's better for their routine if Chad does it as well when he's home, at least most of the time. I don't blame him for deviating every once in a while. He's their dad, and he has to be away a lot for work. There's nothing wrong with him choosing other activities for them to do together.

"Good morning." I smile as I set down my bag on the counter and lean against it to drink my smoothie. "How's the alphabet coming along, ladies?" I ask.

Zoey starts reciting the letters she knows, scrunching her nose and skipping a few. I nod encouragingly, holding back my smile at her cuteness. Scarlett rolls her eyes every time Zoey misses one, and I wonder if that's something she got from Shelby. I've never seen Chad do anything sarcastic or snarky with the girls, especially when they mess up.

"Great job, Zo." I clap when she's done. "Don't you think

that's great, Scarlett? I bet she almost knows as many letters as you did when you were her age. Isn't that cool?"

Scarlett, thankfully, catches that I praised her as well, and her eyes brighten. "You're so smart, Zoey!" she exclaims. Zoey beams, and Chad grins.

"What's up?" he asks, leaning his elbows on the table as he watches the girls continue.

"Thought I'd come over to help out. Your call-outs have been thin this week, and I want to earn my money."

He laughs. "Sounds good. You know you earn your money just by being available, right?"

I wave him off. "Yeah, yeah. But still. I want to be helpful." I will the heat to leave my face. It's not a lie. I do want to be helpful, especially in protecting the girls. From what I've seen so far, I don't think Chad would hurt them. If something happened between him and Shelby that resulted in foul play of some kind, I find it unlikely he'd snap with Scarlett and Zoey. Still, I can't get a case off my mind that I dug into a few years ago. With police closing in on him, a father that had killed his wife killed himself and his two boys. I would hate myself if I let anything happen to the girls just because I wanted to trust Chad amid all the suspicious stuff piling up. Just because Law trusts him.

I try to keep my face neutral as that thought sinks through me and makes my stomach twist. Chad is Law's friend, and me believing he's a murderer can't be good on our relationship.

But I can't just let it go, can I? Not with everything adding up like it is.

"We thought we'd go get lunch and take it to the park to eat," Chad says. "You're welcome to come along, of course."

I nod. "Sounds fabulous. I'm in."

The girls cheer at this news, which makes me feel better. At least they like me enough to want me around even when they have Chad.

———

Chad's on his best behavior while I'm with the girls, of course, so spying on him this way isn't really going to work. I hang out at the house with them for a while longer after we get back, but I mostly just straighten up stuff for when the housekeeper comes in the morning. I head back to my house when he doesn't get called out and take up an advantageous spot on my porch, using a pair of binoculars I bought a couple days ago to watch them through the big windows in the kitchen area and the sliding door in the family room. Maybe buying binoculars is weird, but it's more weird in a cool hobby type of way, not in a creeper way. The items Amazon is suggesting now to go with my binoculars are things like bird identification books and hiking supplies, not rope and duct tape. Besides, I could just as easily be proving that Chad *didn't* do anything to Shelby. And that's good.

From what I can tell, Chad is playing a game at the kitchen table with the girls. I furrow my eyebrows. Does Chad somehow know that I'm on to him and he's putting on the father-of-the-year act? Or was he like this before? The problem is that I've only known desperate-for-help Chad and now calm Chad because I've helped ease the burden he was carrying with being a single parent in a demanding job. I have no idea if he was this kind of dad before Shelby left.

Before she disappeared, I correct myself.

"Are you seriously doing the Peeping Tom thing?"

I startle at the sound of Law's voice, fumbling the binoculars and dropping them on the ground in front of me. I glare at him. "You scared me."

His shoulders are shaking with laughter. "I wasn't even quiet when I came through the gate and walked up."

I pick up the binoculars, sit on them, and eye him with an innocent expression. "I was just checking on the girls." Which is totally true. My motives for spying on Chad are altruistic.

"Mmmmkay." He steps up on the porch and settles next to me on the couch, putting an arm over the back of it. He plays with the ends of my hair, running his fingers through it, and I almost relax into him. But because he didn't say anything about my binoculars and the spying, I pull them out from under me and take a peek into the rooms again.

Except Law sighs when I do. The same slightly irritated one I heard him use when we were talking about this a couple days ago. I ignore the sigh. It looks like Chad is making some mac and cheese. I swing the binoculars over to find the girls sitting together on the couch, watching a movie.

"Carlie?"

I drop the binoculars down, feeling twice as guilty at the concerned look on his face. "I just—"

He holds up a hand. "I understand why everything looks suspicious to you. You're not wrong about how it looks."

I tense. "But?"

"I'm worried. I'm worried that you're so invested in the worst-case scenario." He looks away from me as he says this, and that's kind of endearing. He didn't want to say it, but he did because he cares about me.

"I just have to make sure the girls are safe." But I tuck the binoculars away. Law knows Chad—or at least he thinks he does. He can't see this from my perspective, and I don't blame him for being concerned about me because of it.

"Do *you* feel safe?" Law asks.

I blink. I've never even considered my own safety. Except maybe when I was hiding in the tub. "Chad's never done anything to make me think he's unstable," I have to admit.

"That's not a yes," Law points out ruefully, and all I can do is shrug. He studies me a moment longer but doesn't push things further, even though his eyes are full of things he wants to say but doesn't. "Ivy wants me to convince you to go on a double date," he says, changing the subject and going back to fingering my hair.

"Caleb already tried." I itch to use the binoculars again, but I don't want to disappoint Law.

"It might be good for you," Law says.

"I see that Ivy coached both you and Caleb on what to say." I turn away from trying to see across the yards into the window and back to Law.

"It might be fun."

"It will be stressful. I'll be worried about how I'm acting the whole time. If I'm giving off bad vibes, if Ivy thinks I hate her, if my brother's mad that I'm worried about him getting so deep so quickly with her." I sigh, and my gaze goes back to the window. If Chad's poisoning them at dinner, I've missed him messing with the food anyway.

I shake my head. *If* Chad did something to Shelby, it was very likely a crime of passion, not a premeditated thing. Maybe he told himself that what he did to Shelby was for their sakes somehow. If he does something to harm the girls, it will be because he snaps.

I resist the urge to grab the binoculars again to make sure that neither of the girls is throwing some kind of tantrum about the food.

"That does sound stressful," Law says, bringing my attention back to him. "I won't push it if you don't want to." He curls his finger around a strand of hair lying over my shoulder.

"Thanks." I finally lean back into his arm, and he kisses the top of my head. "Are you worried about them?" I ask.

"Um …"

I turn to look up at him. "Law?"

He still doesn't say anything, and I'm not sure if it's because he doesn't want to stress me out, or he doesn't want to feed into *my* worries if he admits some of his own.

"It's just that Ivy is your best friend, and you haven't once tried to convince me that she's great and she loves Caleb so I should get on board, or something."

He sighs. "I'm worried about Ivy's past." My eyes widen, and he hurries on. "Just her past relationships," he says. "She dated … someone … pretty seriously for a couple years. She didn't want to end it, but she did, because she felt like he wasn't ever going to take it to the next level. So her going from that to telling me she's in love with Caleb in a matter of days is kind of scary for me." He holds up a hand as I open my mouth. *"But* I also trust her. Ivy knows her own mind. I can't imagine her ever getting swept up into something."

My response doesn't change, despite his caveat. "Ivy said she loves him?" I'm falling for Law, for sure. The patient way he's dealt with everything between us, the way he's (kind of) supported me with this thing with Chad and how he hasn't dismissed me outright. I've known him for twice as long, but I can't say that I love him.

I'm not ready to go there yet.

It makes me question what I'm afraid to find out about him. I keep telling myself I know that he's not going to blindside me. I've googled more than I want to admit. Between his mom and his football career, his life is almost an open book. He could be hiding things; I know that. So how much am I *really* letting that affect us?

"Carlie?" Law asks gently. "Can I try something that Ivy does with me?"

I tilt my head, forcing a smile. "Sure."

"What negative thoughts are dancing through there right now?" he asks, tapping my forehead gently with his finger.

The first step in believing what I keep telling myself is being honest with Law right now. "That I'm not letting myself trust you enough to fall in love."

"And how is that serving you?" He's so sincere that I push away the frustration in me that it's not doing any good.

"It's protecting me." I screw up my lips apologetically.

He smiles, brushing the side of my cheek. "And that's okay." He pulls me closer to him, kissing me.

I lean into his chest, wrapping my arms around his neck. Law has this gentleness to the way he handles me that makes warmth seep into every piece of me, enveloping me in gratitude that I found him. And yet the electricity zipping through me makes me forget how important keeping an eye on the girls is. Law's hands press gently into my back, bringing me closer.

"Law," I whisper, pulling a few inches away from him. "I really, really like you."

He smiles, and his lips are so irresistible. I can't help leaning back into him again.

"I really, really like you," he says when we pull away again.

I can do this. I can fall in love with someone totally amazing and get the life I thought I was building with Xavier—only better.

CHAPTER 26
LAW

Camp has been surprisingly good. We've had some other organized team activities before this—OTAs, as everyone calls them—so I've run plays with Jett and the offense already, but something has been clicking even more the last couple days.

Jett calls out a play, and I hide my smile. Given that the defense we're up against already knows what we're doing, there's not a lot of stuff I can hide. Still, it's a fun play. I put a cursory block on the defensive end—no one's wearing pads, after all—and then roll out and run a route behind the line.

Jett passes quickly, before the D-end I hardly blocked gets to him. The pass hits me right in the breadbasket, and I run in the touchdown well ahead of the secondary. I let my grin out now, as Jett jogs up to me and pats my helmet.

"Nice!" he cries, giving me a high five.

"Perfect pass, man," I praise him right back. My heart thumps with excitement.

I can hear Ivy in my head: *How're these thoughts serving you right now, Law?* They're making me eager—like, really eager for the first time since I heard I was being traded to the Pumas and not the Blues. Of course, I think the Blues quarterback is great, but he's no Jett McCombs. I've been pumping myself up for the great things Jett and I will do together, but today I believe it. They aren't just words.

We run a few more plays, some where I just do blocking and others where I catch some good passes. Pretty soon we break up for a short meeting to end the day. It's the last day of the mini-camp, and the next time I see my team in a practice setting like this, it will be for training camp in July.

I drive home still high on those great plays, smiling as I sing along to the playlist Ivy helped me make when I found out about the trade. It's supposed to pump me up, and she even hired someone to lay over some audio of games where I made really good plays. By the time I pull into my street, I hope Carlie hasn't been called in to work. I want to share my excitement with some-one, replay all the great stuff from practice, and I want that someone to be her.

When I pull into my driveway, however, Malcolm's car is parked on the far side of the cement in front of my three-car garage. My brother hasn't visited since I moved to Houston, but he came a couple times when I lived in LA. I'm surprised that he didn't let me know he was coming. We live a lot closer now, but Texas is still a huge state. I think the drive is something like twelve hours. I double-check my phone after I pull into the garage to see if I missed a call or text from him.

"Malcolm?" I call as I come inside.

"In the kitchen," he answers.

I drop my bag in the hallway between the garage and the kitchen and head that direction. He rounds the counter as I come in and meets me, giving me a brief hug before standing back. He's almost as tall as I am, but thinner, probably thanks to our careers.

"What are you doing here?" I ask, noticing that there are a few bags of food from a steak place nearby.

Malcolm goes back to them, opening them up and adding the food to two plates I notice that he's set out. "Sorry for coming unannounced. I needed to get away, and I thought I'd come see what your new place was like. It's nice," he says, grinning at me. I can read the wariness behind that smile, though. "New contract must be a good one," he teases.

I laugh with him. My contract was pretty big news, right behind the news of Jett's huge one. Malcolm knows exactly how good it is.

"Had to get away?" I question.

He shakes his head. "Mom's ramping up her arguments for me to think about a political career. I'm not ready for it." He hands me the plate he prepped for me and some utensils.

I don't tell him that I think that might be my fault. Maybe she actually believes me this time that I have no plans to follow in her footsteps. But Malcolm has always felt like I overshadow the things he does, even when he doesn't come out and say it, and I don't want to add to that.

"And just saying no wouldn't work?" I make sure to smile in commiseration with him. Just saying no to our mom is a difficult task.

He gives a short laugh, and we move to the table.

"Law!" Ivy's voice calls from the front hallway, and I freeze, my gaze going to Malcolm. He stands up, looking like he's on autopilot, as his eyes go wide. My brother is smart, like crazy smart, so he had to have expected this, right? Granted, when I lived in LA, Ivy was still in Nashville, so after they broke up, he didn't risk running into my best friend when he came to visit me.

But Malcolm knows that Ivy came to Houston with me. There's no way he didn't think this through. Maybe he thought he'd be here more than half an hour before she showed up, but still.

"Put your best suit on," Ivy continues, her voice coming closer. "And I mean your very best suit, because I am eloping—" She comes into the dining room just as the last word echoes through the room. She stops abruptly, blinking at the sight of Malcolm standing at my dining room table.

I quickly push back my chair and stand as well. I have no idea what to say to break the tension that has unraveled quicker than an interception followed by a pick-six. Commenting on the fact that I think that Ivy just said "elope" will only make matters worse. Malcolm's eyes might have widened even further. He's gripping the back of the chair with one hand, and he swallows hard.

"Uh …" Ivy says, and she looks frantically to me.

Malcolm stays silent.

I let out a long breath. This is the first time they've seen each other since they broke up a year and a half ago, since Ivy stopped giving ultimatums, since Malcolm let her walk away and then pretended like it never happened.

"I didn't realize you were in town," Ivy finally says, her voice tight and devoid of emotion.

"I didn't tell Law I was coming." Malcolm looks down at the full plates of food on the table.

"I'll let you two get back to your dinner." Ivy nods and spins around, all but sprinting back to the front door.

"I'll be right back," I say to Malcolm in a low voice, and he nods, sitting back down as I jog after Ivy.

She's almost to her car when I catch up. "Ivy! Ivy, wait!"

She stops and turns around, tears heavy in her eyes, but she swipes quickly at them. I reach out to hug her, but she shakes her head and pushes my arm away. "I should've texted or something," she says, her voice trembling.

"You never text or something," I point out.

She takes a deep breath.

I reach out and squeeze her shoulder. "I should've texted you when I saw his car, just as a warning, but you've been with Caleb so much the last couple weeks it didn't even cross my mind." She sucks in a breath at Caleb's name, and I narrow my eyes. "Ivy, were you serious about what you just said, that you guys are going to elope?"

She shakes her head vigorously. "No, no. I mean, I actually

was, but when I walked in and saw Malcolm, I just … It was like a smack in the face. In a way that said I was making a big mistake."

"Ivy …" She spent a year waiting for Malcolm to propose, to commit to forever with her. I love my brother, but I can't watch her do that again.

"I don't mean that I think anything has changed—well, that he's changed." She waves her hand in front of her, and her next breath shudders slightly. "But I can't do something crazy with Caleb—even if I think he's amazing—when Malcolm can still make me feel like this."

I look back to the house and clench my jaw. This feels like the first few weeks after their breakup, being split in two between them. Wanting to comfort Ivy, worried about my brother.

"I'll call you later," I promise.

She nods and gets into her car without saying anything else. I turn and see Carlie coming up the path from the community park with the girls in tow. She waves, but points toward the gate that leads into the main backyard and pulls her hand from Scarlett's briefly to mime sleeping.

I nod and wave back, feeling a little bit sick about how much more complicated this just got.

CHAPTER 27
CARLIE

I plop down on the couch once I get the girls down for naps. I need one too, but I can't bring myself to climb the stairs again to my room here. Scarlett doesn't normally take a nap, but they had a late night last night. And a rough night. Chad had taken them to Main Event with his sister and her family for dinner and playing. Then, of course, he'd gotten called out. He'd sent me a text, just to keep me up to date, saying that his sister was going to take the girls home to stay at her house. I got a call from his sister two hours later, telling me the girls had gotten upset when Chad left and they still hadn't calmed down, and could I talk to them? They begged me to bring them home, and by the time we got everything figured out, it was late. I hate thinking about the look on Chad's sister's face when I came to get them. She used to be one of their safe places. Taking that from her was never in my plan.

Then Scarlett had told me that if Mommy came home, they needed to be here. I've been putting off talking to Chad about this, especially because I'm worried my suspicions will come through, but I can't avoid it any longer. Unfortunately, Chad only came home to sleep for a couple hours before he got called out again.

Footsteps echoing through the house make me jump, my heart thumping hard. I must have drifted off. I slide my feet off the couch, peering into the hallway, where they're coming from, and see an exhausted-looking Chad coming into the kitchen.

"Hey," he says, yawning. He goes right for the coffee maker. "Where are the girls?"

"Taking a nap." I stand. "Probably what you should do."

He chuckles. "And you too. Amie said the girls were really upset last night. I'm sure calming them down and getting them to bed wasn't easy, especially if Scarlett deigned to have a nap today."

I laugh with him. Scarlett is usually pretty adamant about how grown-up she is. "I can stay so you can get some sleep."

He shakes his head. "Go get some rest. It's shaping up to be one of those weeks, and I want you to get your time when you can."

I nod slowly. "Can I talk to you about something first?" I push away the panicky thoughts that I have to address this, but I need to protect the girls in all ways, and that means knowing what to say when they bring up Shelby. I've been able to brush past it so far, but I know in my heart that it's not right to pretend like she didn't exist with them. I really want to believe that she just left, for the girls' sake and for Law. But if Chad is hiding something by refusing to talk about her, I have to get to the bottom of it.

"Of course." Chad pours his coffee and sits at the island, giving me his full attention.

"I think one of the reasons the girls were so upset last night is that they were worried about Shelby coming home while they were gone." I say it quickly and then go on in a rush to explain why. "Scarlett told me she needs to be here in case Mommy comes home."

Chad looks down at his cup, his jaw clenched. "I'll talk to her."

"Okay." I take another deep breath. "I need to know what to say when they talk to me. I can't pretend like Shelby—"

"You don't need to talk to them about Shelby," Chad snaps. "I'll remind Scarlett that Shelby's not coming home, and that will be that."

I shouldn't push further, but I'm taken aback by his tone. "And if she does come back? How am I supposed to handle that if I'm the one here?"

"She is not coming back. I'm positive of that." Chad's voice is so full of anger that I back up a half step. "Go home and get some rest. I'll talk to Scarlett when she gets up." By the end of the last sentence, his voice has mostly calmed.

Sure. I'll go home, but I'll be back. That tone—angry and seething—is exactly what I've been worried about. I can't leave Chad with his girls.

———

My plan to sneak back into the house is waylaid by the fact that I get home to find my brother, in a suit, sprawled across my couch watching the 2007 version of *Northanger Abbey*. I'm so befuddled by it that I stand in the doorway for a full minute trying to understand the scene before me. His suit coat is flung across the back of the couch, the top buttons of his dress shirt are undone, and his tie hangs loosely around his neck. His shoes are by the door, but he's lost his socks somewhere.

"Caleb?"

He looks away from the movie. "Oh, hey."

"What's going on?" I set my bag down. Why is he watching *Northanger Abbey*? He dutifully watches Jane Austen movies with me when I insist, but he's always called them boring.

Caleb doesn't look away from the TV. "Nothing really. Ivy and I were going to elope. I came over here to find you to tell you to get dressed up, no matter what you thought, but she just called it off. Like ten minutes ago or something, so perfect timing."

"You were going to *elope*." I know this isn't the right response, not with my brother looking like I had accidentally jumped on his PlayStation. (It really was an accident!) But I can't help myself. He's known her for two weeks! Eloping? Is he crazy?

"We were. But it's fine, because she saw her ex and realized how stupid we were being and called it off, and now she wants space." He still hasn't looked at me.

My sister emotions are warring with my friend-sister emotions. I mean, thank heavens Ivy came to her senses. Thank heavens *someone* did before they said "I do."

"Wait." My brain catches on something weird, which is also probably not what I should be focusing on either, but there you go. That's my brain, making sure I work out all the details. "Ivy ran into her ex? In Houston? She just moved here."

Caleb finally turns away from the TV, his brows furrowed. "Ivy's ex is Law's older brother, Malcolm. How did he not tell you that? They dated forever. Ivy thought they were getting married, basically begged him, and he wouldn't commit. It's part of the whole reason she moved here." He's so genuinely confused that the whole thing is hard to compute.

Was that the ex who Law was talking about when he said that his brother pretended like she never existed? Why didn't he tell me it was Ivy? "Ivy moved to Houston to support Law. Because it was a difficult move." That's what she told me.

Caleb's confusion only increases, and it makes my stomach do weird, twisty things. "Ivy moving with him because he wanted to get traded to the Blues and not the Pumas is what they tell people, sure. But she wanted to get away, and this was the perfect excuse."

Caleb was about to marry this woman. This woman who he barely knows … except it feels like he knows her way better than I know Law.

"I can tell you need some serious comfort right now—" I tilt my head toward the TV. "—and I'll be right back. I need to go talk to Law."

Caleb frowns. "Yeah. I think maybe you do."

I spin and open the door back up, striding down the steps and toward the gate. Every step makes my stomach twist more. Why wouldn't Law tell me all this stuff? That he's disappointed about getting traded to the Pumas, that Ivy dated his brother? These things should have come up in any of the normal conversations we've had, but they haven't. My stomach flips big time. No, this isn't "oh, by the way, I'm a major drug dealer with ties to a super-dangerous cartel somewhere in South America," but it almost feels worse.

Because I could have sworn that Law was a good, nice guy, and these are easy things to tell me. So what are the big things?

I've googled him enough that I feel pretty confident ruling out major crimes, but the closer I get to his house, the more that confidence falters. For heaven's sake, his neighbor might have killed his wife.

Why does it feel like two small omissions are cracking me apart?

CHAPTER 28
LAW

When Ivy left my house, the closest thing Malcolm got to talking about her was, "Did she just say elope?"

That's seriously the least of what's going on, so I brushed it off with, "I think she was joking." And when I asked him if he wanted to talk about her, he shook his head and went back to eating, changing the subject to football immediately.

After we finish eating, we head into my family room to watch TV, and since I figure Malcolm needs time with his thoughts, I don't push him for conversation. Dealing with Mom about his future and then coming here and seeing Ivy unexpectedly can't have been the break he was looking for.

The doorbell rings, and then a woman's voice calls, "Law?"

Malcolm immediately stiffens, but I recognize it as Carlie's voice pretty quickly. "Does this happen regularly?" he asks dryly. "Women barging in and yelling for you?"

"Not until recently," I mutter, pushing myself up off the couch. I need to intercept her, because the conversation we're about to have really doesn't need to happen in front of Malcolm.

"Hi," she says shortly when I meet her in the entryway. She didn't move far past the door.

Her tone says she's already talked to Caleb.

"Hey. Take a walk with me?" I put my hand on her back, but she slides away. I get that she's probably upset about what just went down, but why am I suddenly in the doghouse? I can't be held responsible for Ivy's actions, so hopefully Carlie will see that once we've had a chance to talk about it. I never imagined that I'd spend so much of my time with Carlie discussing Ivy and Caleb, but here we are.

"Sure." She opens the door and walks out, leaving it open for me.

I expect her to start with something like, "Can you believe they were just going to get married?" So when she whirls on me right after I step down off my rounded stone steps and says, "When you told me that your brother pretended like his ex didn't exist, why didn't you tell me it was Ivy?" it startles me. I flounder for a few seconds, unsure why this is where we're starting this conversation. I have an inkling I won't be moving in to comfort her anytime soon.

"It wasn't the point?" My voice rises, asking her to tell me why this matters. Honestly, the couple times when we talked about it, it was on the tip of my tongue to mention, but the moments didn't feel right. Maybe I knew it would upset her that Ivy had a very serious relationship with my brother and now she was hopping into another one with a guy she barely knew. Maybe I thought it would make Ivy look bad. I'm not even sure, but it doesn't feel like the big deal to me that Carlie's tone says it is.

She blinks. "It wasn't the point? What does that mean? The woman dating my brother—well, I don't know if they are anymore or what—" She closes her eyes and shakes her head. "She dated *your* brother for a very long time, according to Caleb, and you never mentioned that?"

It hits me like a two-hundred-and-fifty-pound linebacker. I kept something from her. My excuse feels so flimsy. "It was Ivy's story. Or Malcolm's. I didn't think it was … relevant."

She throws her hands out. "Not relevant? That my brother was diving headfirst into the most serious relationship of his life, and the woman he was falling hard for spent years waiting for *your brother* to propose?"

This starts to feel familiar, even though I want to push those thoughts away. The way I worried that she'd find something wrong with me, the way she's decided Chad has done something to Shelby. That she would take something like this and fixate on it. I shove my own hands in my pockets.

"Caleb obviously knew," I point out. "That's what's important." What would she have done? Demand he be more careful? Caleb's an adult. I sigh. I recognize why this is important to her. Small things probably feel so much bigger in light of what she went through, and I don't want to be dismissive of that, even though it didn't occur to me before that telling her about Ivy and Malcolm would be *this* important. "I should have said something. I'm sorry."

She presses her lips together and shakes her head slightly. "Why does my brother know that you didn't want to be traded to the Pumas or come to Houston and you never said anything to me?"

I tense. This is another thing that's not a big deal, but she's making it a mountain. She's boiling our relationship down to a few things I didn't say. I may know why they feel so important to her, but it doesn't make it any less frustrating.

"I have nothing to complain about. I'm a successful pro football player who didn't get to play for the team of his dreams? Boo-hoo." I snort. "I guess when you don't pay for the life coaching, you don't have an expectation of confidentiality."

Carlie's not amused. "I guess when your girlfriend begs you to take it slow, she should have no expectation of talking about the real stuff anytime soon."

This is like that linebacker putting a dirty hit right into my gut as he takes me down. Is it any wonder that everyone thinks things can't be totally platonic with me and Ivy when I tell her the things I never even considered telling Carlie? Ivy's always been the one I trusted implicitly, but Carlie never gave me any reason not to share the hard things. She shared her hardest thing with me, and—maybe because I'd already sounded off to Ivy so much about it—I didn't share my hard things with her.

"No, that's not true," I insist. "It's not like that."

Carlie folds her arms. "I have to go. I need to go talk to Caleb. He's watching *Northanger Abbey*." She shoots the last part at me like Ivy dumping him is my fault. In a strange, roundabout way, it maybe is. Malcolm's my brother, and he showed up at my house out of the blue.

"Carlie." I jog after her, the few steps she's gotten, and take her arm gently. "Please, let's not leave things like this."

"I'm done talking," she snaps.

Okay, I really do get it. I messed up by not sharing some things with her, but this isn't fair. "You've already decided then, right? Just like you have with Chad."

She reels back, stunned by my accusation. "What's that supposed to mean?"

I hold up my hands. "I messed up by not telling you some stuff, but you're throwing our entire friendship away because of it. You've decided that what I did is unforgivable."

"I have not." She folds her arms.

I raise my eyebrows, waiting for her to show me she's willing to talk about this. She sucks in a breath and shakes her head, whirling around.

"You're wrong about Chad," I say levelly before she's out of earshot. "And you're wrong about me."

She doesn't turn around, but she misses a step. I thought I was the guy who was going to prove trustworthy to her. Was ignoring the way she latched on to this stuff about Chad just prolonging this fight further down the road? If I had told her about Ivy and Malcolm, or shared about why I didn't want to come to Houston, would it have mattered in a few months when there was something else? A white lie about what restaurant I wanted to eat at? Not confiding my favorite movie or favorite color in a timely manner?

I can try as hard as I want to prove I'm not Xavier, but in the end, I can't force Carlie to trust me.

CHAPTER 29
CARLIE

Caleb tries to talk about Law keeping things from me when I get back, but I immediately move to sidetrack him. I do not want to think about the things Law just accused me of—only thinking the worst of him. He *lied* to me. Yeah, it was by omission, but it's still a lie. Maybe not a big one, but it's the fact that he lied in the first place.

"You just got dumped," I point out.

"Wow. Thanks for reminding me." Caleb shakes his head and sighs, flopping his head back onto the arm of the couch.

"What I mean is, let's focus on comforting you."

He tilts his head back up to look at me, squinting like his twin ESP is telling him that something like that might have happened to me.

Did it? Did I just get dumped? I quickly shove the thoughts away. This is about Caleb.

"Space," he says. "She said she needed space." His voice still holds hope, and I almost rush him and hug him. Maybe more for me than for him.

Instead, I arch an eyebrow and nod toward the screen. "You're watching *Northanger Abbey*." I sit on the couch next to him. "Caleb." I can't help what's coming out next. Maybe if I let it spill out, it will stop pounding through my brain. "What were you thinking?"

He shakes his head. "Stop, Carlie. It wasn't like you and Xavier. Not at all. We told each other everything."

"I thought Xavier and I were saying everything. Although I can see how it might be hard to slip your drug deals into casual conversation." I give a faux-chill shrug, and it works to make Caleb snort with laughter. "You knew about Malcolm?"

He nods. "I knew about Malcolm. I knew that they dated for three years, that she pushed him hard for more commitment the last year they were together, and she finally walked away. She always thought it was their mom, that she wanted Malcolm to marry someone who could help him politically."

"I'm sorry." I put my arms around him. A voice keeps trying to whisper that two weeks, two years, three years, none of it makes a difference. Knowing someone is outside of time.

Caleb puts his face into my shoulder and breathes deeply, and then he shudders. He gulps and holds his breath. I have to hold my own too. I tighten my hold on him.

What if Law *had* told me about Ivy and Malcolm? He's right. Caleb already knew, and all I would have done was harp on my brother more, push him away so that he didn't come here in this moment.

Thought the worst of Law, maybe?

"I'm sorry," I whisper again. Jenna kept saying that after Xavier. When I called her, panicking about the FBI arresting him. How it had to be a mistake. With everything we found out, she just kept hugging me and whispering she was sorry. That's all I can do for Caleb. Strange as it feels to me, I've been here, shattered when everything I thought was real turns out to not be real at all. He was going to marry Ivy. I was going to marry Xavier.

Two weeks.

Two years.

In the end, a heart is just as broken.

————

The fact that Chad doesn't get called in tonight is a blessing and a curse. Ever since our conversation earlier, I'm even more worried about the girls. Which is how the whole story comes out to Caleb, and I convince him to hack into the cameras in Chad's house.

He's resistant at first, probably for good reason. "That's a bad idea, Car. Like, illegal kind of bad idea."

I put my hands on his shoulders. "I have to protect those girls. I *have* to. If something were to happen to them—" I swallow. The idea of it makes me physically sick and tightens my throat uncomfortably. "I wouldn't be able to live with myself," I finish in a quieter voice.

Caleb squints at me. "You really think Chad might have killed her?" He pulls my laptop into his lap but doesn't open it yet.

I might be taking advantage of my brother's vulnerable state right now. He's just been dumped, and this is right up his alley to prove something to himself, like he did with the TA or when he felt helpless in the wake of Xavier's crimes. He's been over to Jenna's GetAwayHome too, installing fancy Bluetooth locks on all the doors and a monitoring system he wouldn't let her pay for. She complained to me over text that she didn't need her family's charity all the time. I was unsympathetic. I might have even sent $10 via Venmo and told her to go buy some fancy cookies. (My bossy older sister used it to have them delivered to me.)

But I can see the wheels turning in Caleb's head with worry for me too, just like with Law. I can't really blame my friends and family for second-guessing my judgment when I've got something like Xavier in my past, but I need them to trust me on this. Yeah, hacking into someone's security cameras is a huge breach of privacy, but if it saves Scarlett and Zoey, even the chance that something could happen to them, is it so wrong?

This isn't about thinking the worst of Chad. It's just better safe than sorry. Why can't Law understand that?

"Probably not?" I raise my voice in question. I can't even decide anymore if Chad's really capable of it, and I feel like I should give him the benefit of the doubt while still being cautious, if that makes sense. I'm *not* just thinking the worst of him. I see that he's a good father. "But it's a lot of weird, sketchy stuff, right?" I say anyway. Law has already confirmed this for me, but if my brother is on board, then I can feel justified even if Law doesn't think Chad did anything.

"Let's just go dig up the body," he murmurs. He stares at me a moment longer, then presses his lips together and slowly opens the laptop.

I shudder. "Law said that too."

Caleb glances up at me but doesn't ask what Law and I talked about. I don't want to go into this with Caleb yet. Every time I think about my fight with Law, my stomach gets all squirmy.

"I can't dig up the body while Chad is home or he'll see me, and I can't while I'm with the girls because that's traumatizing. So I'll eventually tip off the police and let them do the digging." I lean over Caleb to see how he's doing, expecting that since he just opened up the program a couple moments ago, getting into the camera feeds will still take some time. But he's already scrolling through half a dozen feeds of Chad's house.

"He should really use more secure passwords," Caleb says. He hands me my laptop.

I scan through them—one of the hallway outside the girls' room, the entryway, the kitchen and family room area, and then a few of the exterior of the house.

The girls' bedroom doors are closed, of course. It's late. It shows Chad sitting in the family room, watching TV. I set the laptop on the coffee table but don't close it.

I'm going to be watching him like a hawk.

CHAPTER 30
LAW

I've texted Carlie a few times, testing the waters of what happened between us. Once her answer was, *I need to be here for Caleb right now while I can.* Meaning that she spent her time off with him, not me. Maybe it's just that he's really hurting and she wants to be there. Maybe it's how she pushes me away.

I was harsh; I know that. But when I think of the way she looked at me because I didn't tell her two little things, frustration boils inside me. I want to point out that the things Xavier didn't tell her are big, bad things. Not telling her about Malcolm and Ivy wasn't.

It doesn't matter to her. I want to fix things, but I also need to know I can trust her to trust me. This won't work if she doesn't.

I want to be there for Ivy too, but that's become more complicated than I expected. Unfair though it may be, the fact that she spilled her guts to Caleb and it backfired on me is undermining my sympathy for her. I know it's my fault that I didn't share the things I should have with Carlie. It's just easier to blame Ivy.

Then there's the fact that Malcolm is still at my house. He needs me too. I've overheard his end of some conversations with Mom. What he's told me sounds like what she's been saying to me all these years, but Malcolm doesn't shut her down the way I have. Maybe because part of him wants it a little bit.

I have about six weeks before training camp starts with nothing to keep me in Houston. Before I met Carlie, I had planned to head back to Nashville as soon as this minicamp was over, but now I don't want to leave Houston. But if Carlie doesn't want me here, if there's nothing here to save, should I take Malcolm home and help him figure this out? Get him out of Houston and away from Ivy's vicinity? Is that how I can help them both? She left Nashville to stop running into him, to separate their social circles.

One problem at a time.

"Be straight with me," I say to Malcolm on Tuesday. We've been hanging out for four days and haven't had a deep conversation yet. Not about Ivy. Not about Mom. Not about why he up and left Nashville to get away. "Do you want to run for office?"

Malcolm leans his head back against the couch. We've been playing FootballPro, and I've been putting off saying something while we did, because it reminds me of the night I played with Chad and how he pushed off any attempt to talk about Shelby. And that, of course, leads me to think about Carlie and what she's up to. Would she text me for help if she ends up in his bathtub again?

Or worse?

There's not going to be a worse, I tell myself. Carlie has an excuse for her misguided concern for the girls. Chad is my friend. I believe in him.

"I don't *not* want to," Malcolm says warily. "That's the problem. I like the idea of being a change maker like that. It's probably some kind of genetic thing in our blood. But I also know the reality. We've lived with the reality since we were kids."

"You know way better than me," I point out. He's been on Mom's staff since he graduated law school three years ago, and really even before that. "Maybe you start out with something small. City council?" That's not really that small, but in the scheme of national politics, it's a place to start. Gabriella Duncan is gearing up to run for Houston city council next year.

He raises an eyebrow and turns toward me. "What's one little sip gonna hurt?"

"If you think that once you get into it you won't want out, maybe that's the answer. If you're going to fall in love with it, do it. Be the change maker."

"Maybe I talk you into running because you're not as stubborn as Mom, and I can mold you into what I want all while staying in the background. Best of both worlds." He picks up his controller to start another game.

I snort. "Never gonna happen."

We turn our attention to setting up our teams again. On my own, I've earned enough points to trade players. It's flattering that it took more points than average to trade myself to another team. Then I surprise myself by choosing to spend those points putting game-me on the Pumas instead of the Blues. Does that mean I'm actually happy about it now, not just grateful for the chance to keep playing?

Or is it some kind of mental told-you-so? That not saying anything about it to Carlie *isn't* actually a big deal?

"Are we ever going to talk about Ivy?" I ask once the game has started.

"What's there to talk about?" Malcolm tilts to one side as he tries to avoid a tackle. "She's your best friend, and she's never going to be completely out of my life. It's fine. Eventually, when we see each other, it won't be a shock. We'll get used to it."

I purposefully let him run in a touchdown on his next play—seventy yards—and then turn to him. "Why didn't you propose, Malcolm? You guys were crazy about each other. I haven't seen you as happy without her as you were with her."

Malcolm narrows his eyes. "Marry her? How could I marry her? I could never get around the fact that she'd dated you too."

It's too bad I wasn't taking a sip of something, because this would be the perfect time to spray it all over him, sputtering, *What the—*

"Ivy told you we dated," I force out. This is far worse than her telling Caleb everything about me. Did she tell him that too? Carlie was worried about that from day one, and Caleb reinforcing that with stories from Ivy will shatter any chance of fixing things between us. It won't matter what I say. It will be a big lie to her, and I won't be able to blame her for thinking the worst of me then.

Malcolm scowls at me. "No, but it's obvious you guys did in college and probably after. You're together all the time."

Relief fills me first. So this didn't come from Ivy. But frustration rises right back up. "Ivy and I have never dated. Never kissed. Never anything."

Malcolm shakes his head. "You don't have to lie to me for her, Law. Everything's over for us."

I level him with my best glare. "It has never been like that for us. No feelings. Nothing. I swear, Malcolm. I'm not just saying it to protect your feelings or something. It's true."

He still stares at me. "No way." But his tone is filled with disbelief more than anything.

"I don't know how to make you believe me—maybe just beg you to trust me. Nothing has ever happened between me and Ivy, and nothing ever will."

He turns back to the game, lifting his controller and refusing to look at me. I don't know if he believes me. I don't know if he wants to believe me. It might mean that he threw away the best thing in his life because he made a horrible assumption. There has to be more to it than that, but the way his face has paled makes me wonder if that was the biggest reason—that he couldn't bring himself to marry someone he thought I'd dated. Even if he loved her more than anything.

I don't press for more. It's the first time he's talked about Ivy since their breakup, and I might have handed him more than he can handle.

I check my phone, hoping for a text from Carlie asking me to come talk. Can't Jenna take over some of the sisterly comforting? From what Carlie has said, she's spending a lot of time on the GetAwayHome that she needs to get guests into ASAP, but can't she spare a night for her brother?

Probably. But I'm guessing Carlie has her reasons for making sure that it's her.

CHAPTER 31
CARLIE

So far, Chad hasn't said anything about the fact that I spend most days at his house, helping with the girls and around the house. His call-outs the last few days have all been in the middle of the night, so he doesn't question me staying when he gets home because he needs sleep.

The atmosphere does *feel* different, though.

It has to be just me. I'm imagining suspicion in his eyes when I look up and see him watching me or that he seems more tense than usual. This week has been a rough one, and anyone would be off when they're getting as little good sleep as Chad.

I can't get Law's accusations out of my head, and it's messing with my ability to interpret everything.

But *does* Chad suspect that I'm on to him killing Shelby? How else can he be so certain she won't come back? What will Law think of that when I—

I've had to stop myself from thinking about what I'm going to tell Law a lot. He texted me this morning that he's going with Malcolm back to Nashville for a little while. They're leaving tomorrow. He gave me all the details in some lame way of proving that he's willing to tell me everything. I said, *Have fun,* even though I wanted to beg him not to leave. I will text him. We'll talk about this, but not until after I've proven that I'm right and that this isn't just about thinking the worst of someone because of my past trauma. That way, Law will trust *me*.

I'm sitting at the table, doing a math lesson using a Dr. Seuss book, when Scarlett asks, "Do you know my mom, Miss Carlie?"

And Chad walks into the room the same time she asks.

I meet his gaze for a brief moment before turning to Scarlett. "I don't," I say, even though I want to take Naomi's advice and ask Scarlett to tell me about her. I couldn't do that even if Chad wasn't in the room. He asked me not to, and worried as I am, I have to try to respect his parenting decisions. Doing something he asked me not to will just put me at risk of getting fired, and I have to be here for the girls.

I turn another page in the book, reading it to them before asking them to count along with me. I glance up at Chad as I listen to them. His back is to me, pouring coffee, but his muscles are tense.

I turn the page when they're finished counting, but before I can start reading, Zoey says, "Mr. Law knows our mom, doesn't he, Daddy?"

Oof. Double whammy. "Mr. Law has lived here longer than me," I say quickly. *Please, please don't let Chad think I'm encouraging this.* After our conversation the other day, he might think I'm trying to prove a point. His back is still to me, or I would plead innocence with my eyes.

We finish the book without any more comments about Shelby. "What do you guys want for lunch today?" I ask, nodding toward the chart we keep on the fridge to make their requests simple. I slid three choices into the chart this morning while they were still sleeping: sandwiches, chicken nuggets, and corn dogs. I've put off grocery shopping for a few days since I wanted an excuse to be here during the day when Chad was, so we're out of some of their favorites.

"I'll take care of lunch today," Chad says. He smiles at me, but it's so forced I feel like it's a sticker from one of the books I got the girls to help them practice letters. *Oops, wrong one*, I might say to the girls. *This face looks like a frown belongs there.*

I wave him off, pretending I don't notice his fake chill-ness with me. "No problem. It's my job."

"I'm here," he points out, still with that stiff smile.

One glance at the girls says they see through it. Scarlett studies her dad with a slight frown, and Zoey has moved closer to me. My heart thumps, but I keep my expression and my body loose. My body language will scream to the girls that they're safe, if that's all I can do.

"I don't mind." I don't move any closer to the chart, though. That feels like overstepping my bounds by too far.

Chad does, crouching next to the chart and beckoning to Scarlett. "You think I can't make sandwiches, sweetie?" he asks, his tone almost normal.

Scarlett giggles and hurries to the fridge, but Zoey stays next to me. I can't help thinking of a podcast I listened to where they later discovered a three-year-old had seen her mother's murder. She just hadn't had the words to tell anyone about it until much later.

"I don't want sandwiches," Scarlett's saying. "I want chicken nuggets."

Chad slaps his hand over his forehead. "Oh, no. I don't know how to make those."

Zoey laughs now too and hurries over to him, chiding him. "Yes, you do, Daddy! You make them all the time."

I should be relaxing that Zoey seems fine with him, Scarlett too, but I can't get my muscles to obey.

Chad stands, opening the freezer to grab the bag of chicken nuggets. He turns to me, his smile turning false again once it's on me. "I know your brother's going through some stuff. I'll call Amie if I get called out so you can spend some time with him."

It's a dismissal, not offhanded like he's trying to make it sound. If I push any more, his suspicions will just keep rising—but about what at this point, I'm not sure. That I'm talking to the girls about Shelby behind his back and against his express wishes? Or that I think he might have done something to Shelby and I'm on to him?

"Okay." I nod and wave at the girls, grabbing my bag as I head toward the door. I make sure my smile is as real as possible as I leave. The last thing I want is for them to worry.

He didn't do anything to Shelby. I chant it all the way back to my house.

There's no way I'm leaving my house today.

———

I park myself on my bed. I don't want anyone walking in and surprising me while I spy on Chad and the girls all day. When he takes them to the park, I slip onto the path once I'm sure they're past and sit down next to a tree far enough away that he won't be able to tell it's me, but close enough so I can see them. I wear a baseball hat and sunglasses and pull my hair back in a bun, hoping that's enough of a disguise. I pretend to read a book and tell myself he wouldn't do anything to them in public anyway.

"Carlie!" a voice calls, and I look up to see Chad's neighbor on the other side, Mrs. Kay, strolling down the path.

I wave enthusiastically and hope she doesn't call out my name again. The park is busy enough that Chad might not have heard. I risk looking over my shoulder, and his attention is still on the girls.

"Hi, Mrs. Kay," I say with false brightness when she approaches. "How are you today?"

"Melting." She laughs loudly, and a glance over my shoulder says that Chad has looked up now. Hopefully he doesn't know it's me with her. He gave me permission to go to Kemah to see my family, and instead I stick around to hang out at the park by myself? That's not weird at all.

"It is pretty hot," I agree quietly, in hopes that Mrs. Kay will bring her voice down a few notches and stop attracting attention from the whole park.

"Speak up, Carlie," she says. *Stop saying my name, woman!* "I can barely hear you."

I titter. "Oh, sorry. Bad habit. You know, Chad's had a lot of late-night calls, and me and the girls have to try and be quiet while he's sleeping. They usually follow my example if I speak quietly, you know?" I'm rambling, and I didn't increase my volume by much. I can only hope if I keep talking, Mrs. Kay won't be able to shout my presence here to the whole world.

I take Mrs. Kay's arm and pretend to casually stroll away from the park where the girls and Chad are playing. "Is your son coming this weekend like he said?" I ask the only thing that comes to mind. Mrs. Kay actually hasn't mentioned him the last couple times we've spoken, but that never deters her from complaining about his infrequent visits when he just lives in Dallas.

"No, of course not." She gives an irritated *harrumph* and then stops abruptly. "Goodness, Carlie—" I can't help wincing every time she says my name. "I'm going the wrong way. I'm doing the loop of the park clockwise today. It's Wednesday, you know." She says this like it makes perfect sense.

"Oh! I'm sorry." She tilts her head at me because I'm still speaking as quietly as I can get away with in a park. "Well, I need to head back to my house. I'll see you!" I hurry away before she can protest, which I realize is risking her shouting after me again, but maybe I can get back inside my gate quick enough that Chad will decide that Mrs. Kay is going a bit senile.

"I'll see you soon, Carlie!"

Wince

I wave without looking back, and book it back to my yard. It's possible I'm really bad at being a spy.

———

I find a stepstool at the guesthouse and haul it to the back of the fence where I can peer over the fence at them. I also grabbed a pair of hedge clippers that were in the storage box at the back of the house. There's nothing near me to trim, but only Chad will know that. I'm doing a pretty good job of ducking every time he glances this way.

He gets a call at the park that I know is a call-out. He nods officially as he listens. His company is the only call he takes that he uses that nod. I silently will him to have dismissed his suspicions about me, to call me because it's easier.

But when he gets off the phone, he shouts for the girls, waves them over to him, and then makes another call. My phone doesn't vibrate in my pocket.

I slip into the backyard in time to see his car back up and pull into the street. I have no way of knowing if he's really taking them to his sister's house. I don't know if that call at the park, when he nodded officially, was really a call-out. What if he knew I was watching?

I head back to my house and pace up and down my hall. I can't stop thinking of Law's accusation, how he believes I'm really overthinking this, believing the worst about Chad, and that I'm letting all my fears about Xavier color everything. All the stuff with Caleb and Ivy is bringing up old fears and making me paranoid. He's wrong.

But hearing his voice telling me the girls are alright would make me feel better about watching them drive away with Chad.

I could call him. We could talk about all this. He's not leaving until the morning. Since Malcolm drove here, Law's driving back with him. He told me all about how long the drive's going to be —twelve hours—and how Malcolm was crazy for driving instead of flying.

I text Jenna to try to clear my mind about Law.

CARLIE

He should have told me about Malcolm and not wanting to move to Houston.

She already has the full story, and she responds exactly as I expect her to.

JENNA

Of course.

CARLIE

Should I forgive him?

Am I overreacting because of Xavier?

She doesn't answer for long enough that I know she's thinking hard about how to word something.

CARLIE

Am I only seeing the worst in him?

After a few more seconds of the dots dancing, she answers.

JENNA

Maybe you are, but I don't blame you. But I also think he deserves a chance. Do you?

CARLIE

Probably.

JENNA

I plop down onto my couch and watch Chad's house, hoping they come back. What will I tell the police if something happens? When they ask why I didn't say something sooner? I've listened to this story before, to the people who saw all the signs and didn't say anything. The ones who just couldn't believe it was real, and the podcaster swears as they chide people for not saying anything when something was clearly wrong. *Don't be afraid of standing out, especially in a bad situation.* That's what the host would say to me now.

What will I tell Liz?

This is what Law doesn't understand. Maybe Chad is totally innocent. Maybe I'm building things up. *But what if I'm not?*

I must have drifted off on the couch, because the next thing I know, light spills out into the backyard from the family room of Chad's house. I clamber back to my bedroom, checking on the security cameras. Chad's cutting a hamburger into quarters and putting it on two plates. The girls sit at the kitchen table, smiling and legs swinging underneath.

They're fine.

See? Law's voice says in my head. *Overthinking it.*

I stay glued to the computer, though, not even playing a movie on my iPad like I was before. I watch them eat dinner, watch Chad read them books, then put them to bed. He's a normal dad. He loves his girls.

Chad settles in the family room, watching something on TV. He folds his arms and looks as tense as when I left earlier today. I sigh and stretch. I need to pee, and I have to sleep sometime. If I called Law and told him how worried I am, how off Chad's been acting, would he believe me? Or would he just chalk this up to me thinking the worst of people?

I pick up my phone. He could come over, and we could talk, maybe figure out some kind of middle ground. He's friends with Chad and has so much more information on the issue than I do. I could give him a chance to explain why he didn't tell me about how bad he wanted to play for the Blues, or why he purposefully left Ivy's name out when he told me about his brother. I could admit that the way he didn't tell me such small things threw me off, but they're not dealbreakers. I like him too much.

I really, really like him.

But first, I need to pee.

I pick up my phone as soon as I come back, but my gaze

strays to the computer out of habit. I gasp. Chad is striding through the family room, then into the entryway toward the stairs.

He's carrying a shotgun.

CHAPTER 32

LAW

I've been waiting for a text from Carlie all day. My text with the information on when I was leaving and the details of the road trip was preceded by more than a few requests to see her so we can talk. As frustrated as I am, I don't want to end it all because of this. I want this to be the turning point.

All of my texts have been met with the same variations of excuses from before. She's with the girls. She's with Caleb. At least her response to my road trip information was different. *Have fun.*

I don't want to go to Nashville. Telling her all that was my last-ditch effort to shake her up and make her realize I was leaving. Now I'm actually packing a bag and getting ready to take a trip tomorrow morning that I don't want to take. I want to storm over to her house and make her talk to me, but I can't force her to trust me. This will take both of us. I'm falling hard for her, but I can't ignore the issues.

My phone dings—I turned it off vibrate a couple days ago so I didn't miss a text or a call—and I dive for where it sits on my nightstand next to my bed. I accidentally kick my suitcase, which slides off the bed with a crash.

All worth it. The text is from Carlie, the first since our fight that she's initiated.

"Everything okay?" Malcolm calls, and then he appears in the doorway.

"Fine," I say, swiping to get to the text. I glance up to see him eyeing my suitcase. I wave him away and try to make sense of Carlie's text.

CARLIE

Chad has a gun. Come not.

Chad has a gun is pretty straightforward, but is she serious? *Come not* is harder to translate, but my guess, given the first phrase, is *come now*. If she was typing in a hurry, that makes sense.

So I don't hesitate. In fact, I look up to realize that I'm already sprinting out my front door, Malcolm calling behind me, asking what's going on. I don't stop to explain, and I only glance down at my phone as it dings again while I run across my yard and hurdle Chad's four-and-a-half-foot front fence. The texts are from Malcolm, not Carlie, so I ignore them.

Chad's front door is unlocked, which is strange, but I'll think about that later. Chad stands in the entryway, a shotgun hanging at his side. Carlie stands just inside the entryway, as though she came from the back door and through the family room, her hands clasped together in front of her, pure terror on her expression.

"What's going on?" I ask, making Chad whirl on me, the shotgun rising an inch or two before he drops it again.

"Law? What are you doing here?" His expression is one of complete confusion.

I turn to Carlie. "Carlie?"

She points. "I thought—he has a gun—" She shakes her head. "Where are the girls?" She sounds out of breath, so my guess is that she ran from her house.

"Upstairs, asleep … for now." Chad's voice is irritated.

Carlie bolts past Chad and runs up the stairs, toward the girls' rooms.

Chad looks at me, frowning and taking a few steps. "What is she doing? What's going on?" He turns to me for answers, but I don't know what to say. How did Carlie know he had a gun? Was she here when he pulled it? Then why didn't she know where the girls were, and why is she out of breath?

Carlie looks to me when she comes to the top of the stairs. "They're fine. They're safe."

Chad swears. "What's going on?" He does still keep his voice down. Dad first, I guess. The instincts must be powerful.

Carlie comes halfway down, but she's still looking at me. "You had a gun, and I thought—"

Maybe it's just me willing her to stop talking, but she doesn't finish that she thought he was going to do something to the girls or maybe to himself.

"You thought *what?*" Chad snaps. "How did you know I had the gun?"

Carlie draws in a long breath. "The security cameras. Uh … I … I've been watching them."

I stave off my own sharp intake of breath that's almost in unison with Chad's. Probably for different reasons, though. What had her so worried that she'd do something so drastic like spying on him? I mean, Chad is standing in the entryway with a shotgun, so I'm giving her the benefit of the doubt here, to be honest. Something happened in the last four days; otherwise she would have told me. It makes guilt spiral through me. If she was right about Chad and I dismissed it because I assumed she was just thinking the worst of us both, I'll never forgive myself. And I won't blame her for not forgiving me either.

"You've been spying on me. In my own house." Chad's voice has turned calm and official, maybe the way he talks to patients or families. "I'm calling the police."

"No, no, no." Carlie waves her hands at him. "I was worried about the girls. I was just making sure they were okay."

"Why wouldn't they be okay when they're with me?" Chad holds up the shotgun, like this is proof that he'd protect them, obviously. He's not seeing what Carlie is, which maybe makes me believe that he really didn't have anything to do with Shelby's disappearance. He's clueless right now, or he's an Oscar-worthy good actor.

Not that I ever *really* thought he did something, but I'd be lying if I didn't admit to doubts. Especially right now.

"Listen." Carlie holds out her hands, like she's the one dealing with someone not quite there. It's a bit funny—in a that's-not-actually-funny kind of way—that they're both so sure the other one is a criminal. She starts spitting things out in a rush. "There's a suspicious mound in the trees between the houses, and your carpet is different in your master bedroom and you're pretending like she doesn't even exist—no pictures or talking about her."

I see the moment Chad realizes what she's getting at. His eyes widen, and then just as quickly they narrow. "You think I killed Shelby?"

Carlie's voice pitches high. "You're so sure she's not coming back. You told me. How else would you know unless—" Even now, in the midst of accusing him, she won't say it.

Chad whirls on me. "And you?" His eyes snap with betrayal.

Again, I don't know what to say. I didn't really believe it, but I couldn't stop thinking about how Carlie might be right about everything, especially as I went over our fight, questioning all my actions, wondering if I'd acted defensively and just out of frustration. I draw in a breath to point out that she's right. It looks suspicious as all get out.

"No. He didn't think that," Carlie says before I can open my mouth. "He told me multiple times that I had it all wrong."

The way that she defends me makes warmth rush through me. But I can't let her stand here and take all this by herself. "I was worried about you," I say genuinely.

He clenches his jaw and works it for a minute. "Well, let me ease both of your minds. I have this gun—" He lifts it again slightly but keeps it pointing toward the floor. "—because I heard someone trying to get into the front door. And when I got to it, my wife was standing there, trying to use her old keys on the new locks. See for yourself." He nods to the top of the stairs, where Shelby stands with a giant, shiny silver suitcase, gripping the rail and looking like she's about to tumble right down the stairs. "And her drug-dealing boyfriend is waiting outside. Rest easy, Carlie. I'm protecting my girls just fine."

Shelby smiles lazily at me, mascara smeared along the bottom of her eyes, and her blond hair is messy and wild in a bun on top of her head. "Hey, Law," she says, and she plops her butt down on the top step, grinning at all of us.

CHAPTER 33
CARLIE

The woman swaying at the top of the stairs looks like the woman in the pictures, but then again, she doesn't. This one is clearly drunk. Or high. Maybe both. Her cheeks are thin and gaunt, her hair's a mess, and her clothes look dirty and stained.

She eyes me and tips her head to one side. "Are you Chad's new girlfriend?" she asks, and then she laughs. "Sorry to barge in. I forgot some things." She motions to the gigantic suitcase, which I'm guessing contains as many items from her closet as she could stuff in there.

I look over to Chad, who's folding his arms, still holding the shotgun in one hand. "I'm not Chad's girlfriend. I'm the nanny."

Chad snorts, and my face flames. Of course he's going to fire me. I would totally fire me. I kept telling Law about all the things that made Chad look suspicious, but what about me? I hacked into his private security cameras. I snuck into his bedroom to snoop. I went through the phone Shelby left here. I told one of Chad's friends that I thought he killed his wife.

Considering that Shelby is sitting at the top of the stairs right now, I'm definitely the one who looks like a fool. I did everything Law said I did. It's only with great control that I don't burst into tears on the spot.

"The nanny!" Shelby bursts into a fit of laughter.

"I think your boyfriend's still waiting," Chad says dryly, nodding toward the door. Through one of the windows flanking the huge wooden thing, I see a car idling in the section of the driveway that arcs in the yard.

"Oh. Right." Shelby shrugs and stands, gripping the rail again as she sways.

"Let me get that for you," Law says, taking the stairs two at a time and hefting up Shelby's massive suitcase in one hand, his other hand on her elbow as she recklessly descends the stairs.

"Tell the girls hi!" she says in a light voice. Then she giggles and finger-waves at Chad as Law escorts her out the door.

Everything in me tenses to think that this is the woman those sweet girls upstairs call Mommy, who they want to come home. By the anger burning in Chad's expression, this is not new behavior. This doesn't surprise him.

He was protecting Scarlett and Zoey from her, and I have no idea how long he's been doing that. Since long before she left, that I'm certain of. It's written all over his expression in small ways: the tightness around his eyes that speaks volumes of wariness, the sadness lingering in his expression, the frown that isn't quite anger and is maybe holding back emotion. Why didn't I see this possibility?

We both watch through the open door as Law keeps Shelby upright as she toddles down the three steps to the sidewalk in four-inch, expensive-looking heels.

"I'll go pack my things and go to my sister's," I say quietly.

Chad grunts in response.

I spin and hurry back the way I came ten minutes ago, sprinting like the FBI was about to arrest me to get to Chad's house before something bad happened. I push down worries that I don't deserve to have anymore—what will the girls do when Chad has to rush off and I'm not here? All this time I wanted to protect them, but I've probably done the worst thing I could by treating Chad like this. I've ruined my chance here and taken away another person in their life who they trusted—me.

I stride as quickly as I can through the yard and down the path. I push past thoughts of what the mound is—probably a dog, like Law said, or extra landscaping dirt or something. Footsteps pound behind me, and I startle, spinning and expecting Chad to come after me to yell at me, exactly like I deserve.

But it's Law. He puts his arm around me and says softly, "Let me help."

I nod, and we make it up the steps and through the front door before I spin into him and begin crying. "I'm so stupid," I stammer between breaths. "You were right. You were totally right."

"Shhhh, no," he says quietly, pulling me tighter into him. "You did everything you did out of concern for those girls." He leans back just slightly, using a finger to tip my chin up to him. "You got hurt, and with all your heart you wanted to protect those girls from that. Chad will see that when the dust settles. I see that," he says meaningfully.

I shake my head. "He hates me." The words wobble, making me feel even more foolish. And I'm sure Law must feel the same way. I look up at him pleadingly.

"I'll make him understand." His voice is low but threaded with a protectiveness that shoots electricity through me.

A half-laugh, half-sob escapes. "You came so fast," I whisper. Even though he never believed my crazy suspicions, he ran when I called. Even though I hadn't spoken to him in days. Even though I held back trust.

"The second you asked." He pulls me back into his chest and kisses the top of my head. "The *come not* part kind of sent some mixed signals, but I took a chance."

I start to laugh. "Come not?"

"I think you were probably typing quickly."

Now I lean back to look up at him, at the gentle expression on his face, the protectiveness in the way he holds me to him.

"I'm sorry," I say. "You were right, about me only seeing the bad. I don't really care that much about you not telling me that stuff." I shake my head. "I mean, I do. But I made a bigger deal out of it than I should have. I was going to call you tonight."

"I should have said something. I tell Ivy too much—that much is very clear to me now." He puts a finger under my chin, tilting my face up toward him. "Just promise me you'll always give me the benefit of the doubt, the chance to explain. That's all I want, Carlie," he says softly.

Whatever worries I had about those little things he didn't tell me dissolve away. There is full trust in his voice, full willingness to stick by me even through my dark moments. He forgave me so much easier than I forgave him. He is better than I can even imagine, and he is letting me have his whole heart. Happiness chokes me.

"I promise." Tears trail down my cheeks, and Law gently wipes them away, making everything inside me feel like it's going to burst.

"I'll tell you anything you want now," he says softly. "Remember when we did embarrassing moments? I never got a chance." He sways slightly, as though there's music I don't hear. It makes me laugh, and I can't help but love that he's letting me off the hook so simply, even though I majorly screwed up. He deserves me groveling, and I fall for him more because he doesn't require it.

I chuckle. "To be honest, what I need right now is you promising you won't say anything about this to anyone."

He tightens his arms again, almost lifting me off my feet. "I promise." He pauses, and then looks at me seriously. "Carlie, after Xavier … did you ever talk to anyone? Like therapy?" He asks so hesitantly, so carefully. After everything, he's still making sure to be gentle.

Embarrassment dumps through me again. The snooping, the spying … half an hour ago, it seemed justified. Now I hate that I thought something so horrible of Chad when he was just trying to keep from telling the girls that their mother is so high and drunk and whatever that she doesn't care about them. "Um, a couple times? But I thought I was good." I can't look at him. I'm not good, and he knows it.

He pulls me back toward him, holding me close. "This was just drastic," he says softly. "I want *you* to be safe too."

I nod into his chest. "I'll talk to someone. It's a good idea." I pull away enough to look up at him in gratitude and take his chin in my hands. "Thank you for being here for me today, Law." I pull him toward me.

"Always," he breathes as he lowers his lips to mine.

My emotions are chaos, but his touch settles me, makes me believe that me letting down Scarlett and Zoey is something I can think about later, that apologizing to Chad might not fix things but will be worth it, that I can trust Law will never hurt me the way Xavier did, that he's the kind of man who's solid and honest and steady, even when it's hard.

After several moments of kissing, I force myself to pull away. "I should really get out of here," I whisper.

"That's probably a good idea," he whispers back. "But since Caleb is sleeping in your room at your sister's, maybe you should take one of the guest rooms at my house."

I relax against him for one more moment. "Since that means I can put off telling my family the terrible things I've done for another night, I accept that offer." I take Law's hand, and we head for my bedroom to pack my suitcase.

"Full disclosure," he says. "Malcolm is still there, but he's leaving in the morning, and I'll make sure you don't have to face him if you don't want to."

I turn to him before I get my suitcase from the bottom of the closet. "Just Malcolm? What about you?"

He grins and pulls open a drawer. "I never wanted to go in the first place."

CHAPTER 34
LAW

When Carlie heads over to Jenna's the next morning, and after Malcolm has left, I drive over to Ivy's apartment. Carlie told me that she hasn't spoken to Caleb, so I'm not worried about bumping into some kind of reunion. In my gut, I know that they're not getting back together. I'm dreading the moment I have to admit this to Carlie. She probably suspects too. There was a wariness to her expression when she told me how hopeful Caleb still is.

Ivy answers the door in leggings and an oversize University of Tennessee sweatshirt from college, despite the fact that it's almost eighty degrees outside. I step inside and pull her into a hug, but she pulls away after only a moment. Ivy has never been one for long hugs. She's got too much go-go-go in her.

"Hey," she says. "I thought you were going to Nashville today." She plops down on her couch and eyes me.

"I made up with Carlie." This is normally the part where I'd spill about what happened last night, and Ivy waits, obviously expecting it. "She and Chad had a misunderstanding, and she got fired, and she and I ended up talking." That's all she'll get. This is Carlie's story, and this is where I start compartmentalizing what I tell my best friend and what I don't.

It's a beat before Ivy realizes that's all I'm going to say. She pulls in a quick breath. "Oh my gosh, Law. This is it, isn't it?" She's so thrown that I'm not expounding that she glides right over the part about Carlie getting fired.

I tilt my head at her. "Ivy, nothing's going to change about our—"

She laughs sharply and interrupts me, shaking her head. "Stop right there, Law, because everything is about to change. Don't feel bad." Her voice sounds shaky, though, and I hate that. "It would've been the same for me with …" She doesn't finish, and I don't know if she was going to say Caleb or Malcolm. "It was always going to change when you met the right person. Or when I do."

"Yeah." It seems like so little when we've been friends for so long. Eight years, almost a full decade. But she's exactly right. Carlie is going to be my best friend now, and I want her to be. "Horrible time for me to dump you like this." I try to make the pronouncement light, and it gets a chuckle out of her.

"I shouldn't have run away from Nashville," she says, looking down at the couch. Her hands are half covered by the long sleeves, a sure sign that Ivy is pulling in on herself. "I know better."

"I needed you," I remind her.

She shakes her head. "No, you don't. I see all my clients remotely, and I could've helped you just as well without picking up and following you across a few states. I wouldn't have hurt Caleb like this, and I would've eventually gotten used to seeing Malcolm around." She puts her face in her hand, and I move to sit next to her on the couch.

"You don't have to be perfect, Ivy. Leaving Malcolm was hard, and I can't blame you for wanting to just walk away."

"I'm supposed to know better," she says into her hand. "To be better."

I lean back. "Tell me about why you hold yourself to a higher standard than everyone else." I imitate the breezy way she always says this stuff to me.

She drops her hand and glares at me. "Don't life-coach me, Law."

I try not to grin. "Someone needs to."

"You're not certified." But her shoulders have relaxed the slightest bit, and a smile threatens.

"So you can dish it out but you can't take it."

She rolls her eyes. "I have to be an example," she finally says.

"You need to be you—the genuine, authentic you. People will relate to you more if you show you're human and you make mistakes." I can't even keep a straight face as I parrot her words back to her.

She shoves me in the shoulder. "Alright, enough of that. I give, I give." She sighs and leans back against the couch with me. "I'm going to be alright. I bought a new notebook. I'll have this solved and journaled out by this evening." She winks at me.

I chuckle and reach over to take her hand in mine, squeezing it. "The change in our friendship isn't positive or negative, Ivy."

She shakes her head at me, and despite more of her advice being given back to her, there's a sheen to her eyes. She squeezes my hand back. "I know, Law."

Her emotions are likely heightened by all that's been happening the last few days, but it makes the shift in our relationship feel that much heavier. It's not something I would change. I've fallen completely in love with Carlie Gallagher. But as Ivy would tell me, humans always have a hard time adapting to change.

I'm going to miss this, even if I want the next chapter more than anything in the world.

CHAPTER 35
CARLIE

I only stay at Law's house one night before I drive to face the music with my family. Jenna manages to keep a straight face through me telling the whole ordeal and is genuinely serious when I confess to how bad I feel about screwing things up with Scarlett and Zoey. She says a lot of the same things Law already has—being worried about what I've done, asking me to get help, and it's easy to tell her I will when I've already promised Law.

But then she excuses herself to go make dinner, and I hear her muffled laughs in the kitchen. You have to admit, aside from my criminal behavior, you can see how some of it would look funny to an outsider.

I share a look with Caleb. "Good to know you were wrong," he says with a smirk.

"You're an accomplice, you know." I poke him in the arm. "I'm taking you down with me."

He arches an eyebrow. "I leave no trace."

We both chuckle then. The worry that I saw in his expression a few days ago when I asked him to hack into Chad's security cameras left his expression as soon as I promised Jenna I'd work harder on my trust issues. He's my twin, and he'll do anything for me—he's definitely proven that—but he also believes in me and he knows when I'm telling the truth.

"Have you heard from Ivy?" I ask in a low voice. I haven't seen him in a couple days, and I can't help but wonder if Malcolm's departure from Houston has changed Ivy's mind about the space between her and Caleb.

But he shakes his head. "I'm going to go find us an apartment." He pushes himself up off the couch where he was sitting next to Grandma.

I settle into the seat he left behind. "What do you think, G?" I ask. "Did I royally screw that up, or what?"

"You did." She looks sterner than I've seen her in a while, but then she softens and pats my hand. "Don't be so hard on yourself. Besides, you love those girls and you love that job. It will work out."

"Grandma." I sigh out her name and shake my head. "I accused my boss of murdering his wife. I don't think I'm coming back from that."

She threads her fingers through mine and squeezes. "Be patient. I think he'll see it for what it was, especially if you explain where your heart is."

I lean my head on her thin shoulder. "That's what Law said."

"Smart boy."

A couple days later, I'm inexpertly helping Jenna put up drywall in the areas the electrician had to redo. The work is slow, and I know she'd much rather have Devin over here helping. Jett has been banned from helping, since she thinks he'll just spend the whole time trying to convince her to move into the house he bought her. Maybe she's actually just worried she's going to cave.

We're sitting in the middle of the floor, having a quick dinner, when I bring it up. Maybe it'll get me banned too, but I won't let her enforce that.

"Move into the house, Jenna," I say. I try for the same tone that Ava used that night when she was trying to convince her. It just earns me a narrow-eyed glare from Jenna. I put up a hand before she can argue. "If you had known how bad I had let things get, spiraling with Chad and the girls, what would you have done?"

She shakes her head, and she's pressing her lips together and sucking in breaths in a way I know means she's holding back emotion. It makes it build up in my chest too.

"What would you have done, Jen?"

"Anything," she finally says. "Anything to help you."

"Why won't you let us do that? Why won't you let Jett?"

She stares at me for a long time and then finally drops her head, resting it on her knees. Her entire demeanor shows how exhausted she is, and the house is still at least another few weeks away from being ready.

"I don't know," she whispers.

I scoot over next to her, wrapping my arms around her, and she leans into me. "Move into the house," I repeat.

She's quiet for a long time, but she's relaxed against me. "Okay," she says.

––––––––

It's another week before I get a text from Chad.

CHAD BOSS

Law insists that you need a chance to explain yourself. Can you meet me somewhere for coffee?

I smile when I read it. I can imagine Law championing my case, telling Chad there's more to my actions than what he saw that night.

He chooses a place and texts me the address, and I agonize over what to say for the next few hours until our meeting. I make sure to dress professionally, like the teacher he hired, and I walk into the coffee shop with as much confidence as I can muster. Apologies and explanations are all I have left to give to Chad, and I hope, at the least, he can accept that I never really meant him harm.

He stands when I approach the table, and I sit quickly. He follows suit on the opposite side of the booth.

"Thank you again for letting me explain," I say.

His expression is tense, but not angry like it was before. I recognize the caution in it. "Law was persuasive." One side of his lips even ticks up a little, which feels promising.

"First off, let me apologize. Whatever explanations I give you today probably won't make up for everything I did, so I just want you to know that I'm not trying to make excuses. I recognize that what I did was wrong and terrible to you and your girls, and I'm sorry." I clasp my hands in my lap so he won't see them trembling. I want to stay professional, but I also hope that he sees how much I mean what I said. How much I regret the relationships I damaged by my assumptions.

"Thank you." He nods, and his expression softens the slightest bit. Also promising.

So I tell him about Xavier, how I thought I knew him so well and then he tipped everything on its head. How he hid an entire life from me without so much as a hint to what was really going on, and how it all crumbled spectacularly one night when the FBI busted down my door and dragged him away. By the time I finish telling him that, all tension has left Chad's face, and he watches me with interest and even sympathy. Really, we're two people who have been used by the people who should've loved us most.

"Like I said," I finish. "It's not an excuse for what I did, but I want you to know that when I looked back on it, I never really thought you were capable of hurting Shelby. Too much didn't add up to me, but that's because I didn't have all the pieces. That's because there were pieces I didn't necessarily have a right to have. After Xavier, I just relied too much on what the facts in front of me meant and not enough on my heart."

He sits back for the first time since I arrived and studies me. "I should apologize too—"

I shake my head. "Please, don't think that you need to do that."

He holds up a hand. "Maybe you didn't have a right to know some of the things I kept from you, but that doesn't mean it wouldn't have helped if I'd explained that Shelby was an addict and that I feared she was going to harm the girls if she came back. I thought that if we didn't talk about her, they'd just forget, but I was wrong. Honesty toward you and the girls would've been the better path, and you wouldn't have felt like you had to protect them from *me* instead of her."

I let out a slow breath, so grateful for his understanding that I could hop up and hug him. "I didn't talk to anyone about what Xavier did for a long time. Don't beat yourself up too much." I shift to move from the booth. I've done what I came here to do, and I do feel a lot better just being able to properly apologize.

"The girls miss you," Chad says quickly, stopping me from my slide across the seat of the booth.

I hold my breath, tamping down hope that he means what I think he might. He could just be telling me that I was a part of their life and they miss that.

"What you did to help them these last few weeks more than makes up for our misunderstanding."

I can't help the snort of laughter that escapes, and Chad even smiles. "Misunderstanding?" I arch an eyebrow.

"Yeah," he says with a smirk. "Start again on Monday?"

"Absolutely." I nod firmly. Emotion is already working its

way up my throat. Of course I'd hoped something like this would happen, but I didn't believe I deserved this much forgiveness from Chad. I can make it make sense with Law. I think he might have rose-colored glasses on when it comes to me. But Chad? It feels too good to be true. And I'm just going to trust that something can be too good to be true but still right.

"My brother's looking for an apartment for us," I say. "I'll have him find one nearby? I think it might be a better arrangement."

Chad looks like he might be holding back a laugh. "Probably." He slides out of the booth first. I'm afraid my knees might collapse if I try to leave now. "See you Monday."

"See you." I watch him walk from the coffee shop before I put my hands over my mouth and quietly squee for joy. I've missed Scarlett and Zoey so much.

"I'm guessing that went well?" a voice says, and I look up to see Law scooting into my side of the booth, holding a steaming cup that smells sugary and amazing.

I grin and throw my arms around him. "Been spying, have you?" But I'm laughing with joy.

"Cross my heart, I waited until I saw Chad leave before I came in." He puts his arms around my waist. "He hired you back, right?"

I bounce in my seat. "He did. Did you talk him into that too?"

Law chuckles. "That, my dear, was all Scarlett and Zoey. They keep asking when you're coming home."

My throat tightens. I've only known those girls just over a month, but they have my whole heart. I lean up and give Law a peck on the mouth. "When you see them next, will you tell them I'll see them soon and I miss them?"

"Of course." His smile grows. "So, you have until Monday, right?" he asks. "And I'm off for another month. What do you say to Hawaii? Or maybe we try something different, like Mexico or the Caribbean?"

I start backward, eyeing him. "Are you serious?"

"So serious. We could both use another vacation, and luckily, I can afford it. And some." Law pulls me back toward him.

"Okay, but this time, no Ivy." I can't help it. I haven't forgiven her. I don't think it's a coincidence that I haven't seen her since she broke up with Caleb, and I think that's more Law's doing than it is Ivy's.

"Definitely not." He nods solemnly. "Car, I can see how people think that there's something between us, or was at some point, and I see now that I told her so much I forgot to tell you—which is something I promise never to repeat."

I hold up a hand to his mouth as soon as he takes a breath, stopping him. "I don't think you feel that way about her. I did, before she started dating Caleb. She broke my brother's heart, Law. I should be more forgiving, especially given how forgiving you and Chad have been when I've done something far worse, but he's my brother. And I get the feeling that she's not coming back to Caleb." I raise my eyebrows in question, and Law nods reluctantly.

"I don't think so either," he says. "She's moving back to Nashville—but not for Malcolm," he hurries to add when I scowl. "She says she's done running away, she's ready to try new things with her life-coaching business, and she wants to be closer to all her people." He shrugs, and there's a hesitancy in his expression that makes me tilt my head at him. He grins. "I love that you know me twice as well as she does with half the effort," he says softly.

"What is it?" I ask.

"Our friendship is naturally changing—new chapters and all of that. She was never going to be in Houston forever, so this makes sense."

My heart squeezes. "Change is hard."

"How about a distraction?" His smile returns. "You choose an island, and we'll go."

I grin back. "You *are* being serious."

"What's it going to take to convince you, woman?" He uses the arm around my waist to pull me impossibly close to him.

I laugh. "Cozumel?" I suggest. Mexico is close enough that we won't have to spend too much time traveling.

He nods, pulling out his phone and not letting me out of his arms. "First class?" he asks, glancing up at me.

More laughter bubbles up. Is this real? I keep finding ways to contrast Law with Xavier, proving to myself over and over again that Law is the better man, hands down. Xavier was filthy rich—literally *filthy* rich—but he didn't spend a lot of that on me. On us. He kept his spending in line with a financial advisor who had money to spare.

"Duh," I answer, staring at him while he books flights for today—*today*—to Mexico. I lean over and kiss his cheek, lingering and enjoying the moment. "You're amazing, Law."

He turns so our faces are millimeters apart. "This might be too fast for you, and I understand, but I want you to know." He says the words so gently, so carefully. "I love you," he says softly, and then he smiles and adds, "Don't be scared."

The words have made warmth erupt inside me. I shake my head. "I'm not scared," I whisper back. I lean into his kiss, which is long and sweet, but more on the chaste side, considering we're sitting in a coffee shop and there's a decent chance someone's taking a picture of Law.

He scoots me back against the wall and adjusts so he's between me and any possible picture takers, which seems silly. I'm the one who should be hiding him. But heat shoots through me as he curls himself over me and puts his lips to mine, definitely not worried about picture takers.

"Good," he murmurs. "Because next time we're just going to dig up the body."

I can't help laughing, but Law keeps kissing me, and the truth is, I'm pretty sure I love him too.

EPILOGUE

CARLIE

Six Months Later

I never get to go down on the field to see Law after games. I have to wait with the other wives, girlfriends, moms, or partners, in the family room. But today Ava and Gabriella have tugged me through a series of hallways, past security guards that nod at us and smile, and down into the tunnel to watch the final plays of the Pumas' first playoff game of the season. They're killing the Arizona Cobras, and the smile I've seen on Law's face every time he comes off after a fabulous play says he's enjoying it.

Supposedly there's some kind of family thing on the field today, but Ava and Gabriella are the only other significant others here with me.

"Everyone's spread out," Gabriella says, squeezing my arm. "Julia organized the whole thing. She wants us to come out a few at a time from different places for more of an effect."

Julia is the coach's wife. Because I'm only Law's girlfriend, there's a whole world of the players' wives that I'm not a part of. There's a hierarchy here that I still don't completely understand, but thankfully Ava and Gabriella don't mind that I'm *just* a girlfriend. Maybe because they're convinced that's not going to last very long.

I smile to myself. I hope it doesn't last very much longer either. Law is perfection, and despite my demanding schedule with Chad and the girls, plus his football schedule, we're together every spare minute. And every minute is better than the last. Thanks to Caleb, our house is just minutes away. I lamely protested when I did the mental calculations for approximately how much of the rent Caleb must be paying, but then Law got in on the argument and I didn't last. Minutes away from Scarlett, Zoey, *and* Law? How could I say no?

Besides, what kind of example would I be to Jenna, who we finally got moved into her new house next door to Jett?

But until my status changes, I'm on the outs with all the stuff that happens behind the scenes with the players and their families and the special events stuff, like today. I peer out of the tunnel without coming into view. I can't see other nonchalant wives, fiancées, or moms around the field, but maybe they're better at blending in than I would be. That's probably why I got stuck in the tunnel.

Jett kneels the ball for the last play, and we join in the cheering erupting around in the stands. Ava jumps up and down, clapping, even though Jett can't see her back here. He's totally going to notice that she's not in the stands where we normally sit, so he's going to know something's up. Colby too. These women who've become my best friends this season have unnatural connections with their husbands. In a sea of people, Jett can find Ava in an instant. It's enough to make my heart tremble every time I see it.

"Okay, go, Car," Ava says, nudging my back. "You're supposed to go first."

I spin on her. "You're joking. I don't even know what we're doing."

Gabriella pushes at my shoulder. "You'll figure it out. Promise. Go," she says urgently. "Just find Law. After that …" She shrugs, insinuating that it will be obvious from there.

"Oh, here, don't forget your shirt." Ava shoves the rolled-up material into my hand. They're special shirts, made for if we won this game.

I grab it before I turn and run out of the tunnel, feeling ridiculous. I tell myself again that I'll know what to do in a few minutes. I hate being the outsider. *Please propose soon*, I mentally will Law. My answer should be obvious to him by now.

I sprint onto the field, eyes darting every which way for any other women coming out with me, but I don't see anyone yet. It's not a surprise; the field is crowded with players. The women here will be dwarfed by the huge linemen milling around.

Suddenly a cheer roars through the stadium and the crowd around me parts to reveal Law just a few feet from me. A glance at the big screen tells me why. The camera is on us, and ever since someone published pictures of us basically making out at that coffee shop months ago, we've been Houston's Tom Holland and Zendaya.

Then Law drops to one knee.

I squeal, sprinting the final steps to him and basically running him over as I throw my arms around him.

He rises quickly, like I'm nothing to lift in his arms even though he just played sixty-plus minutes of football. I wrap my legs around his waist, and he holds me against him.

"I guess that's a yes?" he shouts above the growing roar of the fans.

I laugh-slash-cry, wrapping my arms around his neck and burying my face in his neck. "A million times yes, Law. Of course."

"You were supposed to let me ask, and then you were supposed to put on the T-shirt. Ava and Gabriella are going to be so disappointed that the plan didn't work how they thought."

I lean back to look at him. Then I kiss him, still keeping my hands locked behind his neck. "Sorry." My tone is completely unapologetic.

Law grins, then releases me so he can bend and pick up the T-shirt I dropped when I all but tackled him. He unfurls it and waves it around, yelling, "She said yes!"

I hop up and down in excitement, although I do appreciate that the T-shirt is cute—a giant "YES" printed in the Pumas logo font.

The crowd starts chanting, "She said yes!" and Law sweeps me up into his arms again to kiss me soundly.

"I've been waiting for months," he says when we break apart and he rests his forehead to mine.

I take a handful of his jersey and grip it. "What took you so long?" I tease.

"Just wanted to make sure I took things slow."

I shake my head and laugh at him. I've found the safest place I can think of in him, and I've known it for months too. He's not perfect. There have been, and there will be more, times when he messes up. When I mess up. But we're going to make it through that every single time, because we trust each other with every-thing. "I love you, Law Card."

He lifts me up to him, holding me so that my head is above his. "I love you too." Then he kisses me and spins me around, and it's the best moment ever.

I can't think of a better start to Law's first championship run.

———

Would you like a bonus epilogue for Carlie + Law?

Want more Houston Pumas Sports Romance? Read The Comeback *now!*

ACKNOWLEDGMENTS

Every book takes a village. Sometimes a small city. To my usual book-critiquing besties: Kaylee Baldwin, Kate Watson, and Gina Denny. You ladies are always polishing and shining my work and making me look good. XO

To my editor at Covenant, Kami Hancock, who also had a hand in helping to edit this one in its short time there.

To my critique group: Jen Atkinson, Gracie Ruth Mitchell, Susan Henshaw, Kaylee, Kate; and my sweet little sister Savanna Cornia for all their additional thoughts as I prepped this for publication. And as always, my Zoom Sprint group for keeping me on task. Yeah, that's what we'll call that…

To my readers in my Instagram and Facebook communities, thank you from the bottom of my heart for sticking around so long.

To my family, my awesome husband and three cool boys. I'm so glad to call you mine and have you on this adventure with me. My sisters and mom, who are always helping with brainstorming. To the whole Savage and Clark extended clan for your support.

And to my Heavenly Father. I am so blessed to have this talent and the community it brought me to.

MORE FROM RANEÉ S. CLARK!

LA Rays Sports Romance
Best Friends, Backups & Something More
Mistletoe Kisses & Something Merry
Layla Meets her Match
Presley's Christmas Catch

Houston Pumas Sports Romance
The Comeback

Love in Little River
Roxy's Song
Dating Dru
Catching Coy
Hallie's Hero
June's Forever
Addy's Prince Charming
Battling Ben
Finding Taylor
Love in Little River Prequel Novella
(Available free to subscribers)

Playing for Keeps Series
Playing for Keeps
Double Play
Love, Jane
Meant for You

Historical Romance
Beneath the Bellemont Sky
The Heiress and the Boy Next Door
A Lady's Promise

Get a FREE novella!
Sign up for Raneé S. Clark news and get *Roxy's Song*, the first
book in the Love in Little River series for FREE!
SIGN UP HERE!

Thank you so much for reading Carlie & Law's story! If you
enjoyed the book, please consider leaving a review on Amazon.
Reviews are vital to the success of a book, so thank you!
Follow me on social media for news about my writing and more
football + Jane Austen books!

LISTEN FOR FREE!

You can listen to Love in Little River audio for FREE on
YouTube!

Roxy's Song
Dating Dru
Catching Coy
Hallie's Hero
and
Battling Ben
are now available!

AUTHOR BIO

In a house overrun by boys, it shouldn't come as a surprise that Raneé loves football and enjoys watching and playing other sports as well, like basketball and baseball. When she's not chauffeuring three busy boys to various activities (and sometimes while she is!), Raneé is either writing, reading (usually romance), obsessing over clothes in the form of her online boutique, or figuring out how to get a Crumbl cookie in rural Wyoming. When her real-life love interest can drag her away from imaginary worlds, she doesn't mind spending some time with him in the great outdoors that he loves.